DARK KNOWLEDGE

Clifford Browder

ANAPHORA LITERARY PRESS

BROWNSVILLE, TEXAS

Anaphora Literary Press
1898 Athens Street
Brownsville, TX 78520
https://anaphoraliterary.com

Book design by Anna Faktorovich, Ph.D.

Printed in the United States of America, United Kingdom and in Australia on acid-free paper.

Editor: Ezra Koch.

Cover Images: "South Street from Maiden Lane, New York, in 1828" by William James Bennett. The Edward W. C. Arnold Collection of New York Prints, Maps and Pictures, Bequest of Edward W. C. Arnold, 1954.
"Navio Negreiro" by Johann Moritz Rugendas. 1830. Wikimedia.

Published in 2018 by Anaphora Literary Press

Dark Knowledge
Clifford Browder—1st edition.

Library of Congress Control Number: 2017911487

Library Cataloging Information
Browder, Clifford, 1928-, author.
Dark knowledge / Clifford Browder
234 p. ; 9 in.
ISBN 978-1-68114-367-5 (softcover : alk. paper)
ISBN 978-1-68114-368-2 (hardcover : alk. paper)
ISBN 978-1-68114-369-9 (e-book)
1. Fiction—Action & Adventure. 2. Fiction—Historical—General.
3. Fiction—Thrillers—Historical.
PN3311-3503: Literature: Prose fiction
813: American fiction in English

DARK KNOWLEDGE

CLIFFORD BROWDER

for Nancy —
a glance at a dark chapter in
our history

Clifford Browder 12/21/20

Also by Clifford Browder

André Breton: Arbiter of Surrealism (Droz, Geneva, 1967)

The Money Game in Old New York: Daniel Drew and His Times (University Press of Kentucky, 1986)

The Wickedest Woman in New York: Madame Restell, the Abortionist (Archon Books, 1988)

The Pleasuring of Men (Gival Press, 2011)

No Place for Normal: New York / Stories from the Most Exciting City in the World (Mill City Press, 2015)

Bill Hope: His Story (Anaphora Literary Press, 2017)

Acknowledgments

To research the background for this book I consulted materials at the New York Public Library and the library of the New York Historical Society, using primary sources whenever possible. I am grateful to the staffs of both libraries for their assistance. I am also deeply grateful to my publisher, Anna Faktorovich, and to my editor, Ezra Koch, for without them this book could not have happened.

1

I had never quite liked my uncle, and he had never quite liked me. But I had two good reasons to see him, an invitation and a question, so I was bound for his office on South Street. Bowsprits of anchored sailing vessels jutted high in the air overhead, stevedores hustled huge bales and barrels and crates onto wagons, and iron-wheeled drays clattered on cobblestones amid smells of whale oil, sawn wood, and brine. These were the sights and sounds and smells that three generations of my family, the Harmonys—tough, keen, hardbitten men—had known and reveled in, as they set out for rampageous adventures in hot distant places. The very thought of those adventures always sparked me, fired me up.

After a few minutes I stepped into the ship chandlery that still bore the sign, HARMONY BROTHERS, even though my father had left the firm years before. Knowing me, the salesmen nodded but left me alone. I loved the sight of those mysterious instruments that I would never use—barometers and sextants and quadrants—and the smells of cordage, paint, canvas, and oils. Buoys and bells dangled from rafters, big windlasses sat heavy on the floor, cutlasses and axes gleamed. Gingerly I ran my finger along the cutting edge of a cutlass, imagining the heroic purposes such weapons might be put to—Grandpa Harmony battling boarders from a British man-of-war, or Great Uncle Noah fighting off hordes of pirates in the Sunda Straits, before succumbing to their poisoned darts—while a few feet away a salesman spieled on to a customer about the latest model of bilge pump. The chandlery was a world that even close up felt distant, a world that my grandfather had exposed me to early with robustious tales of battles and pirates and typhoons, a world that beckoned and enticed me but in the end shut me out; it was and wasn't mine.

In the office next door, I told a clerk I wanted to see my uncle. Just what his business was, aside from the chandlery, I couldn't be sure; I knew he was a shipper of goods and a shipowner, but precisely what he shipped or owned escaped me, since he kept mum about it. Around me in the front office were crates and bins offering samples of goods;

in back, clerks perched on high stools penned entries into ledgers at a counter.

"Good morning, Cousin Chris. We haven't seen you down here for quite a while."

It was Cousin Dwight, Uncle Jake's older son, tall, heavyset, with a wisp of waxed mustache curled over his lip like a snake: for a Harmony, a bit of a dandy. But a hero, too: in Mobile Bay the ironclad *Tecumseh* had been blown to bits out from under him, leaving him splashing about in the water, one of the few survivors, with shots whizzing and booming all around—an incident that, as he told it, prompted Admiral Farragut's famous cry: "Damn the torpedoes—full steam ahead!"

"Good morning, Dwight. I was hoping to see your father."

"He's with a customer. Is there anything I can do for you?"

"Thanks, not really. I need to see Uncle Jake."

"So how's the scholar? Learning all kinds of things, I'm sure." (A touch of irony; Dwight hadn't been to college, didn't miss it.)

"Well, classes are suspended for the summer."

"Just lolling around, then?"

"Not really. Ma has me sorting out Pa's old papers in his desk."

"Anything interesting?"

"Old bills long since paid, sewing machine announcements, hotel brochures from 1863. He never threw anything away."

"I see. Pa will be with you shortly, I'm sure."

Dwight retired into a back office, probably miffed because I wouldn't deal with him. We'd never got on. I found him pushy and aggressive; he thought me soft.

Suddenly Uncle Jake's voice thundered forth from his back office. "If they think that, they can kiss my royal ass. My terms are clear; I won't renegotiate. If that's not good enough, the deal is off—do you hear?—off! I don't need those shit-their-britches, and you can tell them that from me. Go to hell, all of you! Good day!"

His voice had boomed; the whole room heard. The clerks didn't even look up, just kept on pushing their pens. Then a silk-hatted older man came out of Uncle Jake's office, a troubled look on his face, and hurried off. Uncle Jake stepped into the outer office in shirtsleeves, his eyes flashing under heavy brows, his face as red as his square-cut beard. When he saw me, his features softened.

"Chris, boy, how are you? Come in, come in."

He waved me into his office. I took off my silk hat with the band of crape; we sat. Over his desk hung a large print of the clipper ship *Falcon*, which on its first run in the early fifties had made record time to California and been hailed by all as a wonder; part owner, he never let anyone forget it. A hard man, as hard and keen as the cutlass I'd just touched in his chandlery.

"Pardon my Dutch, Chris; I was a bit het up. You're how old now?"

"Twenty, sir."

"Old enough to have heard talk like that before. Men at sea, with no women around, talk like that too much. Not that you've been to sea or ever will be, unless of course you've changed your mind."

"Uncle Jake, I'm not meant for the sea."

"True enough: too thin, too slight. Not your fault, but once out of the harbor, you'd heave your cookies in the deep."

Years before, when Grandpa Harmony had taken all the kids in a small boat to see the lighthouse at Sandy Hook, I'd retched over the side all the way. Dwight of course told his father, and the two of them had been reminding me of it ever since.

"Be that as it may," said Jake, "don't mention my cussing to your ma. It might make for rowdy weather between us."

"I won't, sir. I promise."

"How is she, by the way? Haven't seen her since the funeral."

"She's getting used to Pa's not being around, but it's tough for all of us. She's putting up a thumping-big monument in Woodlawn, and lights candles in front of his daguerreotype, talks to him sometimes, prays a lot."

"Like me, when I lost Emmie. Didn't pray much, but I talked to her, at first."

Suddenly his eyes cut into mine. "So, Chris, what can I do for you?"

"First of all, sir, Ma wants to invite you and Dwight to dinner next Sunday, if you're free. She's still in deep mourning but is willing to see family."

"I should think so. Moping around won't bring Mark back. Tell her Dwight and I will be delighted to come. Maybe about three?"

"Three would be fine, sir."

"Chris, your pa and I had our differences at times, but Mark Harmony was a decent man. Too decent for his own good."

"Yes sir. Ma asked me to clean out his desk. Right off I found a diary. The very last entry in it, written the day before he died, thanked the Lord that he'd been able to see his family through the financial convulsion of the last decade and the tribulations of this one. 'In spite of earlier doubts and fierce misgivings,' he wrote, 'thank God for the Venture.' We can't figure out what he meant. Would you have any idea, Uncle Jake?"

His features tightened ever so slightly, and he looked away. "The Venture?"

"Yes sir, with a capital V. We think it might have been some stroke of business he pulled off just before the war. He'd lost a deal of money, but after that everything was fine."

"I'm afraid I can't help you, Chris. I know nothing about any Venture. That's old stuff. Does it matter?"

"Well, it might help me with the family history I'd like to do someday. With classes over for the summer, I thought I might get started, maybe go through the stuff in Grandpa's chest."

"Chest? What chest?"

"The sea chest with all Grandpa's papers. It came to us when he died, and it's been sitting in the library ever since. Pa meant to sort it out but never did."

"Chris, I should have been told about that chest. Old Biggs was Caleb Harmony's executor, but Biggs left it to me to go through my father's personal effects."

"Ma told you about it at the time. You shrugged it off, said you were busy."

"I was, and then I guess it slipped my mind. I'd like to have a look at it."

"I'll tell Ma, sir. Maybe when you come next Sunday."

"To really look into it, I'd need to take possession." He was fingering a gold penknife; something was up.

"Well sir, I'd kind of like to hold on to it. For the family history, you know. I really mean to write it."

"Chris, this family doesn't need a scribbler; we're doers. Forget the history. Don't look back—that's dead. Always look ahead!"

"But Uncle Jake, the Harmonys have been everywhere, done everything. It's a roaring good story, it's prime. If it isn't recorded, it'll soon be forgotten. That's where I come in. I'll make sure the Harmony name lives on. Because you're heroes, all of you, and you ought to be remembered!" (This was laying it on pretty thick, but with Jake you just about had to.)

"Chris, life at sea isn't all glorious adventure. It's hard, it can twist your gut. It's ugly sometimes, and sometimes just plain boring."

"Then tell me, Uncle Jake. I'll put that in, too."

"No you won't!" He slammed his fist hard on his desk. Papers flew; the *Falcon* hung crooked on the wall. Then, calmer: "For God's sake, Chris, don't mess with things you know nothing about."

"Well, sir, I still think you're all heroes. Even Rick. How is he, by the way?"

Asking about his younger son always put Uncle Jake off. Rick was a bit of a scamp, going off to dubious exploits at sea and then turning up when least expected, spouting tales of adventure and woe.

"How should I know, Chris? I'm only his father. He's been gone a year and a half without word. He could be drowned or in Timbuctoo."

A hint of regret? I couldn't tell. Then suddenly he eyed me cannily, spoke softly.

"You're a shrewd little bastard, aren't you? I hadn't realized."

I smiled. "Just curious, Uncle Jake. Rick is family. I like to keep up."

He rose quickly from his desk. "See you next Sunday, Chris. Dwight and I will be delighted."

We shook hands. He was barking orders at a clerk as I left.

When I got back to our brownstone on St. Mark's Place, Ma called my sister Sal and me into the sitting room. Sal was my twin, a brisk brunette with eyes of green agate. She and I shared everything, could often read each other's thoughts, which was sometimes fun and sometimes just a mite awkward, since there are things a fellow's sister doesn't need to know.

"I've been reading your father's diary," said Ma. In deep mourning, she stood tall and stark in a dress of lusterless black. "There are two entries you might find of interest, since they have to do with a 'Venture.' Here they are." She cleared her throat, read.

"16 October 1858. Another row with Jake over the Venture. He's not telling me enough. What have I got into? He assures me all is well, substantial Profits will result. How? From what? A Mistake from beginning to end, but I'm committed, it's too late to pull out."

She showed us the entry, paused to let us absorb it, then took back the diary, flipped through some pages, resumed.

"9 August 1859. Good Profit from the Venture; Jake has settled the Accounts. He promises even more Profits, but I insisted that I want my share now and won't be involved in any further Transactions. I'm out of it, thank the Merciful Lord, and will have no further Dealings with Jake."

Again, she showed us the entry and waited while we absorbed it.

"Your father was not a happy man. I had no idea. I'll inform you if I encounter any more entries that seem relevant."

With that, she left us. That was Ma's way: quiet, dignified, but when she spoke, you listened.

We pondered in silence for a moment, then I told Sal about my meeting with Uncle Jake.

"So Uncle Jake was in some 'Venture' with Pa, but now he won't admit it."

"Exactly."

"So he's a liar. And he wants to take possession of the chest." She scrunched up her features in a frown.

"Mr. Biggs asked him to sort out Grandpa's personal effects."

"Will Ma let him have it?"

"She might be glad to get rid of it."

The chest had been dumped on us when Grandpa died and had been sitting in a dark corner of the library ever since. Ma wanted to store it in the attic, but Pa clung to it, promising to sort through the contents, which of course he never did. In desperation Ma covered it with an old shawl and a burnt china mug, and we all forgot about it; it had hunkered down in the shadows.

"Look," said Sal, "you'll need it for that family history you've been threatening to write."

"That's what I told Uncle Jake, but he said forget about it, always look ahead, never back. Grandpa Harmony told me once that I was much too young for such a hefty undertaking, and Pa just plain damped me down, ordering me to stick to my studies."

"So nobody in the family wants you to write that history. Yet it's a dandy story, it's keen."

"That's what I told Uncle Jake. We owe it to the family, the city, and the nation."

"Why doesn't he see it that way? And why does he want to get his paws on that chest?"

"There must be something in it he doesn't want us to know about."

"Then it's high time we had a look in there ourselves."

"Pa told me not to mess with it until I got my degree."

"Oh rats! We're going to have a look, right now!"

That said, she hustled me into the library, whisked off the scarf and the mug, and with my help, the hinges creaking, opened the musty old chest. Loose papers spilled out amid a smell of dried ink and decay.

2

"What do you make of it?" asked Sal.

Snatching up loose papers from the chest at random, we'd been reading in silence for at least twenty minutes.

"It's what in pidgin English is called a chow-chow," I explained, having picked up the term in my readings. "A mix of stuff, a muddle. Loose pages from journals and letters, bills of lading, lists of port expenses, ships' manifests. Grandpa must have tossed it all in the trunk and forgotten about it. But it's super. For a historian"—so I now termed myself—"a devilish hot smash of a find!"

"Look at this," said Sal, thrusting at me a sheet of paper yellowed with age.

Rec'd from brig Resolute, J. Hawkins, master, 1 hogshead fine French brandy adressed to Harmony & Biggs, New York, containing preserved remains of Noah Harmony, deseased of Panama fever, Chagres, 11 Sept. 1823, age 31 yrs, 5 mos., 3 days, recovered from sea by said brig off Barnegat Light, having presumably washed overbord from another vessel, identity unknown, and now duly delivered hear for Christian burial, God's will be done. Caleb Harmony, 16 Oct. 1823.

Sal looked perplexed. "So Great-Uncle Noah was shipped home in a hogshead of brandy that was lost at sea and then recovered and delivered as addressed?"

"I guess. Quite a postmortem adventure!"

"I thought he died fighting pirates in the Sunda Straits."

"So did I."

"Grandpa said his ship was becalmed, and suddenly thirty whatchamacallits—"

"Thirty proas."

"—Attacked from all sides. He died a hero fighting pirates."

"A pistol in one hand, a cutlass in the other."

"And not from some silly old yellow fever."

"Killed the pirate chief with his last breath, and was buried at sea with full honors."

"So do you believe it now, or not?"

"Well, Pa warned me more than once to take Grandpa's stories *cum grano salis.*"

"Please, no Latin."

"With a grain of salt."

"Grandpa lied?"

"Pa didn't quite say that. He said Grandpa liked to spin a good yarn."

Sal frowned. "You mean like those silly dime novels you used to read?"

"I outgrew them long ago. This is something else again."

"And these," she said, brandishing a loose page covered with a neat, tight hand. "Aren't these journal entries from when Grandpa was rounding Cape Horn? They aren't just a yarn too, are they?"

> *July 4. Terrible gale to westward; no thot of celebration. Mountinous seas, violent hale and snow skwalls. Strange hissing and singing sounds heard in the roar of the wind, abundant wild fowl, monstrous whales. One man overbord, reskew impossible; may the Good Lord receeve him in his Grace. Crew stedfast, passengers terrified. I prey to God we find good wether soon. Little progress. Lat. 56° 20' S., long. 65° 27' W.*

I glanced at the page she was holding. "No, those entries are solid, they're for real. He always said that rounding the cape was the toughest sailing he'd ever known."

"Snow and ice in July?"

"In the southern hemisphere it's winter when we have summer."

"Oh."

"That was early in his career; I can tell."

"How?"

"His handwriting is still quite legible. Later it became a god-awful scrawl."

My first job one summer had been as office boy at the Mariners' Bank, where Grandpa had become president. They hired me because I alone could decipher his script.

"But the stuff that really gets me," said Sal, "is Grandpa's letters to

Grandma about the China trade. This one, for instance."

> *When our ship rounded a bend in the river, I was thrilled to see a long line of vessels ankored side by side, perhaps a hundred of them, each flying its national flag. This is Whampoa, the port of Canton. Proceding upriver in a small boat, I marveled at the thik swarm of craft—clumsy-looking oceangoing junks with sharp prows painted with huge eyes to watch for the devils of the deep, river junks manned by near naked koolies pulling on long sweeps, and mandarin patrol boats with red sashes around the muzles of their cannon. As we approached the confined district outside the city where, by the grace of the Son of Heaven, forin devils are allowed to reside and trade, we picked our way thru a hord of sampans with barbers, juglers and storytellers drifting past us, and pedlers hawking bird cages, and wives cooking over open fires on the stern while hens and ducks in wikker baskets clucked and skwawked insessantly. It was a feast of life, my dear Sarah, a mix of sites, sounds and smells like I have never encountered in all my roavings on the far seven seas.*

Sal read it over twice. "Yes, that must have been a bang-up sight to see."

"There'll be more," I said. "We've just scratched the surface. But so far, nothing about any Venture, and nothing for Uncle Jake to get worked up about."

"That letter congratulating Grandpa on becoming president of the bank, what's that all about?" She showed me yet another loose paper.

> *Dear Caleb,*
>
> *Well, you old dog, you have survived storms and earthquakes and Chinamen and British men-o'-war to get yourself into the Chamber of Commerce, and now, to further dazzle the lubbers, you strut in clean cuffs and glossy patent leathers as the president of a bank. Congrats, old salt. Needless to say, I am devoured by envy, hence this hurried hodgepodge of a letter.*
>
> *Ah, Caleb, if you can holystone yourself, you sly Presbyterian, so can I. Gideon of old I shall no longer be. I shall trade my sea togs for finery, put on the sheen of Virtue, and tread its narrow Lane. You have sprigs, and sprigs of sprigs, as do I. For their sake—and our own—we*

must shed our naughty ways. Rechristened, I shall strut not a prince, but a king. Embrace me, fellow royal. Cleansed of our past, we

I put the letter down. "From some old pal of his, I guess. The rest of it is missing."

"He makes it sound like Grandpa had to become respectable. Wasn't he always?"

"Maybe not in the eyes of bluebloods. He smelled too much of the waterfront. Once he became a shipowner, that changed."

"I still don't get it. The whole letter, I mean."

"Neither do I: a *mysterium immensum.*"

"In English, please."

"A big mystery. But 'sprigs of sprigs,' that's us."

"Us?"

"His grandchildren."

"Oh. And in the letter of his to someone about supplies—a copy by a clerk, I suppose—why does he put 'rum' and 'hats' and 'soap' in quotation marks?"

"I hadn't noticed."

She showed me the letter; the first part was missing.

20 "rum" casks, 50 lbs lumber, 1 crate "hats," 3 boxes "soap." Daily exercise and song are highly recommended; an upturned kettle can serve as a drum. Also recommended is a familiar diet of rice, pepper, palm oil, potatoes, and corn. Beware of diseases of a febrile character and the flux. Allow substantial sums for gratuities, and at all times have on hand the two sets of papers. I wish you Godspeed; the prospects are bright.

—C. Harmony

I read it again, twice. "Yes, quote marks. But why?"

"It's like saying, 'I don't really mean these things; they stand for something else.'"

"They're code words?"

"Exactly," said Sal. "There was something he couldn't just say right out."

"But what?"

"We'll have to find out. Maybe this is what Jake's worried about."

"Maybe. And maybe you've been reading too many novels."

"Grandpa's papers are better than any novel. Misspellings and all, they're real, they're the Harmonys, they're *us.*"

That said, she scooped up more papers and resumed reading. I did, too, and started sorting them into piles. In time, I hoped, we'd gather together all the scattered pages of the letters and journals, and then organize them in chronological order. Meanwhile it was a rich, haphazard feast. We read until dinner, when Ma's entreaties pulled us away from the chest. After dinner we went back to it and read until bedtime.

"So?" said Sal finally, with a yawn.

"It's juicy, it's prime. But the more I read, the less I understand."

"Me, too. There's always something implied, something not spelled out."

"Fascinating. But let's not get carried away."

A ship with reefed sails and VENTURE on its bow, foundering in mountainous seas where whales broach and plunge, with sheets of gray water flying over it, its masts and decks coated with ice. Sinking in a squall, it becomes a junk with huge eyes on its prow, its cannon ringed with red sashes, while clucking hens strut on the deck. Nearby, rising silently out of a floating hogshead, Noah Harmony looms, wasted and delirious, his clothes stained with bloody black vomit, his skin a sickly yellow, as slowly, accusingly, he points the skinniest of fingers: Why do you disturb me? Why?

I woke up in a sweat.

3

"Pa, were you a cabin boy at fifteen?"

"No, at sixteen."

"A ship's master at twenty?"

"More like twenty-two. So long ago. Why do you ask?"

"Just wondering."

"You've been listening to Grandpa, haven't you? The so-called family motto: cabin boy at fifteen, ship's master at twenty."

"Well… yes."

"Don't worry about it, Chris. Not everyone is meant for the sea. I wasn't."

"But you went to sea for quite a spell, didn't you?"

"Six years. That was my youth, and I wouldn't trade it for anything. But then I'd had enough. I wanted to come ashore, snug down, get married. And I did."

"Uncle Jake didn't, though, did he?"

"He got married, but he didn't quit the sea. Not for a long, long time. It was in his blood."

"He sure is Go Ahead, isn't he? A real wide-awake, a hustler."

"Yes, Chris, he's all that and more."

"Like Grandpa."

"But Grandpa has a mellow side, too; Jake doesn't. Oh, Jake can be charming, all right, but at heart he's a mean, hard man. Keep smooth weather between you; you wouldn't want him for an enemy."

"No, sir."

"You wouldn't want that at all. And there's a difference between his side of the family and ours. They have adventures and tell tall tales, but don't believe everything they say. We live quieter; we have the burden of truth. Remember that, Chris. It's important."

"Yes, Pa. The burden of truth."

"Let that be your ballast, your anchor. In the long run it'll keep you safe."

Uncle Jake and Dwight came to dinner by carriage, which Ma considered just a bit flash, since we didn't keep one. They had a hint of pomade in their hair, and both sported gold cuff links and a diamond tiepin. Ma used our best dishes, a set of blue-and-white chinaware that Grandpa had brought back from Canton long ago. Jake and Dwight raved about Ma's roast turkey, which Jake carved with a flourish, eyes flashing, announcing, "The nearer the bone, the sweeter the meat!" They ate with gusto, pronouncing Ma's turnips and spuds delicious and her plum cake "confoundedly good." Ma's cooking was superb, but I thought their praise just a bit much. Throughout dinner, and afterward in the parlor as well, they regaled us with stories. Dwight told about running the Vicksburg batteries with Farragut and his fleet in '62, and Jake told how years before on the brig *Hunter,* bringing palm oil and ivory from the Guinea coast, he took command when the captain and mates were stricken with fever, and sold the cargo for a roaring good price in New York.

"You know how I never come down with fever, not in Africa or in the Americas either? I took the advice of a Spanish gent who'd been in those parts many a time: soak your feet in brandy, wear thick wool socks, avoid night air and the noonday sun. Other poor devils took sick, turned yellow, and wasted away, but I was in fine fettle."

Finally, he sent Dwight to fetch their carriage; a look passed between them. Then, to end the evening with a bang, he entertained us with a host of anecdotes about old merchants and skippers he had known. This was Uncle Jake at his best. He had us laughing one minute, and shocked or all but in tears the next. Yet as he talked, he kept fingering his gold penknife, which struck me as odd. When he launched into yet another yarn about a sailmaker who married three ladies of property—albeit one at a time—and had even Ma, who was kind of straitlaced, laughing to the point of tears, Sal slipped quietly out of the room. Moments later we heard her shout, "Chris, they're stealing the chest!"

I was on my feet in a flash. Darting into the hallway, I found Dwight and Uncle Jake's black coachman Luke lugging Grandpa's heavy chest toward the open front door, while Sal shouted and protested. Making a flying leap, I landed on the chest, which under my weight crashed to the floor. Luke stepped back in astonishment, but as Sal and I yelled "Thief!" at the top of our lungs, Dwight's look of surprise changed to rage. Lunging, he pummeled me with his fists. I tried to hit back, couldn't, so I huddled up and fended off his punches as best I could, while still yelling "Thief! Thief! Thief!" By the time our cries brought Ma and Uncle Jake from the parlor, and the cook and the maid from the kitchen, my face was bloodied-up and pretty much a mess.

"Stop it, Dwight!" yelled Jake.

Dwight stepped back, breathing hard, scowling.

"Thief!" I cried, pointing at Dwight. I was sitting crumpled on the floor, one eye shut, nose bleeding.

"Sal," said Ma, "fetch a wet towel and help your brother stop the bleeding. Annie and Meg, get back to the kitchen. Dwight and Jacob, what's this all about?"

The servants left. Dwight started to speak, but his father cut him off.

"Martha, I was only taking what's rightfully mine; I didn't think you'd care. But Dwight's too free with his fists; I'll deal with him later."

"Jacob, that chest isn't yours."

"I'd be doing you a favor to take it off your hands. What do you want with all those old papers?"

"More to the point, Jacob, what do *you* want with them?"

"Just a matter of winding up some loose ends from Pa's estate. Dull legal stuff. Those papers may or may not be relevant."

Ma eyed him something fierce. "The chest stays here. Put it back where you found it."

Jake's features tightened, but at a nod from him Dwight and the coachman lugged the chest back into the library.

"And now, Jacob, you and your minions can leave." She said "minions" with a sting of contempt.

"That chest is mine, Martha, and I mean to have it."

"Jacob, you are not a gentleman."

"Martha, I never said I was. But thanks for the dinner. I hope you'll make it into half mourning soon; Mark would approve. When you do, I'll welcome you back to the land of the living."

Preceded by his "minions," he flashed a sour smile and left.

Sal came with a wet towel and dabbed my face; I was surprised by the splotches of blood on the towel: roses, a whole bouquet. Then she ran to a front window, looked out.

"They're going," she reported. "They've gone."

"Did they put the chest back exactly where they found it?" asked Ma.

Sal ran to the library, looked. "Yes, Ma, they did."

"And that's where it shall stay. Christopher, I advise you to take up boxing, I don't think Dwight is done with you. As for the chest, the two of you must go on searching it. Jacob's worried about something; find out what it is."

"Yes, Ma," we chorused.

"Sal, put some salve on your brother's wounds. Annie and Meg will see to the dishes. I'm going to bed. I suggest that you two do the same."

Of course we didn't.

"Dwight really hates you," said Sal, as she put on the salve.

My bleeding had stopped, but the sight in one eye was a blur. "I guess he does.

I didn't know it until today."

"Me neither."

"But why? I've never done him hurt."

"He's jealous, because you were Grandpa's favorite."

"I wasn't! He liked all of us."

"Dwight was the oldest, biggest, strongest, and fastest, and we all knew it, but Grandpa liked you best."

"Why?"

"You were the youngest of the boys, not as big and strong as the others. You had a wonderful smile, an even temper, and you loved to hear his stories."

"We all did."

"Yes, but as Dwight got older, he got bored with them, he fidgeted. He didn't want to hear any more about Grandpa's adventures; he wanted to get out and have adventures of his own."

"He did. Look at all he went through in the war."

"But he's still jealous. Take Ma's advice, learn to box. I'd love to see you punch him in the face."

"So would I."

"Chris, you're a hero. The way you jumped right on that chest!"

"I feel like mush."

"You're a hero."

"And I've never been in a war."

"You're in one now!"

4

"Head down, Harmony, head down; you're begging for a punch. That's better. Elbows close in together, to protect your chest and gut. Now, jab with the left, then follow with the right. Jab—jab harder, *harder!* Remember, you're out to do damage. Think of your sparring partner as your worst enemy, and act accordingly. That goes for you, too, Hunter; live up to your name. That's better, both of you—jab hard! Duck, Harmony, duck! He's out to land one, duck! Now both of you, footwork—it's like a dance. Keep moving, don't stand still. That's it, good! Feint a bit, both of you; don't telegraph your punches. Head down, Hunter. Harmony's developing a mean left hook, watch out. Hey, hey, that's it, guys, mix it up! Wow, what a wallop! Time, time, you two, break it up. Hunter, he really bashed you. No one's a boxer until he's been bloodied up a bit. You today, Harmony tomorrow. Harmony, you're not in this just for the sport of it; you've something in mind. So be it, we may yet make a boxer of you. Hunter, here's a rag. Stop that bleeding; you're messing up my gym. Congrats, you two. Bloody Monday it is!"

"Venture… Venture…" Professor Stevenson pursed his lips, tapped his fingers on his desk, and pondered. "No, Mr. Harmony, that word doesn't pluck the strings of memory. Or does it? Perhaps the faintest resonance, but I can't place it. I second your mother's surmise: your father was probably involved in some kind of commercial enterprise that prospered. *Fortunatus mercator!* In this city it's only professors who remain invincibly impoverished, toiling to live, living but to toil. Does this Venture business really matter?"

"It bothers me a bit, sir. There's something I should know, but don't."

"The fate of all researchers. Probe, Mr. Harmony, probe."

Tie askew, Professor Stevenson peered at me through wire-rimmed glasses, his pink face framed by silver-gray muttonchops. We were in his office at the university, its walls covered with big maps of North

America at various dates, and framed replicas of old documents in several languages.

"Yes, Mr. Harmony, delve into that chest. It sounds like the richest of troves."

"You think my project of a family history is valid?"

"Absolutely! Who hasn't heard of Caleb Harmony? Even me, in my musty little scholarly den. His funeral was well attended, was it not?"

"I'll say! Half of South Street came: shipowners and builders and other merchants, captains and able seamen, and sailmakers and riggers and carpenters, as well as high muckamucks from the Mariners' Bank, and even some people from the Custom House. Every countinghouse on South Street had its flag at half- mast, and many of the ships in the harbor as well. He'd been hugely successful at sea and was known to everyone on or near the waterfront for decades."

"So there you are. If you have access to his papers, you're cut out for the job. Maritime history is an engrossing field of study, though not mine own. This will be more than a family history. It will sketch out a whole phase of this nation's recent past: the age of sail, now doomed—*tempora mutantur*—by the advent of steam. Make it the center of your life."

"I'm not too young for the job?"

"Of course you are, dear youth. But you're not going to write it now, while still an undergraduate. You're going to start accumulating sources, and that can take years. But it will give your life a focus, a purpose. *Labor omnia vincit.*"

"Sir?" My Latin had limits; I couldn't fake it any more.

"Mr. Harmony, we expect all our students to have Latin."

"Yes, sir. But you see, sir, I've been concentrating on your field, history, so my Latin is just a bit rusty."

"Hmm, yes, alas. I said, 'Work conquers all.'"

"Yes, sir. Aptly put. Quite so."

"Now about another matter, Mr. Harmony: did I hear you say earlier that over the summer you've taken up boxing?"

"Yes, sir. I've just started. With Tiger Wilson, one of the best. I have yet to get the hang of it, though I did land a punch yesterday. A whacking good one, too."

"Boxing? Whatever for?"

"I may need it, sir. I told you about my cousin, Dwight."

"Hmm, yes. Well, all right. *Mens sana in corpore sano*, and all that. It can balance out your studies, I suppose."

"It's good exercise, sir. Unless you have a better suggestion. What do you do, sir, when you feel like exercising?"

"I lie down until the feeling goes away."

"So what did he say?"

Sal and I were sitting on the library floor, sorting out the papers in the chest.

"*Tempora mutantur.*"

"Oh, come on, Chris. Don't start in with your Latin."

"That's what he said: 'Times change.' The age of sail is giving way to the age of steam. A family history will tell the story of sail, with Grandpa Harmony smack in the middle of it. A long-term project. I should make it my *sine qua non.*"

"Come on."

"The center of my life."

"Is his opinion important?"

"You bet! He's a professional historian, and highly respected. A real old-style scholar, more into the past than the present. A bit absent-minded, he's usually got a button dangling, misplaces his specs. The students love him. They call him Old Muttonchops."

"He sounds a bit fusty and musty."

"Not if you like history. I'm taking another of his courses this fall. Once classes resume, I'll have less time for the chest."

"Then I'll keep at it alone."

"You won't have time either. The summer's almost over. With Ma in mourning, we're sure not going anywhere, but she says you can have gentlemen callers."

"I know. She wants to marry me off."

"You're only twenty."

"She got married at eighteen."

"So who'll be calling? The usual collection of louts and freaks?"

"They aren't all freaks."

"They are."

"So who am I supposed to see, Mr. Finicky?"

"Dan Hunter."

"What's that?"

"My sparring partner at the gym. I walloped him a good one a week ago, and yesterday he walloped me back."

"A rich and intense friendship."

"Well, we're chums. He's intelligent and not bad looking. So shall I bring him around?"

"All right, bring him around. And now that we've got my life squared away, what about yours? Will you be calling on Little Miss Muffet?"

"Moffat. No, I doubt it."

"A bit treacly, that one. Sarah Throgwhistle?"

"Throgmorton. No, not her, either."

"Good! In dancing class she maimed her partner's feet. So who *will* you be dazzling this season? Miss Twinkletoes Moore, I suspect."

"What have you got against her?"

"Nothing at all. She's the *crème* of the *crème.* A gumdrop. A honey crisp."

"Look, *tempus fugit.* Let's get back to Grandpa's chest."

"All right, but no more Latin."

"Labor omnia vincit."

A cushion smacked my face.

As we left the harbor with our cargo of spices, coffee, arrack and sandalwood, the consul, who had feested the ships officers the nite before, wished us Godspeed and bade us a fond farewell. To catch the tide, we set sail in the evening to a lite breeze from the land. A full moon had just rizen above the mountains and shed its silvery lite upon the bay. Small craft hawled us seaward, the native rowers singing all together as they rowed, dipping their oars into likwid silver, then raising them all together to rain drops of tiny diamonds into the fosforessent sea. It was, my dear Sarah, the most magical scene I have ever witnessed in all my roavings, and has made of me, a plain Yankee sailor, a poet. Even the sharks that hawnt those waters joined in, darting here and there, leaving streeks in their wake like flashes of white forked litening. It was pure enchantment.

*****

5 April 1846

Dear Pa,

We just spoak the brig Pluto bound for New York off the Carolinas, so I am sending you this letter. I have thot long and hard about what you toald me just before I left. Since you and Biggs have broak up your partnership and your lawnching Harmony & Sons, Mark and I are honnored to be your partners. But—doant make Mark your agent, he is too nicey neet, too dainty. Let him run the chandlery. After this trip I will come home and kwit the sea and be your agent. I can handel the ruff ones like Captain Williams and the slik ones like Martinez, I can handel them all. This business takes a strong gut and I got it.

When I lode cargo in Havana I will have a look at Martinez & Co. and da Cunha and the lot. It cant hurt, we need sownd contacts there. I will see the consul too. They say he is all rite—some are, some arnt.

Pa you old devil it will be a privelege to work with you. Give my best to Ma and Mark but doant make him your agent. The less he knows the better. I doant know what he knows, maybe lots, maybe nothing. Write me care of Martinez & Co., Havana. Things are going grate, we will prosper fine. Your loving son, Jake

"Grandpa Harmony really was a poet, wasn't he?" said Sal. "That description of the harbor at night."

"Yes, it really grabs you."

"Where do you suppose that was?"

"Somewhere in the East Indies. That was way back."

"How can you tell?"

"His handwriting is still quite legible."

"And Uncle Jake's letter—he can't spell at all."

"It's funny, he had more education than Grandpa—not a lot, but more—yet Grandpa's spelling is better, and his letters are a sight more fun to read. Grandpa saw things, heard things, described them."

"But they were keeping something from Pa, weren't they?"

"Grandpa and Uncle Jake? Maybe."

"Jake says, 'The less he knows, the better.'"

"Hmm, yes. Another mystery."

"I'll bet it all ties in together—Havana and this Captain Williams and Martinez and da Cunha."

"You've been reading novels again."

"It means something, but we don't know what."

"It could mean anything."

"Something dark. Something sinister."

5

Fall came; classes resumed; I had less time for the chest. Meanwhile our war with Uncle Jake and Dwight made for awkward Sabbaths, since we all worshipped at the same church, First Presbyterian, that spanking big Gothic stone structure on the Fifth Avenue at Twelfth Street, with the huge square tower that soared. Their pew was well up front, and ours about halfway back, so we didn't sit together, but we were bound to meet in the aisle or outside the church after service. When we did, they nodded civilly to us, while Ma gave them the barest scrap of acknowledgment; you could have sliced the frost with a knife. "Jacob is not a gentleman," Ma remarked to Sal and me more than once; for her, there was nothing more to be said. Then, one day, a letter came.

Dear Aunt Martha,

As soon as I got home and got the usual hullabaloo with Pa and Dwight out of the way, I learned about your loss. I was shocked. Uncle Mark was a good and decent man, wise, kind, and understanding. I'll miss him terribly. I've always been more cozy with your branch of the family than my own. You folks are so—well, <u>livable</u>. My side of the family have an edge to them, they're pushy and loud, so Go Ahead it hurts. I hope to come see you soon. I have presents for you all and tales to tell. I've been everywhere, done everything and more or less survived. God bless you all!

Your scapegrace loving nephew, Rick

Ma showed us the note. "He hasn't changed one bit!"

"I want to hear his tales," said Sal. "We can invite him to dinner, can't we? Please, Ma, he's family. That's okay, even in mourning."

"And *I* want to know if he's heard about the chest," I put in. "I'd like to know his reaction."

"Of course, we'll invite him to dinner," said Ma. "He's a sweet boy, though a bit wild and impulsive. Dear Mark wouldn't begrudge us a little fun. He was always fond of Rick."

So she invited him to Sunday dinner. Him alone, of course. Which was fine by Sal and me, since it would cut into the soupy gloom that had settled over the brownstone ever since Pa's sudden death from a heart attack—the same gloom that had gripped us once before, when my brother Nathan died in the war.

"Haloo, Aunt Martha! Haloo, cousins Sal and Chris! Here's the black sheep, back from his latest tussle with the deep, frisky as a flea, as full of deviltry and pluck as ever!"

Lean and wiry, he came in white duck trousers, a check shirt open at the neck, a blue jacket, and a straw hat—the very image of Jack Tar spruced up for a spree on shore. His face was bronze from the sun, his eyes bright, his curly black hair untamed by any comb.

Hearty greetings, kisses and hugs all around. A sober moment, while he repeated his condolences to Ma, then a quick shift to quips and jokes, he wasn't one to linger into grief. With a flourish he handed out gifts: a carved sandalwood box for Ma, a silk fan from Paris for Sal, and a piece of black coral from Key West for me; we were dazzled.

Then he regaled us with a slew of wild stories: flying fish that landed on the deck; huge icebergs drifting past his ship and flashing green and blue and silver in the sun; and how in Constantinople a Greek skipper, a pal of his, had rescued a captive Christian lady from a harem by helping her descend from a window at night by a silk ladder, so he could smuggle her away to safety at sea.

"Now Rick," said Ma, "that harem tale is a bit too tall for me to swallow."

"It's as true as Holy Writ, Aunt Martha. In those parts, strange and wondrous things can happen!"

He then demonstrated the dozen or more knots he could tie, danced a hornpipe while Ma was in the kitchen with the cook, and when he learned of my boxing lessons, proposed to spar with me in a cousinly way.

"C'mon, Chris. I learned to box while in jail in Marseilles, where I'd landed after a bit of a row with my skipper, but that's another story. C'mon, up with the mitts!"

I clenched my fists, assumed a boxer's stance.

"Don't you two dare—I forbid it!" Ma announced, as she came

back from the kitchen. It was, after all, the Sabbath, and we were in that holy of holies, the parlor.

Back in the parlor after dinner, when Rick took a breather from his yarns, we told him about Grandpa's chest. He was shocked.

"They actually tried to steal it?"

"Yes, Rick, they did," said Ma. "While your pa sat right here in the parlor, distracting us with a bunch of stories—good stories, but not nearly as wild and outrageous as your own."

"Wow! That means they're flat out desperate. There's something in that chest they don't want you to find."

"But what?" I asked. "We're more than halfway through it, but still don't have a clue."

"Loose papers of all kinds," added Sal. "Letters and journals and lists of supplies for ships. Prime stuff, a lot of it, but nothing to get them all fired up."

"Let me help," said Rick. "I've been at sea, you haven't. Maybe I'll spot something you've missed."

I leaped at the idea. "Bully! When can you start?"

"Now!"

"No you don't," said Ma. "It's the Lord's Day. No time to go poking about in old chests."

"Tomorrow, then," said Rick.

"Tomorrow," I agreed. "I've classes all morning, but I'll be home by three."

"This is capital," said Rick. "The Skipper and Dwight have called me a ne'er-do-well, a scalawag, a black sheep, and a sight of things not to be repeated in a parlor. I'd love to foul their anchor!"

"Another thing, Rick," said Sal. "In Pa's desk we found a diary. In the last entry he thanks the Lord for having survived bad times and rebuilt his fortune. He ends with the words, 'In spite of earlier doubts and fierce misgivings, thank God for the Venture!' We have no idea what venture he's talking about. Does that mean anything to you?"

Rick thought a moment. "The only Venture I ever heard of was a racing yacht that won a lot of prizes in the fifties. For a while it was the talk of the town."

"So that's it," I said, "a yacht!" Because Pa capitalized so many words, it hadn't occurred to me that "Venture" might be the name of a vessel. "But Pa didn't own it, did he?"

"Not back then; it belonged to some members of the Yacht Club.

But after that it dropped out of sight. I think they sold it. But wait a minute, there's a print of it on the wall in the Skipper's office: a real beauty of a ship, built for speed. So at some point Pa must have been at least part owner."

"Rick," I said, "in that very office I asked Uncle Jake about it, and he said he knew nothing about any 'Venture.' Yet right there, maybe four feet away, there must have been a picture of the yacht!"

"Now I'm really curious," said Rick. "I'll check the records at the Custom House. They'll give the names of everyone who's ever owned the yacht, and when. Hey, you folks have given me a whale of a task. This could be great fun!"

Finally he got up to leave.

"Rick," said Ma, "if things ever get too hot at home, you've always got a berth right here. You can have Nathan's room."

Rick choked up. "Thanks, Aunt Martha. That means a lot. Thanks."

I saw him to the door.

"Okay, Chris, I'll poke about tomorrow and come by in the afternoon to give you a report." Then he lowered his voice. "By the way, mate, how old are you?"

"Almost twenty-one."

"And still a virgin?"

I blushed.

"We'll have to work on that. For now, take this. I got it in Havre. It should bring you luck."

He pressed a small packet into my palm, winked, and left. The packet contained a French Secret, a thin-skinned sheath that on other occasions he'd assured me made possible the most rambustious pleasures without any risk of the pox. That night I had some pretty wild fantasies.

6

Following chapel, Monday morning I had classes in Modern History, Logic, Belles Lettres, and Moral Philosophy, this last a heavy course required of all seniors. When I got home at three, Sal was in the library already, and Rick came a few minutes later. Straight off he announced the results of his trip to the Custom House.

"The schooner *Venture*, 180 tons, was sold to Jonathan Biggs on March 28, 1858, and was sold by him to Jacob Harmony on June 17, 1858; no subsequent record to date."

"What does that mean?" I asked.

"Jonathan Biggs is the son of Grandpa Harmony's old partner, Hiram Biggs. For some reason, Pa didn't want his purchase of the *Venture* to be known, so he had Jonathan Biggs acquire it first, then sell it to him later."

"I don't understand," said Sal. "Wouldn't both sales be reported?"
"They'd be recorded at the Custom House, but chances are that only the first sale, ending the yacht's career as a racer, would get reported in the papers. So Pa got the *Venture* on the sly. Maybe his brother was part owner, but he's not listed in the records."

For me, it was still a mystery. "But they never raced it, did they?"

"Never, or we'd have heard."

"So what did they want with one of the fastest schooners afloat?"

"That's what I'd like to know. And what's become of it since?"

"Yet your pa has a print of it right there on the wall in his office."

"Not any more, he doesn't. It's gone; I checked."

"He took it down?"

"Of course. Probably right after you came nosing around."

"Why did he put it up in the first place," asked Sal, "if he doesn't want his ownership known?"

"Maybe habit, maybe pride. It was quite an acquisition. And he probably figured no one would ever come sniffing around. I'll look into it some more. Now let's get at that chest."

Over the summer Sal and I had sorted many letters, journals, ships' manifests, and bills of lading into separate piles, so Rick started going through the piles, while the two of us resumed sorting out the few loose papers still in the chest. No tall tales today, Rick was all business.

"No, no, this isn't a bill of lading, it goes with the manifests… Another letter from Canton. Great stuff; I'll read it later… This one is from Hiram Biggs; let's put all those together… Copies of letters to a Captain Matthews of the schooner *Charity.* What was that all about?… The brig *Fearless,* the schooner *Mary D…* A letter from Pa to Grandpa—the less your pa knows, the better. Hmm… More crates of soap; I wonder why… Lots of stuff for fast schooners, hmm… Canton, Guayaquil, Valparaiso—the old boy sure did get around… Hey, this goes with that. Now we've got the whole letter. Listen!"

He read us a letter that I recognized; we'd seen the last part, but not the first.

"Dear Capt. Matthews, A few more words before you sail. I have no worries about officials here; that has all been seen to. The consul in Havana is not to be relied on; Señor Martinez will advise you. Given your experience, I have no need to caution you about the voyage going and returning. Many merchants here are active in the trade, but most of them are callous in the extreme. As a God-fearing man, I cannot be, so I urge you to make ample provision for the comfort of the passengers, without, of course, compromising the security required on such a voyage. Interference at either end is possible; you know what to do. If you have any last-minute requests, please contact my son Jacob at our South Street office; he acts as my agent. By now you should have on board 20 'rum' casks, 50 lbs lumber, 1 crate 'hats,' 3 boxes 'soap.' Daily exercise and song are highly recommended; an upturned kettle can serve as a drum. Also recommended is a familiar diet of rice, pepper, palm oil, potatoes, and corn. Beware of diseases of a febrile character and the flux. Allow substantial sums for gratuities, and at all times have on hand the two sets of papers. I wish you Godspeed; the prospects are bright. —C. Harmony."

"That's the one with words in quote marks," said Sal. "We thought it odd."

I nodded. "Yes, like a code."

"Rum… hats… soap…" mused Rick. "That's more rum than you need for a run to Havana. And why 'hats'? And all this 'soap'? And lumber? A familiar diet with palm oil—familiar for whom? And why two sets of papers?"

He pondered a moment, then tensed.

"Holy God! It's beginning to make sense. I hope I'm wrong; I may be. I don't like it. I don't like it at all."

"Don't like *what?*" Sal and I chorused.

"I can't say till I'm sure. Is old Biggs alive—Grandpa Harmony's former partner?"

"I think so," I said. "I haven't heard otherwise. Why?"

"I've got to see him, and maybe some other people, too. Did Grandpa have a confidential clerk?"

"I don't know."

"I'll ask around. I need to see him, too. You kids have no idea what we're getting into."

"Tell us!" said Sal.

"Later, if I'm right. Then you'll know soon enough, and wish you didn't. But if I'm wrong, the less said the better."

He grabbed his sailor's cap and was off like a shot.

He was back the next day, going through the chest with Sal, even before I returned from classes.

"I hit a head wind, I'm stymied," he announced. "The confidential clerk is dead. And when I tried to see Hiram Biggs, his daughter-in-law informed me that he's old and feeble, doesn't see anyone. She all but slammed the door in my face."

"Seeing him is important?" I asked.

"It's crucial."

"Sal, hasn't Peter Biggs been calling on you?"

"He's taking me on a drive in the Park tomorrow."

"He's Hiram Biggs's grandson, isn't he?"

"I think so."

"And lives with him and his parents in their brownstone?"

"So far as I know. I've never been there."

"Is he sweet on you?"

"What a way to put it!"

"Well, is he?"

"Sort of. He comes around a lot."

"There's our solution, Rick. Sal will use her wiles on the grandson and get you in to see the old boy himself."

"Sal," said Rick, "that would be smashing."

"Look, you two, what am I supposed to do?"

"Charm him," I said. "Bat your eyelashes, smile winsomely, then pout, then smile again. Girls do it all the time." Which was asking a lot of Sal, whose manner had an edge to it; demure she wasn't.

Her green eyes sliced me with a glance. "What do you know about girls?"

"Enough. But maybe you *can't* do it. Maybe you just don't have the knack."

"We'll see about that. As long as it's for a good cause."

"A crackajack!" said Rick.

Her jaw set. "I'll wrap him around my pinkie."

She did. After the drive in the Park, she informed us that Peter Biggs would be expecting Rick and me at four on Thursday at the brownstone.

"He says his pa will be at his South Street office, his ma has some meeting at her church, and the maid will be out on errands. But get there at four on the dot. I can't be there; I have another engagement."

"Another smitten swain?"

She stepped on my toes, hard.

"Ouch! Watch out, Rick. She's a terror!"

"Sal, this is capital. Thanks a lot."

"How does Peter feel about it?" I asked, rubbing my foot.

"Wobbly," she said, "but he'll do it. He'll do it for me."

Rick and I got there on the dot. It was a big brownstone with a high stoop on East Twenty-second Street near Madison Avenue. Peter Biggs met us at the door, a tall young man, kind of scrawny, with neatly combed sandy hair. A bit slack for Sal, I thought: no fire, no grit. Introductions followed.

"This is going to be ticklish. Grandfather is very frail, and not used to having visitors. His mind isn't clear. He has good days and bad ones; it's pretty chancy. But Sal says you're doing an important history, and he'll be in it."

"He sure will," said Rick, with a trace of a smile. "We'll try not to rattle him."

"I'll take you up. You'll have less than an hour. You've got to be gone before anyone gets back. I could never explain your seeing him."

He led us up the stairs to a bedroom in back, knocked softly on the door.

"Grandfather? Grandfather, it's Peter. Can I come in?"

A murmur from behind the door.

"Wait here," Peter whispered. "I'll try to prepare him."

He went in, leaving the door ajar. I cast my eyes about the hallway, noticed fine carpeting, fancy lamps, a window of stained glass admitting shafts of multicolored light. South Street had been good to the Biggses. Then Peter motioned us in.

We found a shrunken old man wrapped in shawls and slumped in an armchair, his jaw quavery, who stared vacantly with dull gray eyes.

"Grandfather, these are the gentlemen I told you about: Rick and Chris Harmony. They're cousins, and grandsons of your old partner Caleb Harmony. They'd like to talk to you about the book they're doing."

"Caleb Harmony…" The old man looked puzzled, probed his memory. A flicker of recognition; he smiled. "Yes, I knew Caleb."

"You owned a lot of ships, didn't you, sir?" asked Rick.

"Oh my yes, lots of ships." His voice was soft and dreamy.

"They went to distant ports—Canton, Valparaiso, Rio, Havana…"

"Oh yes, we did business everywhere. Caleb was very Go Ahead. Cabin boy at fifteen, ship's master at twenty. Later, a king on 'Change." The old man was perking up; he seemed less vague.

"You did business with Brazil and Cuba, didn't you?" asked Rick.

"Did business everywhere. Hardly a port in the world we didn't reach."

"But often Brazil and Cuba. A special trade with them, was it not?"

"Oh yes. Coffee from Brazil, sugar and hides from Cuba."

"Nothing else from Cuba? Or to it?"

"Segars from Cuba. Silks and velvets to it, furniture, machinery, shoes. Oh, everything." A smile of satisfaction.

"Nothing else?"

"Everything."

"Your agent in Cuba, wasn't it a Señor Martinez?"

"Lots of agents. Can't remember them all."

"You and Caleb owned many ships, did you not? The brig *Fearless*?"

"Maybe. Can't remember."

"The schooner *Mary D.*?"

A puzzled look, then a frown. "No. No *Mary D.*"

"The schooner *Sea Eagle*? The schooner *Charity*, Captain Matthews, master? With rum and hats and soap?"

The old man stiffened; his eyes flashed. "No! No!"

"Please stop," said Peter Biggs. "You're upsetting him."

"Crates and crates of soap! Why, Mr. Biggs, why?"

"Leave me alone!" yelled the old man. "Go away! Go!"

"We'd better leave," said Peter Biggs. "You've excited him."

I tugged at Rick's sleeve. "C'mon, let's go."

"Lots of soap, Mr. Biggs. *Why? Why? Why?"*

The old man was twisting in his chair and screaming. Peter Biggs and I grabbed Rick and all but dragged him to the door.

Now Peter Biggs himself was in a fit. "Why did you do that? If he keeps screaming, there'll be hell to pay!"

We were hurrying down the stairs, with the old man's screams echoing behind us.

"I had to," said Rick.

"Please go," said Peter Biggs at the front door.

"I'm sorry," I said lamely.

"I hadn't bargained for this. Please go!"

We left; the door slammed shut behind us.

"Why did you do it?" I asked, as we went down the stoop. "He's a feeble old man. You upset him, and we didn't learn a thing."

"We learned plenty."

"What?"

"Everything."

"Then tell me!"

"Not here. Sal has got to hear it, too. We learned everything, and it's as bad as I feared. It's awful. Stupendously awful."

When we got home, we found Sal in the library. Rick shut the door, lowered his voice.

"We just saw old Biggs, and when I mentioned crates of soap, he panicked and ordered us out."

"Rick," I said, "you badgered him. It was cruel."

"I did what I had to do. This settles it. Now I'm certain."

"Certain of what?" asked Sal.

"Of what this is all about—the chest, the *Venture*, everything. Grandpa Harmony and my pa, and Biggs and maybe your pa, too, were in this thing together. Not all of the time, but some of the time, mixed in with their other operations. They did it a lot."

"Did what?" Sal and I demanded.

"They were slavers."

7

"They weren't!" Sal was yelling, even before I could absorb what Rick had said. "Not Pa and Grandpa Harmony, they couldn't be, they weren't!"

"Rick, are you saying that our family brought slaves over from Africa?"

"Exactly."

"But wasn't it illegal?"

"Of course, but they did it anyway, and so did lots of others. A great way to make money."

"They brought them to this country?"

"Maybe, maybe not. They probably brought them to Brazil, until the government there cracked down, and they certainly brought them to Cuba, where there's a slave market to this day."

"I don't believe it," said Sal. "Prove it!"

"I've talked to some old salts on the waterfront," said Rick. "They make no bones about having put in a stint on a slaver, say almost everyone did it at one time or another. It was hardly a secret."

I was amazed. "Right here? In New York?"

"Here above all, up until the start of the war."

"That doesn't mean *our* family did it," argued Sal. "You haven't proved a thing!"

"Old Biggs was Grandpa's partner. When I brought all this up, he was terrified."

"Could he be prosecuted?" I asked.

"No, no one's prosecuting slavers now for what they did way back. But he doesn't want a tarnished reputation. He wants to die like Grandpa, a respected South Street merchant, mourned by family and friends."

"Even if Biggs did it," said Sal, "that doesn't mean Grandpa did."

"Grandpa's letter to Captain Matthews makes it clear. It mentions rum, lumber, hats, and soap, with all but lumber in quote marks. That's how the stuff was labeled. The so-called 'rum' casks really contained water—lots of it, for hundreds of slaves. The crate marked 'hats' probably contained an unassembled boiler or stove for cooking tons of food. The lumber was for building a sleeping platform tween decks for the slaves, and the boxes marked 'soap' must have contained shackles and chains, since the slaves would be fettered the whole trip over, even when they slept."

I felt sick.

"I don't believe it, I don't!" insisted Sal.

"The 'gratuities' mentioned in the letter were bribes to customs officials so they'd clear the ship for sailing. The two sets of papers meant that the ship would leave under the American flag with one name, then on the African coast change its name and become a slaver under another flag, maybe Spanish or Brazilian. The only real risk was that the British or American navy might catch them after they'd taken on slaves. Some slavers got caught; most didn't."

"What about the *Venture*?" I asked.

"A racing yacht, swift enough to outrun the fastest cruisers, steam or sail. Fast schooners were especially in demand."

"What's become of it?"

"Who knows? Under another name, it may be operating still. Maybe the Skipper owns it, maybe not."

"*Our* pa can't have done this!" Sal protested.

"Him I'm not sure about. The *Venture* belonged to my pa for sure, but your pa was his partner."

"Pa didn't know!" she insisted. "They kept it from him. Uncle Jake said in a letter, 'The less he knows, the better.'"

"It's hard to believe he wasn't wise to what his brother was up to. After that crash in '57 he needed money, and here was a sure-fire way to get it. Slaves that cost fifty dollars a head on the Guinea Coast brought four to six hundred dollars over here: a tidy little profit."

"Still, he might not have known," I argued. "You haven't linked him to those other deals, only—maybe—to the *Venture.*"

"Agreed," said Rick. "Maybe he knew not to ask questions. Maybe. But I'll bet he knew about the Skipper and Grandpa. He had to; he was no fool."

"I still can't believe it," said Sal. "It was a dirty business!"

"Ah, but *they* didn't get dirty; they left that to others. They bought the ships, outfitted them, hired captain and crew, and got cozy with the customs people. They never saw the slaves marched on board in shackles, or lying side by side—hundreds of them—with only three feet of headroom. They didn't smell their unwashed bodies or their shit—pardon me, Sal—or face the risk of revolt, or dump overboard the corpses of those who didn't make it. They just pocketed the profits."

Sal was fighting back tears, and I just sat there, stunned. I had grown up during the war and idolized my brother Nathan, who had fought and died to save the Union and put an end forever to slavery, that abomination long since abolished in the North. The whole dirty business of slavery was in my mind confined to the South, a benighted land afflicted with a scorching climate and, until recently, lazy planters whose bullnecked overseers cracked whips over the backs of long-suffering slaves. The mere thought that anyone in the North—citizens of New York and maybe even my own family—had been in any way involved left me in a daze.

"So much for family pride," said Rick. "I'm disgusted and goddamned angry. Tonight I think I'll get drunk."

"Don't tell Ma," said Sal. "She couldn't bear it. Even if Pa wasn't directly involved, she just couldn't."

"Rick," I said, "I don't know if I can believe this. You're guessing about the *Venture,* and about that letter of Grandpa's, too. I need facts, solid facts." The historian in me was perking up.

"Look, those shackles had to come from somewhere. From ship chandleries, of course. Go to Harmony Brothers on South Street and talk to the salesmen. I bet they'll tell you plenty. And if that doesn't convince you, I'll introduce you to some of the old timers I talked to on the waterfront, maybe even some who shipped on a Harmony vessel. You'll learn a vast deal more than you want to."

After Rick left, Sal and I hardly spoke, not then and not at dinner; Ma wondered what had come over us. That night I had a jumble of dreams: rum casks and soap crates and shackles, and Pa and Grandpa, and the wind-filled sails of a schooner, and tween decks, a mass of black bodies packed tight.

"Pa, you didn't, did you?"

"Of course not."

"Rick says—"

"Don't worry about what Rick says. A likable scamp. Tells tall tales. Don't believe anything he says."

"He's pretty convincing."

"Lots of liars are."

"I don't think he's lying."

"Maybe just leaping to conclusions. Wild ones. Unfair ones."

"Maybe so. It was a dirty business, wasn't it?"

"Foul."

"That's why you couldn't."

"That's why I couldn't."

"You didn't even know."

"I didn't even know."

"Pa, remember how when I was little, in bed at night I'd moan, and you'd come, and I'd ask you for a 'be-sage' and a tickle?"

"I remember."

"That felt so good. I'd just drop off to sleep."

"I remember."

"I wish you could do it now."

"So do I."

"A 'be-sage' and a tickle."

"Yes."

"I'd just fall asleep."

"You'd just fall asleep."

"Good night, Pa."

"Good night, son. Sweet dreams."

"Hello, Chris, what can I do for you?" asked the salesman at the chandlery.

"Mr. Fowler, do you sell shackles?"

"Of course, a whole line."

"Can I see them?"

He led me past the barometers and anchors and oilskins over to a counter where several kinds of shackles were displayed: pairs of iron bracelets with a short chain linking them.

"They're needed on every ship," said Fowler. "Mutinies do happen. The leaders are put in irons."

"Back before the war, were they ever ordered in quantity? Hundreds, for instance?"

"Before my time, Chris. Let me fetch Stokes; he's been here for ages."

He went off and soon returned with an older man who had spent much of his youth at sea.

"Good morning, Master Chris. So you want to know about shackles?"

"Yes, Mr. Stokes. For a history class of mine. I guess you used to get some pretty big orders."

"In the old days, six hundred or a thousand at a time. We'd get 'em from an iron manufactory, who'd deliver 'em to the ship's agent on the dock."

"Slavers, Mr. Stokes?"

The old man smiled. "Master Chris, that word was never spoken. We took orders, didn't ask questions."

"That was way back in the time of Harmony & Sons?"

"Yes, way back. Whatever a ship needed, we supplied. If they needed large quantities, we ordered 'em."

"My grandfather was in charge back then, of course. So he knew all about it."

"Your grandfather, may he rest in peace, knew everything. He kept a pretty close eye. Had a mind like a steel trap. But a tender heart, even so."

"Tender?"

"He forbade us to stock thumbscrews. You know, those devilish little thingamabobs for torture. A ship's agent who wanted shackles often wanted some of them, too. But Caleb Harmony had his principles: shackles yes, thumbscrews never. Lost some business, but he didn't care. A real merchant of the olden time; they don't make 'em like that anymore."

"No, Mr. Stokes, they don't. Thank you."

I left, more shook up than ever.

When I got home, I found a note from Rick: "Chris—A big row with the Skipper and Dwight. Can't take their bilge any more. I'm shipping out. Good luck. See you whenever. Rick."

I told Sal.

"He's cut out just like that?"

"Yep."

"He was going to help us."

"Yep."

"You can't ever count on him, can you?"

"Not for long."

"So where does this leave us?"

"On our own, dear sis, dealing with something dirty, something foul."

8

"Grandpa, you didn't, did you?"

"Cabin boy at fifteen, ship's master at twenty."

"The brig Fearless, *the schooners* Mary D., Sea Eagle, *and* Charity*—they weren't slavers, were they?"*

"Smart ships all, fast sailers."

"Those boxes marked 'soap,' were they shackles?"

"At sea you take only what's absolutely needed."

"Were slaves really packed in tween decks, with only three feet of headroom?"

"I always required ample provision for the comfort of the passengers."

"It was an ugly business, Grandpa."

"Life at sea is often ugly."

"Did you send them to Brazil and Cuba, when it was illegal here?"

"I wished my captains Godspeed, whatever their destination."

"I loved your stories, Grandpa—doubling Cape Horn in a gale, the harbor at Canton, the pirates, the earthquake at Lisbon. I'd love to hear more."

"I wish I could, Chris. I wish I could."

"Grandpa, I love you!"

"Chris, I love you, too."

"I feel so ashamed!"

"I'm sorry about that, Chris. Real sorry."

"If I write about it, it will bring disgrace to the family. Say you didn't, Grandpa, say you didn't!"

"There are no atheists at sea."

I mulled things over in my room. Everything there—the old maps on the walls, the prints of sailing vessels and scenes of the waterfront, and the carefully crafted ship models I had made as a boy—bespoke my interest in ships and the sea, not as an aspiring mariner, but as a future historian. Some of the maps and prints were birthday gifts from Grandpa Harmony, who knew I was keen on such things. Also, displayed right there on a table in the corner was his bequest to me in his will: a marvelous ivory chess set from China with elaborately carved pieces, some red, some white, representing warriors in outlandish garb. To his other grandsons he had left his nautical instruments, and to Sal a beautiful silk and sandalwood fan, but to me he had given this chess set, a rare item of great value, in hopes that I would learn chess and, in so doing, stretch the muscles of my mind. I had yet to learn, having no one to teach me, but I often contemplated the set, studying the intricately carved ivory figures and imagining the strange faraway world of Canton, described by Grandpa in his letters and stories.

Indeed, the old man and his voyages were all through the house. In the parlor, where his massive gilt-framed portrait dominated the room. In the silk-screen Chinese landscapes with birds and butterflies and flowers that fancied up the parlor's walls, and the blue-and-white chinaware that filled the china cabinet. In the embroidered white silk scarves that Ma and Sal had both worn on occasion, and in Ma's room, in the elaborate lacquerware sewing box with ivory needlework tools. All these mementos from the China trade we had valued as a rich heritage, but now that heritage was tainted. Had money from the slave trade helped finance those voyages to Canton and Grandpa's other enterprises? Had dirty money helped to buy the homes of his sons, including the very one I lived in? And would the family history that I proposed to write reveal all this and bring disgrace to the Harmonys? I was in an almighty dilemma and a funk.

"Well, Mr. Harmony, isn't this a fine kettle of fish! You set out to research a family history, and you find out that they were up to their ears in slaving."

"Maybe, sir, just maybe. I'm not totally convinced. My cousin tells tall tales."

"A bit of skepticism is always healthy. But if they were involved, how would you feel about it?"

Professor Stevenson wiped his glasses, put them back on, peered quizzically, his pink face framed by muttonchops.

"The very idea of it—the mere possibility—pretty much wipes me out. I'm rampageously shocked and ashamed."

"Understandable. And yet, you say, there's a fair chance that your father was not involved."

"Yes sir."

"But your uncle and grandfather were."

"So far, the evidence is vague. Cousin Rick may be leaping to conclusions."

"As for the uncle, that would-be thief of sea chests, it would hardly be surprising. But your grandfather, Caleb Harmony, that grand old man of the sea, it would be downright disturbing. You were fond of him, I gather."

"Very fond."

"Tell me about him."

"A bully old man. He took all his grandchildren, my sister Sal included, for walks along the waterfront. He took us on board ships and taught us about masts and sails and such, and even had us peek in the holds."

"He knew everyone on South Street, I gather."

"Captains and common seamen greeted him, and even wharf rats and beggars. He took us to shipyards and showed us caulkers and joiners at work, and sailmakers stitching sails in their lofts. Those were bully fine times."

"And told you tales as well?"

"Marvelous tales about the China trade and pirates and mutineers—about everything!"

"And now you learn he may have been a slaver as well, and if you go on with the family history, it could all come out."

"There's that risk, sir. What should I do?"

"*Magna est veritas.* You must at all costs go on with it. The truth, whatever it is, will come out sooner or later. Better sooner, and with you as the teller."

"Come what may?"

"Come what may. History is at war with myth. Myth tells us what we wish had happened; history tells us what did. In the long run, alas, myth usually wins. People don't want facts, they're afraid of them, and often understandably so. But our job as historians is to be ruthless in presenting facts. We can interpret and theorize, but always based on facts. So forge ahead, seek out the facts. With an eye to a rather impressive precedent, I say, *Fiat lux.*"

"Sir, it will eat up my time. My studies may suffer."

"Hmm, yes, a good point. This is your senior year, just a few more months to go. Shelve the project for now, stick to your studies. They'll give you a solid basis for your research. Then, as soon as you've graduated, throw yourself into it. Talk to people on South Street, anyone and everyone who knew your family. Some won't talk, some will. I'll point you to an unusual source myself—someone with useful information."

"Who, sir?"

The professor smiled slyly. "Not now, my young friend, not until you graduate. You're lucky, Mr. Harmony, you've found your subject early. So did I, when I was just your age. I knew that I would spend my life studying how three great empires—the Spanish, French, and British—struggled to dominate this continent." He gestured toward the big maps on the walls of his office, showing those empires in North America at various dates. "Out of that struggle our republic was born. The epic sweep of that conflict still dazzles me."

"My story isn't so grandiose, is it?"

"Your story is darker, more sinister. It's about greed and corruption. Maybe your family will be vindicated, maybe not. What a challenge! I envy you. Full steam ahead! *Ad astra per aspera*."

"Sir?"

"Through the rough ways to the stars."

"Yes sir, aptly put. I guess I've found my mission."

"Mr. Harmony, you've found your obsession."

"So what did Old Muttonchops say?" Sal asked, when I got home.

"Ad astra per aspera."

"Stop it."

"As soon as I graduate, full steam ahead."

"You won't graduate till June."

"Meanwhile, in my spare time, I can be reading in Pa's library. There's a lot there I still haven't touched."

"So what do I do, twiddle my thumbs?"

"Finish sorting out the papers in the chest. But we can't keep this to ourselves any longer. We've got to tell Ma."

"Everything?"

"Everything we know so far."

"When?"

"Now."

So we called her into the library and told her all that we had learned from Rick, and what certain papers in the sea chest might mean. She listened quietly, didn't interrupt us once. When we finished, a long silence followed. She sat stock still in her chair with a puzzled, then a determined, look on her face. Finally she spoke in a low, calm voice.

"This is very difficult. Jake, maybe—maybe—but Grandfather Harmony? A man so wise, so kind? I've always been an abolitionist, and so were my family, the Winslows. Quietly, without agitation. We believed that to own other human beings like property was as degrading for the masters as the slaves. When President Lincoln began freeing slaves, we rejoiced."

"Pa, too?"

"Him, too. I am convinced that he was in no way involved. As for your grandfather, and even Jake, I shall believe them innocent until we know beyond a doubt otherwise. Go on with your research, learn everything you can. I don't just ask the two of you to do this, I *enjoin* you. You owe it to your father and us all. Learn the truth and speak it, no matter whom it hurts."

She rose and left the room, leaving Sal and me to our commitment, our obsession.

9

I treasured my brother Nathan's war letters. Some were addressed to the whole family, but in the ones he sent to me he really spoke his heart. I was honored that he would open up to his kid brother. The first ones told of the send-off parade down Broadway past cheering crowds, the trip by boxcar south, then drill, drill, drill at camp, target practice, and the regiment's eagerness to have a muss with the Rebs: "Won't that be a lark!" But after that his mood turned somber.

Dear Chris,

Well, I got my wish—here we are in Dixie. They've been marching us all over the place, no one knows quite why. We're camping now, and with winter coming on, probably won't get a crack at the Rebs till spring. The food is awful—beef that stinks and biscuits you can break your teeth on. Thank God for the coffee, we drink it black, strong enough to float an anvil. The talk here is pretty free, and a lot of the boys get tanked up on the tar water that the commissary claims is whiskey, but don't worry, I'm keeping shy of the oil of gladness. I still read the Bible that Ma gave me, and it will see me through.

Most of the boys think abolitionists are a bunch of shit asses (yes, Chris, that's exactly how they put it), and claim the Army puts the Negro first, the mule second, and the white man last. But I tell you, when a bunch of us visited a plantation and saw stocks and chains and whips and thumbscrews, we became abolitionists on the spot. And if that wasn't enough, we met an escaped slave who'd walked fifteen miles with an iron yoke and a ball and chain, so's to get to "Massa Lincum's sojers." When we got that stuff off him, we saw that his ear had been cut off to mark him, and he'd been branded, and his back was ridged with pus-oozing wounds from a whipping. God damn these slaveholders and every son of a bitch who ever defended their "peculiar institution" or in any way helped make it possible! This war is going to put an end to it once and for all. The Rebs can holler and fight all they like, we're going to break their balls. Write. Write soon! Write often! Love,

Nathan

So as regards the family history, Nathan was of the same mind as Professor Stevenson and Ma: no matter what, full steam ahead! I often went into his room, which Ma had kept just as he left it. On one wall, framed, were the Ten Commandments, and on another, the Declaration of Independence. Arranged neatly on a shelf were mementos of his two years at sea: *Paradise Lost, A Pilgrim's Progress,* a compass, a sailor's cap, and a small silver cross with a chain. He had shipped out to Mexico and the Caribbean as a cabin boy at sixteen and would probably have gone back to sea, if it hadn't been for the war. Dwight and Rick enlisted in the Navy, but Nathan, who always had a mind of his own, preferred the Army. His death in battle shattered us. His room was like a shrine; Ma had offered it to Rick, but the idea of anyone else living there struck me as sacrilege.

God damn these slaveholders and every son of a bitch who ever defended their 'peculiar institution' or in any way helped make it possible. For Nathan, a God-fearing man, strong words. Now, like never before, they were burned into my brain.

"The chest is gone—they stole it!" Sal screamed at me, the moment I got home from classes.

"Some expressmen came while Sal and I were out," Ma explained. "Meg let them take it."

"I didn't know," said Meg, almost in tears. "Oh ma'am, oh Master Chris, they acted so nice and regilar, like you was expectin' 'em. I'd niver a let 'em take it, if I'd known!"

"It's our fault, Meg," said Ma. "We should have warned you. Don't fret yourself into a frenzy."

"I didn't know!" wailed Meg. "I swear I didn't know!"

It took the three of us to reassure Meg and send her back to help Annie in the kitchen.

"Of course, Uncle Jake sent them," said Sal. "He must have known Ma and I would be out."

"Well," said Ma, "it can't be helped. So now, Chris, what do we do?"

"Nothing. Go on as we were, and wait."

"Why are you so flat-out calm?" asked Sal. "We'll never see Grandpa's papers again."

"That's what you think. Come!"

I led them to the library, rolled up the top of Pa's desk, and inside, stacked neatly in separate piles, were the papers. Sal rushed to the desk and verified that all Grandpa's stuff was there.

"Then what was in the chest?" she asked.

"Pa's papers from the desk. Old gas and water bills, clippings of ads for coal stoves and water heaters, scribbled notes about dentist's appointments and taxes due..."

"In other words, trash," said Ma. "That man never threw anything out."

Sal brightened. "So you switched the stuff in the desk and the chest?"

"On a hunch, just to be safe."

"When?"

"Last night, before going to bed. I forgot to tell you. So Uncle Jake and Dwight have Pa's stuff—worthless—and we still have Grandpa's. To muddle them up them further, I mixed in with Pa's stuff a few items in Grandpa's handwriting—lists of ship's stores, receipts for rope and hardware, stuff we don't really need. It'll take them days, even months, to figure out what I've done, and maybe they'll never catch on."

Sal gave me a hug. "Chris, that was egregiously brilliant!"

Ma smiled one of her rare warm smiles. "Well done, Chris. But from now on, Meg and Annie will be instructed not to open the door to anyone in our absence. No exceptions!"

"The fun now," I said, "will be to see what they do next. I have a hunch we'll hear from them soon."

Dear Chris,

I was shocked to learn what Pa had done. I didn't know he'd try again to get that chest, and I don't approve. Who needs it anyway? It seems to be more your Pa's stuff than Grandpa's, and has nothing to do with Grandpa's estate. I've told Pa point-blank that he's in the wrong and owes you an apology, and that he ought to return it. I hope he'll be in touch.

Chris, I too owe an apology. When you jumped on the chest that time, I got angry and laid into you. For that, I'm sorry. I really thought your ma wanted rid of the thing, but that's no excuse. I've got a mean temper that I'm trying to learn to control. Chris, family feuds are the worst. Let's bury the hatchet and start fresh. Drop me a note or say hello Sunday after church. —Dwight

I read Dwight's note to Ma and Sal.

"Do you believe him?" asked Sal.

"Not much. They haven't caught on, think there's nothing in the chest to worry about, so why not smooth things over?"

"Well," said Ma, "we can give him the tiniest benefit of a doubt. Maybe, just maybe, he doesn't even know about the slaving. Rick didn't, after all. Speak to him next Sunday, see what he has to say."

"But keep up those lessons in boxing," Sal advised.

In point of fact, I had. My studies were taking most of my time, but Dan Hunter and I still managed a session a week with Tiger Wilson, who claimed my left hook showed some promise—a thought that spunked me up.

When I saw Dwight briefly after church, he was all over himself with apologies, and after that, so was Uncle Jake. Jake's mea culpa came in a letter to Ma that promised the return of the chest, and sure enough, three days later it was delivered to our door, Dwight and Luke the coachman lugging it up the stoop and down the hall into the library, where under Ma's supervision they deposited it. Sal and I watched, Sal standing on guard in front of the roll-top desk, its top down, its papers out of sight. As Dwight left, he chatted with me a moment on the stoop.

"How's the family history coming?"

"It's not—not until I graduate. My studies take all my time."

"I'd like to help. I can introduce you to some people."

"You can?"

"Of course. For a start, come calling with me on New Year's Day. Your ma won't be receiving, since she's still in mourning, but surely you can make calls."

"Dwight, that's months away. I haven't thought that far ahead."

"Come along, Chris. I guarantee you'll find it interesting."

"Well, I'll think about it."

On that note, we parted. On New Year's Day ladies received gentlemen callers, and gentlemen went out making calls on ladies. To date, my calls had been on ladies from the church, neighbors, mamas of girls

I'd met at dancing school, and wives of some business acquaintances of Pa's; I'd never made calls with Dwight. All through our childhood he had tried to make me feel puny, soft, and useless, a tagalong who was barely tolerated, yet now he suddenly wanted my company. He was up to something. I wanted to know what it was.

10

All that autumn I was at grips with Plato, Aristotle, the Gospels, and Saint Paul, not to mention Milton and Shakespeare and Swift. And at the suggestion of my sparring partner Dan Hunter, the two of us saw a performance of *The Black Crook,* a wild extravaganza where a hundred cuties in flesh-colored tights danced up a storm, flaunting two hundred very shapely legs that I'll admit we kind of ogled. More respectably, I was keeping genteel company with Miss Ruth Ann Moore—Sal's Toothy Ruthie—while Sal was being courted by several young men, including one named Gus Miller, a lumbering sort of fellow I had christened Gorilla Gus.

"He's not a gorilla," she insisted. "What happened to that thug of a boxer you wanted me to meet?"

"Dan Hunter? He's been bewitched by another fair charmer. Once he comes to his senses, I'll bring him around."

"So what am I, the choice of last resort?"

"You, dear Sal, are the pot of gold at the end of the rainbow, Eve before the Fall, the Bower of Bliss."

This might have earned me a cushion in the face. Instead, she merely singed me with a glare.

Our Christmas was quiet: a home dinner with just the three of us, following an exchange of gifts. To our embarrassment, since we had sent them only a greeting card, Jake and Dwight gave us a silver tureen.

For the New Year's Day calls with Dwight, I put on my best tan frock coat and a silk cravat, but he outshone me by far, having donned a fawn frock coat with a black velvet collar, a red waistcoat, and a glittering watch chain, tiepin, and studs. We went on foot, calling first on my dancing class damsels and their mamas, whom Dwight was also acquainted with, and then on some ladies from church. Tall and heavyset with a snaky mustache waxed at the tips, Dwight charmed both young and old with his elegant manners and tales of misadventures at sea.

Late that afternoon, as the last feeble sunlight yielded to flurries of snow, Dwight led me down to the lower Fifth Avenue, the precinct of Old Money. This puzzled me, since the Harmony boys were strictly New Money, and New and Old rarely mixed. But he escorted me up the stoop of an imposing brownstone that reeked of good taste.

"My fiancée's family," Dwight whispered, as we entered the parlor."You're engaged?"

"Almost."

This was news to me, but before I could question him further, the hostesses approached, and Dwight presented me to Mrs. Adrian Van Zandt and her daughter Susanna, who greeted us warmly. Dwight chatted with the stately mother, while the daughter, fluffy in taffeta, set her sights on me, calling me "Cousin Chris" and explaining that, while they weren't quite officially engaged, she hoped to bring her folks around in time. She seemed to be a bit in awe of the Harmonys, who had sailed everywhere and done everything, and of me as a young scholar, to boot.

By now I had grasped it: inspired by Dwight's tales of the sea, Miss Susanna was far more taken with the Harmonys than were her Knickerbocker parents, and to persuade them further toward an engagement, she could mention me as a scholar in our ranks. A budding historian, in their eyes, was far more acceptable than a grubby ship chandler or able seaman. So I dished out snippets of stories about pirates and earthquakes and rescuing a Christian lady from a harem (Rick's tale; I was laying it on pretty thick). In no time mother and daughter were begging me to come back and regale them with Harmony adventures, which I had to promise to do.

Dwight watched all this with the broadest of grins and, once I had done my bit, indicated that he was ready to leave. We did, after due thanks to our hostesses, and assurances that I would come again.

"You made a hit, Chris," he said as we descended the stoop. "I knew you would. Now for something different, something I think you'll appreciate."

"What?"

"You'll see."

Back on the Avenue he led me to a grandiose freestanding brownstone with a steep stoop and monumental entrance. Lights blazed within, and a flock of carriages waited at the curb, with more arriving every minute. We mounted the stoop and were met in the vestibule by a mulatto butler, who took our wraps and calling cards and ushered us in.

The moment I set foot in the parlor, where a host of guests were babbling, I noticed a silk-screen landscape on the wall, blue-and-white porcelain on the mantel, silk scarves draped over upholstery, and carved ivory figurines and lacquerware displayed on little tables and whatnots. It all said *China trade.* I felt a rush of excitement.

Coming toward us was a handsome dark-haired woman in gold-embroidered black satin with a garnet brooch set with pearls.

"Dwight, how good to see you! Your father left only ten minutes ago, having assured me you would come."

"I always save the best till last. Louise, this is my cousin Chris. Chris, this is Mrs. Rivington, equally famous for her charm and her receptions."

I bowed slightly. "Good afternoon, Mrs. Rivington. I'm delighted to be here. Your parlor fascinates me. It speaks of the China trade."

"Of course. My father was long engaged in it. This house is full of his mementos." Her voice was low and musical; it caressed me.

"Perhaps he knew my grandfather, Caleb Harmony, who was also in that trade."

"My father knew everyone. We must talk of it, Mr. Harmony. Dwight tells me you're writing a family history."

"I'll start researching as soon as I graduate in June."

"Come, let me show you something."

She led me down a hallway into another room bright with gaslight. On the walls were prints of sailing ships and nautical charts and maps, while all around were finely crafted models of ships, small camphorwood and lacquerware boxes, a compass and other instruments, and a skipper's cap hanging on a peg.

"This was my father's study or, more accurately, it's a reproduction of it. When I moved here a few years ago, I brought all the items from his study in our old house and installed them here. It commemorates him. When I come in here, I feel that he's still with me."

"It's marvelous. Like my father's library at home, but even richer, more cluttered. I get the feeling here of the old sailing days, now past."

"You *are* a historian, aren't you? Dwight expects great things of you, as I'm sure all your family does. I know you won't let them down."

"I'll do my best. Did your father leave any papers?"

"Not a one. He must have destroyed any that he had, I don't know why. What you see here is all that remains."

"Fascinating."

"Feel free to linger, while I rejoin my guests. Then come for refreshments, with coffee or tea or wine, as you wish."

"Thank you. Yes, I'll stay a minute, if you don't mind."

"Not at all. Browse to your heart's content."

Smiling, she left, a hint of her perfume lingering in the air. She was vastly, stupendously charming.

For a few minutes, I studied the old maps, marveled at the detailed accuracy of the ship models, fingered the intricate lacquerware of a box, and from another box sniffed a faint scent of camphor. Then, scanning the prints on the walls, I imagined myself back in the olden days before steam. I could almost see canvas billowing in the wind, the lookout perched high in the rigging with a spyglass, the crew holystoning the deck under the watchful eye of the mate, the captain pacing the quarterdeck, alert for any cry of "Sail ho!" or "Land ho!" from aloft, determined to bring safely to port his precious cargo of silks and tea from Canton, or silver from Mexico, or coffee from Brazil, plowing that free thoroughfare of all nations, the vast, restless, phosphorescent sea.

"Chris, come have some refreshments."

Dwight's voice jolted me back from my reverie. Returning to the parlor, I nibbled plum cake topped with raisins and hesitantly put my lips to my first glass of wine. Dwight, being well known here, mixed with any number of guests, while I just watched and listened. Over the babble of talk the hostess's voice rang clear.

"No, gentlemen, don't speak to me of gold. Once bitten, twice shy. I'm perfectly content to hoard my darling little treasury bonds, thank you; so tame, so safe… Oh yes, I've seen Old Sixty Millions on Harlem Lane, and what a sight it is! Mountain Boy and Mountain Girl, they race like the wind… Of course, I remember the *Falcon*; young though I was, I had an interest in it. New York to San Francisco in ninety-one days, three hours—remarkable! In fifty-one, I think. Two thousand tons, over twelve thousand square yards of sail. I saw it leave. It glided over the water like a thing alive! … "

The *Falcon*, I recalled, was a clipper that Uncle Jake had been part owner of. there was a print of it in his South Street office. Old Sixty Millions was Cornelius Vanderbilt, the richest man in the country, famous for racing trotters on Harlem Lane. This woman could talk gold, racing, clippers, and theater and politics as well. She even expressed grave concern about events in Europe, where the French had been walloped by the Germans, and Paris was now under siege; she knew about it all. Louise Rivington was like no woman I had ever known.

After an hour Dwight was ready to leave, though I would gladly have stayed longer, reveling in my second glass of wine.

"I do wish you well with your history," Mrs. Rivington said as we departed. "Keep me informed, Mr. Chris. I'll help in any way I can."

Aware again of her perfume and her glittering red brooch set with pearls, I thanked her, we left.

"You impressed her," said Dwight. "I think she'd really like to help."

"Who is she?"

"The daughter of a well-known shipowner who started out poor and ended up a real merchant prince."

"That's who *he* was. Who is *she*?"

"His heir, and the shrewdest woman in this city. She's done quite well on her own."

"How?"

"She invests."

"In what?"

"Ships, gold, stocks, whatever."

"There's a husband?"

"I've never laid eyes on him. Maybe he exists, maybe not. Who cares? Get to know her. She has connections."

To this I made no comment. Nor did I tell him that one of the ships pictured on the wall in the study was the brig *Fearless*, which Rick had mentioned as a slaver. Or had I imagined seeing it? I'd seen and heard a lot that day; I needed time to sort it out.

Our visits over, we parted. I went home all worked up with a jumble of impressions in my head. Ma and Sal were waiting in the sitting room, eager to hear my report. I recounted in great detail our calls on the dancing schoolgirls and their mamas, the church ladies, and the Van Zandts, about whom they plied me with questions.

"Yes, Dwight's all but engaged. They're Old Money, the best manners and all, nothing flash or swank. The mother couldn't be nicer. A mite hoity-toity, but with all that Knickerbocker breeding, I guess it's not her fault."

"And the daughter?" asked Sal.

"Thinks her family a bunch of old fogies, wants new blood—Harmony blood—to liven them up. But for all that, well bred and charming."

"Hmm," said Sal. "A honey crisp."

"If I'm going to see them again," I said, "I'll have to work up some stories."

Ma frowned. "Ah, those Harmony stories! Well, Dwight's aiming high. I suppose we should wish him success."

"You and he are chums now, aren't you?" said Sal.

"For the moment, yes. We'll see."

"Just hearing about all those people has worn me out," said Ma. "I'm going to bed. I trust that you will, too."

"Yes, Ma," we chorused, but Sal held me there after Ma went upstairs.

"You haven't told half of it. I smell wine on you. I'll bet you had a glimpse of the *demimonde.*"

"The what?"

"Chris, don't you know anything? You've been spending too much time on moral philosophy and logic."

"That's what you think."

"The *demimonde* is the world of *demimondaines.*"

"Thanks for clearing that up."

"Loose women, kept women, that sort of creature."

"And how does a respectable young lady like yourself learn about such things?"

"From the girls at school. Some of them had been to Paris."

So I told her about Mrs. Rivington, and she fired off a battery of questions. It soon became clear that there was a lot I didn't know: her maiden name and the name of her father; where she grew up and how she acquired her fortune; who and where her husband was, if indeed he existed; how she had come to know Dwight and Uncle Jake; and who those guests were who had flocked to her reception.

"A mystery woman," Sal concluded. "A *femme fatale.* Be careful."

"Careful of what? She's charming, she's unique."

"Hmm."

"Look, unless maybe, just maybe, a year from now on New Year's Day, I doubt if I'll ever see her again."

"Of course not."

"So that's that. Okay?"

"Okay."

"Okay."

11

My graduation in June was splendid: the academic procession in gown and mortarboard, the president's hour-long address (with snippets of Greek that flew right by me), the chaplain's closing prayer, the award of the diplomas, and hearty hugs from Ma, Sal, Dwight, and Uncle Jake. Then suddenly, the perfume, the musical voice:

"Congratulations, young Mr. Harmony. Here's wishing you the very best!"

Mrs. Rivington had appeared out of nowhere in a stylish pillbox hat trimmed with beads and lace, and an elegant striped satin dress that made heads turn. Not having seen her since New Year's, I was flummoxed and could only stammer an acknowledgment. Uncle Jake introduced her to Ma and Sal, who nodded.

"I persuaded Mrs. Rivington to come," he explained, "knowing her interest in Chris's research."

Mrs. Rivington smiled her warmest smile. "You must be very proud, Mrs. Harmony. Your son is graduating magna cum laude and can now begin his research. He will leave his mark, I'm sure."

"Thank you," said Ma. "You are very kind."

She turned to me. "Yes, Mr. Harmony, I know some people who might help you. Please call on me. I'm home most afternoons; Thursday is my day."

"Thank you. I will." My heart was thumping.

After only a few more words, Mrs. Rivington departed, doubtless aware that the family would be returning to St. Mark's Place for a celebratory dinner. I said good-bye to my fellow graduates and to Professor Stevenson, who now pronounced himself willing to help me launch my project. Then, diploma in hand, having doffed the mortarboard and gown, I was ready to leave.

"Haloo, graduate! Haloo, folks! Look who's back in town, with scars to show and tales to tell! Chris, you looked freaky in that outfit. Congrats, scholar, you've done your learning, so now you can start to live. Well, gang, don't stare, it's just the old black sheep, full of punch and spit, who from all his toil and troubles hasn't learned a thing and wouldn't want to!"

Rick was back, in white duck trousers and a red shirt open at the neck, his low-crowned sailor's hat pushed back atop his unkempt curly locks. Ma smiled, Sal and I grinned broadly, Dwight and Uncle Jake glared.

"You might have let us know you were coming," said Uncle Jake.

"Now Pa, can I control wind and tide? I'm just off a wormy hulk that was hell afloat, with a growly captain and a lubber of a mate, so here I am, ripe and randy for a bit of fun. Aunt Martha, did I hear you say something about a family dinner? Bully for you, if you did. I've had it with salt beef and biscuit!"

So when we got home, another place was set at the table.

Before dinner I opened my graduation presents: from Uncle Jake and Dwight, a watch with a solid gold chain; from Ma and Sal, coral studs and a silver tiepin; and from Mrs. Rivington via Uncle Jake, who presented it, an ivory statuette of a Chinese lady in a long, flowing gown, holding in one hand a spray of flowers, and in the other a mirror—an elegant gift that I marveled at.

"Who is this Mrs. Rivington?" Ma asked.

"A shipowner's daughter whom I met last New Year's," I explained. "I hardly know her."

"A shipowner herself," Dwight added, "and quite charming. She has connections in shipping circles and has offered to help Chris with his history."

"I see," said Ma.

At dinner Rick regaled us with a slew of stories. Recently, while crossing the Atlantic, he had been washed overboard during a storm in the notorious Devil's Blow-hole and thought his time had come. "As I was tossed about in the sea, clinging to a broken spar, I saw my whole life pass before me in a flash—what a mess!—and the Great Mariner jabbing a mean finger at me for all my faults and sins."

"So you prayed for forgiveness," said Ma, "and have come at last to the Lord. Heaven be praised!"

"Not quite, Aunt Martha. Before I could utter a prayer, a huge wave rose up and dumped me back on deck, soaked through but safe and sound. So the Lord will have to wait!"

Ma frowned, the rest of us laughed.

After dinner Uncle Jake and Dwight left by carriage, but Rick lingered with me on the stoop.

"You're not going with them?" I asked.

"Hardly. I'm staying with a ladylove. But it looks like the Harmonys are living up to their name. You've made your peace with the Skipper and Dwight."

"A lot has happened since you left. Where have you been, by the way?"

"Everywhere and nowhere. Tell me what I've missed."

So I told him how I had switched the papers, how the chest had been taken and returned, and how Dwight and I had made New Year's calls together.

"So as regards slaving, you're giving everyone the benefit of a doubt."

"For now, at least."

"And how does this Mrs. Rivington fit in?"

"She wants to help me."

"Why?"

I shrugged.

"Chris, when people offer to do something, they always have a reason. We'll have to find out what hers is."

"'We'?"

"Of course. I'm dealing myself back in."

"You won't take off again?"

"Not soon. I'm much too snug with my ladylove."

"Does she have a name?"

"Lots. But aren't you nosy!"

"Oh, all right."

"Okay, scholar, I'll be in touch. I've great plans for us both. See you soon!"

And he darted off.

"This Mrs. Rivington says that Thursday is her day," Ma observed, when I rejoined her and Sal in the parlor. "What exactly does that mean?"

"In Paris, Ma," said Sal, "ladies have a day when they're always at home to receive callers."

"This isn't Paris," said Ma. "So, Chris, she wants you to call on her."

"I guess."

"Well," said Ma, "as of a month ago you and Sal are of age, so it's not for me to tell you what to do. She and Jake seem to be well acquainted. And she and Dwight as well. And with those clothes, she certainly loves attention."

"Ma, what are you driving at?"

"She's not a good woman."

"How can you say that? You just met her and didn't exchange ten words."

"I sense it."

"Sal, do *you* get that?"

"No, I get something else."

"What?"

"She knows her way."

"What does that mean?"

"I don't know, but I'm sure of it. That woman knows her way."

Rick had told me he had great plans for us both, which turned out to be a night on the town. After all those months of studying I was ready for it, and set off dressed to the nines, with the French Secret deep in my pocket. He took me first on a tour of the Bowery, with its jostling crowds and sidewalk bands, climaxed by a visit to a lager beer saloon and my first taste of beer. Next we went to a fancy dance hall where, inspired by more beer, I did some crazy fandango with a girl named Gladys, until Rick pulled me away to what's known as a pretty waiter girl saloon, at which point my recollections get kind of hazy: a waitress in a short skirt and jingling boots bringing us more beer at a table; me stomping about on the dance floor with a blonde named Nora or Cora or Dora; Rick whispering to me, "Sport, go to it!" Then a drab little room in back, money handed over, clothes shed, a tangle of limbs and groans, and on a stand right by the bed—yes, I'm sure of it—a Bible.

Rick saw me home, I don't know when or how. Waking up with thunder in my brain, I concluded, from the played-out feeling in my groin and the disappearance of the French Secret, that I had managed to lose my virginity. Sal read me at a glance, but since Ma was attending some meeting at church, I was spared a lecture on how well conducted people behave. No need, if this was fun and vice, I wanted no part of it. I plunged back into my project with a vengeance.

I began with Pa's library, whose black walnut bookcases were crammed with books on navigation and sailing, naval histories, and memoirs of ship's masters of the olden time. From an early age, I had devoured many of them, greedy for stories of typhoons and mutinies and scrapes with pirates in distant corners of the seas—just the stuff to kindle up a young boy's imagination and make him dream of wild adventures. And now, with school behind me and a new purpose in mind, I searched out any books that I had missed. And some of what I found wasn't pleasant.

...After we had got the whole lot chained and under hatches, blacks in two canoes came alongside the brig, begging to be taken with us into slavery, so they could rejoin their kin in the hold. They looked sickly or old, so the Captain took only three, then gave orders to get under way. The others in the canoes followed us and tried to climb aboard, but we pushed them off and, when they persisted, fired a six-pound shot that demolished one of the canoes and left the survivors wailing and screaming. This sat hard upon my heart. "Jared," the Mate assured me, "the old man knows his business."

...At this factory we dealt with Don Pedro Blanco, one of the most successful factors on the coast, who assured us that Dahomans, Ashantees, Foulahs, Mandingoes, and Felletahs, by preying constantly on one another, kept the market well supplied. His barracoons were filled with stock, for his friend and ally Baba, a Foulah king, had arrived with a caravan just two days before, delivering over a thousand naked prisoners to the factor. We did our business quickly, trading powder, rum, tobacco, and cheap trinkets for 735 slaves—as many as we still had room for—plus a little gold dust and ivory. We then put quickly to sea, lest a British sloop-of-war reported in the area get sight of us—always a risk, since Her Britannic Majesty was as determined as ever to suppress the trade.

...When the fire broke out amidships, we knew that all was lost. Quickly we hacked off spars and the bowsprit and lashed them together for a raft, and hoisted out the boats, while fire smoldered tween decks amid the screams and pleadings of the poor wretches shackled below. With the boats safely off, and the last of the crew, myself included, scrambling down ropes to the raft, the Mate, who was a decent sort, lifted the hatch gratings and flung down the keys to the shackles. As we pulled away from the brig, negroes began appearing on the deck, where flames engulfed them. Seeing our two boats towing the raft, some leaped overboard and swam toward us in

desperation. Fearing to be swamped, we fought them off with handspikes and knives. For miles around, the sea was illumined by the flaming brig, and we could make out all too clearly the bobbing heads of the negroes, who one by one vanished under the waves. When, the next day, we were picked up by a Brazilian slaver, we gave thanks to the Almighty.

. . . There is no way to stop the slave trade but by breaking up slaveholding itself. Whilst there is a market, there will always be traders. Men like me do the rough work, but we are no worse than the Christian merchants who supply the money and ships, or the Christian planters who keep up the demand for cheap labor. If all the names involved in this foul trade were known and published, many a prosperous and seemingly respectable merchant family in our greatest ports would be exposed and disgraced. May God forgive me for my crimes, and may the story of Jared Chase, forty years a slaver, as told to the Reverend Simeon Oakes of New York, do some good in this world that now, with the keenest remorse, and in the last stages of consumption, I am leaving.

Jared Chase's firsthand account of the slave trade fired me up. I determined to confront anyone who had ever been linked in any way to the trade. I would make them talk about it, make them speak their guilt. And I knew just where to start.

12

"So you are Christopher Harmony, a grandson of old Caleb of honored memory. What can I do for you?"

Jonathan Biggs eyed me just a bit warily across his desk in his ground-floor office on South Street whose sign announced, JONATHAN BIGGS, COMMISSION MERCHANT. Clerks on high stools nearby scratched away with their quill pens at accounts and bills of lading.

"Sir, I'm doing a family history. I'd just like to ask a few questions."

"You were to my house once in my absence, I've been told, assaulting my ailing father with just that sort of questions. It upset him terribly."

"I'm sorry about that, Mr. Biggs. That was my cousin Rick's doing. I had no idea he'd get so rambustious. I really regret it."

"Well, what do you want to know?"

"The schooner *Venture*, sir. According to Custom House records, you bought it from some members of the Yacht Club on March 28, 1858, and sold it to my uncle, Jacob Harmony, on June 17, 1858."

"And what if I did?"

"I'm wondering why you sold it so quickly. Perhaps you had an understanding with my uncle?"

"That was a private matter. If you need to know about it, I suggest you ask your uncle."

"No offense intended, sir. I'm just trying to get information for the history. Do you have any idea what became of the *Venture*? So far as I know, my uncle never raced it."

"I know nothing about that whatsoever."

"Such a famous racer. It's strange how it dropped out of sight."

"I repeat: I know nothing about it."

"Thank you, sir. Your father, Hiram Biggs, was a longtime partner of my grandfather."

"Of course. That's common knowledge."

"Heavily involved in the China trade, were they not?"

"Up to their ears."

"And the Latin America trade?"

"Likewise."

"And the African trade?"

"Probably. There was always a great demand for gold dust, palm oil, and ivory."

"Anything else?"

"Skins, beeswax, honey."

"Anything else?"

He shot me a sharp glance over his fiercely waxed mustache. "Nothing else. Nothing at all."

"Thank you, sir. I believe they owned the schooner *Charity*, Captain Matthews, master?"

"They owned many ships. I don't recall the names or the masters."

"Perhaps in the Cuba trade, dealing with a Señor Martinez?"

"I couldn't say."

"Shipping rum and hats and soap. I know that from Caleb Harmony's letters. Many crates of soap. I gather there was quite a demand down there for soap."

"I suppose there was. Mr. Harmony, are all these questions necessary?"

"Yes sir, very necessary, and I appreciate your cooperation. One does wonder about all that soap. Perhaps those boxes were mislabeled. Perhaps they contained something else."

He rose abruptly. "I can't help you, Mr. Harmony. I know nothing about these matters. Please don't bother me or my family again. If you do, I'll have to take legal action. Good day!"

And I was ushered out.

Shipped by the grace of God in good order and well conditioned, by Jared Chase in and upon the good schooner Friendship, whereof is master under God for this present voyage Jared Chase: 380 slaves on the proper account and risk of Don Miguel Martinez, merchant in Havana, being marked and numbered, to be delivered in like good order and with due caution at or near the aforesaid port of Havana. In witness whereof the master of said schooner has affirmed to a Bill of Lading of this tenor and date. And so God send the good schooner to her desired destination in safety. Amen. Dated in Kabenda, Congo, February 19, 1845.

"I am delighted to meet the grandson of the illustrious Caleb Harmony, one of the most prosperous and enterprising merchants to have ever graced this port. Please be seated in this, my humble office, Señor Harmony, and let me know how I can be of service to you. A *cigarillo*, a cigar? But no, you do not smoke. Not even our superb Cuban tobacco. Vices come with age."

With a gracious gesture Señor Miguel Martinez motioned me to a chair in the Pearl Street office of Martinez & Co., Importers. He was a tall, thin man with glossy black hair and a neatly trimmed mustache and goatee, wearing a ruffled shirt and a coat with braided cuffs. He gave off a faint hint of cologne.

"Señor Martinez, I'm researching a family history that will also be a maritime history of this port for the last half century. Caleb Harmony's correspondence mentions a Señor Martinez, presumably his agent in Havana. I'm wondering if you are related or know anything about him."

"Unfortunately, I entered the import/export trade too late to have dealings with your esteemed grandfather. My father, of course, was here before me, as well as in Havana, and later installed me here as his agent. What was this Señor Martinez's first name?"

"Possibly Miguel."

"Which explains why I have the honor of your visit. My father too was Miguel, and there he is." He gestured toward a gilt-framed oil portrait on the wall, showing a handsome gentleman of years with a slick mustache and beard.

"A very distinguished gentleman," I observed.

"Yes, indeed. Don Miguel was what we call *un hombre muy decente y refinado*, a true *caballero*, a gentleman. I am honored to be his son and successor. What kind of business did he and your grandfather presumably engage in?"

"The African trade."

He stiffened slightly. "I see. Palm oil, gold dust, ivory, and such."

"Yes, and such."

"You do not by any chance mean black ivory?"

I felt a tingle of excitement, shrugged. "Who knows?"

"In that case, my dear young friend, I have to disappoint you. Though this illegal trade is regrettably still tolerated in Cuba, neither my father nor any member of our family has ever engaged in it. We consider it—how shall I put it?—disreputable."

"I see. Would you know any other Martinez with an office here who might have knowledge of such matters?"

"None whatsoever. Martinez is a very common name, as is Miguel."

"I know. I've talked to three others here already."

"With no results, I gather?"

"None at all."

"Unfortunate. But you must realize that we Cubans primarily import your cottons and manufactured items, sending you in exchange sugar, molasses, tobacco, and our world-famous cigars. Such legitimate concerns keep most of us occupied; we have no time or interest in the nefarious trade you ask about."

"Much of it was carried on by American slavers, but they had to have contacts in Cuba. The slave ships rendezvoused with small schooners or other craft offshore, transferred the slaves, and made off quickly, so as to elude British or American men-of-war patrolling those waters."

"You are better informed than I, who know nothing of such matters. Señor Harmony, I wish you well in your endeavor but most regrettably cannot help you. Allow me to give you a parting gift."

He stood up and with a gracious gesture showed me to the door, planting several slender cigars in my breast pocket as he did so. For all his courtesy, I sensed that he was glad to get rid of me.

Tuesday, April 14. Men employed tending slaves and cleaning out the slave rooms; awful stink. Delivered 1 puncheon of rum, purchast 1 girl slave for myself.

Friday, April 17. Died a man slave with a dysentery, been sick but a short time. No. 13. Myself unwell with fever and ague.

Monday, April 20. Found a dead man slave, having been in a consumptive state a long while; should have looked more closely before purchase. No. 14. Myself improving but weak. May God allow us to complete our purchases and get away from this pestilential coast!

Friday, May 1. Held here by the sight of a British man-of-war on the horizon, whose vigilance we must slip past. A slave boy jumped overboard and drowned himself to get clear of a pain in his bowels occasioned by a dysentery. No. 15. Myself taken sick with a severe fit of ague and fever. How the factors here survive I do not know. May the Good Lord deliver us from this hellish hole and grant us a fair wind home. If it so falls out, I swear that I, Jared Chase, ship's master, will quit forever this foul coast and trade and live out my years as an honest man. To die here is doom and desolation.

"Did I know Caleb Harmony? By God, what a question! Of course I knew him! Who on the waterfront didn't? A wide-awake type, if ever there was one. All was fish as got in his net."

A sharp-featured man with iron-gray hair, Captain William Matthews, sipping the whiskey cobbler Rick and I had offered him, had a faraway look, seemed disposed to reminisce. With Rick's help, I had found him at the elegant Astor House bar on Broadway, a prime meeting place for ship's masters and shippers, contractors sniffing about for contracts, and Go Ahead types of every kind, who hobnobbed noisily by gaslight, smoking fat cigars. This being my first experience of a bar, I tried not to gape at the ornate pillars, handsome tile flooring, and busts of chesty females. Having introduced me, Rick had distanced himself discreetly, so the captain and I could talk one to one. When barely sipped, the brandy cordial that Rick had ordered for me had flamed in my throat; it sat all but untouched on the counter.

"You sailed his ships many a time, I gather?"

"Indeed I did. To Callao, the port of Lima, and to Guayaquil, which, God bless 'em, boasts the handsomest women on earth. And to Buenos Aires and Rio and a hundred other ports. Harmony & Biggs were constant and heavy shippers of goods. Likewise Harmony & Sons."

"To Havana?"

"Aye, to Havana, too, and often."

"Dealing with a Señor Martinez, I believe?"

"Señor Martinez?" He searched his memories a moment. "Yes, possibly."

"While avoiding dealings with the American consul there?"

"That depended on the consul and the cargo. They could devil you up, for sure."

He took another sip of his cobbler, savored it, seemingly unaware of the babble of talk all around us. Farther down the bar Rick was watching discreetly.

"What kind of cargo, captain? To Havana, that is."

"Any blamed thing in demand down there. Carriages, furniture, machinery, cordage, cotton, and crates of good hard liquor."

"But didn't ships leaving New York also carry casks marked 'rum' and boxes marked 'soap'?"

"Rum and soap?" His features tightened and he shot me a glance. "Kid, what kind of a course are you charting?"

"I just want to know about the trade of that time."

He lowered his voice, looked sly. "You mean the slave trade, don't you?"

"Yes sir. Attitudes here have changed since the war and emancipation. I want to get back into the mood of that time and understand how things worked."

"They worked, all right, but with risk. A slaver could be caught at this end by a U.S. revenue cutter, or off the African coast by a British or American man-o'-war. If boarded while going over, the large quantities of water and food—far more than needed for the crew—gave 'em away. Coming back, it was the niggers themselves. Since slavers didn't have the men and guns to fight off a boarding party, all they could do was make a run for it, and some pretty wild chases resulted."

"Then why take the risk?"

"Greed, pure and simple. On the eve of the war, a prime male slave costing forty dollars in Africa brought at least tenfold that in Havana. How else could you haul in jack like that?"

"What if you got caught?"

"Damned inconvenient, with a loss of profits and maybe the ship, but nothing more. Here in New York judges and marshals could be bribed—a few hundred for a marshal, a thousand or two for a judge."

"I see. Sir, were respectable merchants involved in that trade?"

"Some yes, some no. It depended."

"Maybe some that you knew?"

"Quite a few."

"I can see how that might have been—the money and all, and so many others doing it."

"Plenty of 'em. And some big names, too."

"I see. Captain, was Caleb Harmony in that trade?"

A long silence, then a canny smile, a soft-voiced reply. "Maybe he was and maybe he wasn't."

"Well, I guess it wasn't for just anyone. All those risks you mentioned."

"And yellow fever, and at this end of it, in the Caribbean in late summer, hurricanes. Many a ship was lost, with not one survivor."

"So it must have taken courage, as well as plain old-fashioned Yankee know-how."

"You can say that again."

"A real adventure. Sir, were you in the trade?"

Another silence, the smile persisted. "Maybe I was and maybe I wasn't."

"I'm not out to judge anyone, Captain Matthews. I just want some facts." (Rick had advised me to take this tack.)

"Yes, you nosy little bastard, and I've given you facts aplenty."

"Yes sir, thank you, sir. But you see, sir, your name appears in some of Caleb Harmony's correspondence, with mention of a Señor Martinez in Havana, sums for gratuities, and two sets of papers."

"My name? Captain William Matthews? If you say that, I'll have to break your jaw." He clenched his fists, glared.

"Well, sir, the letters say 'Captain Matthews.'"

"It's a common name, you green little lubber. There's dozens as bear it."

"I know, sir, I've interviewed six. But frankly, sir, you seem to fit the bill best."

His eyes flashed. "Are you trying to make trouble? If you are, hard work you'll have of it."

"Sir, I don't want to make you or anyone trouble. I'm just trying to learn how things worked back then."

"You've put your oar in here enough. I've said all I'm going to say, and maybe too much. Clear out!"

While the captain turned back to his cobbler and took a quick swig of it, I decided to haul anchor with my jaw intact.

"Thank you, sir. Very helpful. No offense intended."

I left. Rick followed me out and caught up with me on the street.

"Well?"

"It's him! He's the one!"

"He admitted it?"

"No, he was cagey."

"Then how can you be sure?"

"He knows a lot about the slave trade."

"So do you and I lately. That doesn't make us slavers."

"It's him! I'm sure of it!"

"Why not any of the six others of that name you've talked to?"

"They stayed cool as custard. This one got worked up and threatened me. He gave himself away."

"If you're right, it doesn't look good for Grandpa."

"It sure doesn't. But at last, after all these false starts, I'm beginning to learn something."

"So what now? What do we do next?"

"I want you to go through all Grandpa's papers and look for anything suspicious—things that Sal and I may have missed. Especially anything that mentions a Captain Matthews or a Señor Martinez."

Rick smiled. "Hey, squirt, are you ordering this old sea dog around?"

"You bet! It's not just Harmonys but a whole lot of others as well. The more I learn, the angrier I get. I'm going to expose them all, no matter who gets hurt. And you, dear cousin, are going to help. I'll need all the help I can get."

13

The address I had been given proved to be an old three-story frame house on Twenty-Second Street near Tenth Avenue, with peeling paint and shutters that hung crooked. I rapped the brass knocker, waited. Creaking on its hinges, the door was opened by a gray-haired man with bushy sideburns, round-shouldered, slightly stooped.

"Mr. Harmony? Come in, young man, come in. I've been looking forward to your visit."

His clasp was warm and cordial.

"Good afternoon, Dr. Dalrymple."

He waved me into a dim hallway lined with bookshelves crammed with books.

I followed as he shuffled in slippers down the hall and gestured toward an open doorway.

"My study should serve our purposes, I think. Please come in and find a seat, if you can."

I entered a high-ceilinged room where light slanted in through smirched windows to reveal a jungle of books. Books crammed bookcases and shelves, cluttered tables and chairs, and sat in stacks on the floor. Some looked new, others had tattered bindings and broken spines. Framed maps and portraits and documents hung on the walls, and here and there among the books loomed assorted objects, including an ancient pistol, an old leather fire hat, and a silver tankard with a hinged top. Over a cluttered desk appeared a sign: TO KNOW THE PAST IS TO UNDERSTAND THE PRESENT.

"Try that chair, Mr. Harmony. It's comfortable and more or less intact. You can move whatever you find there."

He indicated a high-backed chair covered with glossy black haircloth. From it I removed a box of dusty arrowheads and a pile of theater bills from thirty years before.

Far from putting me off, all this mustiness and clutter whetted me up pretty keen.

"Well now," said my host, settling in a worn armchair by his desk, "my old friend Ernest Stevenson tells me you've embarked upon a fascinating project, a family memoir that will probably expand into a maritime history of this city in the present century, with a link to the slave trade."

"Yes sir. The slave trade aspect isn't certain, but it's a hot possibility."

"And why would you want to besmirch your family name, and the memory of your grandfather Caleb Harmony, our revered old master of sailing, with such a revelation?"

"If it's true—and I hope it isn't—it deserves to be known. I have the impression, still unverified, that a lot of the fortunes in this city were made by trading in slaves. If so, that's shameful. It shouldn't be kept in the dark."

"And you will pursue your research until you know about your family and the trade, one way or the other?"

"Yes sir. Come what may."

Dr. Dalrymple had lit a pipe; its smoke drifted toward me, bringing a heady but soothing aroma.

"Admirable. Go at it tooth and nail. I have no knowledge of your family, though I met the famous—I'll even say legendary—Caleb Harmony once, when he addressed the Historical Society on the fading days of sail. His stories enthralled us."

"They've enthralled me, too. I've heard them since the age of three."

"I envy you that. Now as regards the slave trade in New York, here are some items I've located. I'm sure there are more lurking in this clutter, if I can only find them."

He handed me three framed newspaper clippings that looked to be over a hundred years old.

TO BE SOLD

A healthy young Negro wench about twenty-three years old, has had the Small-Pox and Measles, can spin, knit, cook, wash, and iron, speaks English and Dutch. She is sold only because she gets too many children. With a bit of Discipline, will make a very good drudge. Enquire of Adolphus Schuyler, Pearl Street.

RAN AWAY

from Benjamin Clark of Brooklyn, a lusty Negro fellow named Caesar, tall, about 18 Years of Age, speaks Kikongo but very little English, wearing a cheap cotton shirt and tow trousers; has taken with him a Musket mounted with Brass. Whosoever brings said Negro fellow and Musket back to his Master shall have three pounds Reward. Enquire of the printers.

TO BE SOLD

A parcel of likely Negro boys and girls from 9 to 11 years of age, docile and cheerful, promising to make good slaves. For foresighted Purchasers, an excellent Investment. Enquire of Abraham Hays, Maiden Lane.

Even a glance at the clippings chilled me to the quick. Here in my very own city people had once thought nothing of buying and selling other human beings. And this foul business had been ended nationwide only recently!

"Yes, Mr. Harmony, there has always been a slave trade here—until a few years ago, that is—because there has always been a demand for slaves. They were here from the very start, helping build New Amsterdam's houses and barns and windmills, and the roads later known as Broadway and the Bowery. Ah, the romance of old names!"

His eyes shone as he warmed to his subject. Once again, his voice and the aroma of his pipe carried me along.

"Broadway, the *Heere Straat* or Broad Road of Dutch days, following an old Indian trail that had been there for centuries. Canal Street, where there was once a canal. Wall Street, where they built the wall to keep out the Indians. The Bowery, from a Dutch word meaning "farm," where Peter Stuyvesant's farm was located. Old Peter's ghost is still said to haunt St. Mark's Church in the Bowery, where people claim to have heard his wooden leg clomping in the aisles. What a thought: the old man still with us today!"

For a moment, he seemed lost in reflection, while his pipe smoke caressed my nostrils. A spellbinder.

"Dr. Dalrymple, we were talking about the slave trade and slaves."

"What? Oh yes, so we were. And how they helped build the Bowery and Broadway. Broadway has always been the thoroughfare where sooner or later everybody goes. Slaves too in the olden times, which may have let them meet together and plan the conspiracy of '41."

"There was a conspiracy here in 1841?"

"Dear me, no, young man, in 1741. If conspiracy there was, some have doubted it. There was a series of suspicious fires; the slaves were suspected. Hundreds were arrested, seventeen hanged, and thirteen burned at the stake. A dubious affair, much less certain than the revolt of 1712."

"There was a slave revolt in this city?"

"Yes, indeed. One night they set out to burn down the city and murder every white person in it. Nine whites died, and some twenty slaves were hanged and three burned at the stake, one of them roasted for hours in torment. Another was broken on the wheel."

"That's all of it pretty awful."

Dreamy until now, his features suddenly acquired a look of intensity. "Never underestimate the fear of a slavemaster, who can never feel secure, or the smoldering anger and hate of a slave who longs for freedom. Hannibal and Quanimo and Mingo and Quacko paid a high price for their revolt."

"What strange names!"

"Quacko from an African word for Wednesday, when he was born, and Quanimo for Saturday. And before them there was Simon Congo and Domingo Angola and Jan Guinea and others, their last names indicating their place of origin. I tell you, young man, there's often a whole history contained in a name."

Mingo, Quacko, Simon Congo, Domingo Angola: a whole world of people who had toiled and endured and plotted.

"History, sir, can be a bitter pill to swallow."

"Well said, Mr. Harmony. Which may explain why so many want to forget it. This Go Ahead city delights to tear down the old and build up the new. So be it, but we shan't let them forget, shall we, Mr. Harmony?"

"No sir."

Was he enlisting me in a conspiracy of his own? An elegant idea, I thought.

"I gather there were once a lot of slaves in this city?"

"Before the Revolution, one resident in five was a slave."

"What happened to them all? There aren't nearly that many blacks here today."

"During the Revolution the British offered freedom to the slaves of patriots. When the British left, thousands of slaves went with them. It was the end of an era."

"Maybe that was all to the good."

"Yes, but the slave trade persisted. Come, let me show you something."

Shuffling again in slippers, he led me back out into the hallway and through another doorway into what should have been the parlor, but with its hodgepodge of books and historical debris seemed more a repetition of his study.

"Here is one of my most prized possessions, an engraving dating from 1642."

Hanging on the wall under glass was a large print with a banner proclaiming NIEUW AMSTERDAM at the top. It showed a town of clustered houses with ships anchored offshore in the background, and in the foreground a caped and booted Dutchman in a conical, wide-brimmed hat, stern-faced, gesturing with authority, while a team of half-naked blacks toted burdens up from the shore, their heavy loads balanced on their heads. I stared in fascination.

"There! That says it all. A thriving commercial hub with white men in charge, and blacks doing most of the labor. That's how it was from the start!"

Though they were not depicted as unhappy, I didn't envy Simon Congo or Jan Guinea their work under the eye of this dour master. Of course they would seethe with hate.

As he led me from the room, Dr. Dalrymple brushed against a stack of loose papers that scattered on the floor; I helped him retrieve them. The very first one I picked up grabbed my attention.

Rec'd by the grace of God, our saviour Jesus Christ, his Saints, and the

Blessed Virgin Mary, in satisfactory condition, by Don Miguel Martinez in and upon the schooner Charity, William Matthews, master: 583 slaves, duly marked and numbered, on the account of said Don Miguel, commission merchant of Havana, transferred with due caution in small craft to various points on the north shore of the Island of Cuba. In witness whereof said Don Miguel affirms to this Bill of Lading, acknowledging that the good schooner has safely reached her desired destination. Blessed be the name of Our Saviour. Dated in Havana 26 March 1854.

A thrill shot through me. Here at last was proof linking Don Miguel Martinez Sr. not just to any Matthews, but specifically to the William Matthews I had interviewed. Since I already had a letter connecting "C. Harmony" to a "Capt. Matthews" and a "Señor Martinez," it looked bad, very bad, for Grandpa Harmony.

"Dr. Dalrymple, this document is of capital importance to me. How did you ever come by it?"

"Which document? Oh, that bill of lading. I got it with a whole bunch of papers—they're all there, in no particular order—from a captain who came knocking on my door, knowing I collected old documents. He needed money, of course. That was several years back, and I have yet to really sort out what I got."

"Would you be willing to part with this for a consideration?"

"I rarely do that. I'm a collector, not a dealer. I buy to possess, to keep."

"Perhaps we could do a trade. For this paper I'd be willing to give you a print that my grandfather gave me, showing a clipper ship of the early fifties. It's in A-1 condition, nicely framed."

"A clipper ship? I love prints of clipper ships. Let me see this document."

He scrutinized it, shrugged. "Interesting, but of no special concern to me. Bring me that print. If it's in good condition and not a duplicate of a print I have already, it's a deal. When can you show me the print?"

"Now!"

Before he could say a word, I was out of the room and the house, racing to St. Mark's Place to get the print. I was back within the hour, print in hand, puffing, all of which amused him.

"Ah, the vigor, the impetuosity of youth! Well, let's see the print. Hmm, very nice, and not a duplicate." He scanned it closely, turned it over, and scanned the back of it as well. "Mr. Harmony, that document is yours. I much prefer to own this print."

We shook hands, each well satisfied with his acquisition. Then, at my host's suggestion, I examined the other documents in the batch he had bought from the captain, but found nothing relevant.

Erasmus Dalrymple rarely found a ready listener for his ramblings, so when he did, he clung to him. We talked some more, with my host skipping from subject to subject, mentioning in turn the last visit of General Lafayette (he had met him), Jenny Lind's famous Castle Garden concert (he heard it from a rowboat in the harbor), and a long-vanished Negro Burial Ground. He was scatterbrained and brilliant, tossing out scraps of history like shiny rare coins that I clutched at, though many of them flashed in the air and were gone. But my mind was jumping, eager to get home and scrutinize again the bill of lading, so finally, pleading other engagements, I cut things short.

"Good-bye, sir. I've learned a vast deal. Thank you."

"Good-bye, young man. Keep at your work. Cling to it, savor it, honor it. And by all means come again."

Hurrying home, I rushed to my room and examined my new acquisition. What did it mean? How far would it take me in my journey toward the dark truth of the Harmonys and slavery? I dreaded to know, yet I had to. Yes, I was obsessed.

14

Quanimo: *We are their drudge.*
Mingo: *We built their houses and barns and roads.*
Quacko: *Under the lash!*
Simon Congo: *Stolen away from our homeland.*
Domingo Angola: *Stripped naked and shackled and branded and herded like cattle.*
Jan Guinea: *Crammed into foul-smelling ships and brought to this new land to do their labor.*
Quanimo: *Brothers, are we agreed it is time for vengeance?*
Mingo: *And for justice!*
Jan Guinea: *And for freedom!*
Quacko: *Let us plan carefully.*
Simon Congo: *And secretly.*
Domingo Angola: *They do not expect this, for they think us mindless brutes.*
Quanimo: *For that, brothers, they shall pay.*
Mingo: *We shall burn their fort, and their houses as they sleep at night.*
Jan Guinea: *And their churches, especially their churches, since they pray to their God for safe voyages to bring us into bondage.*
Simon Congo: *We shall burn the whole wicked city.*
Quacko: *And scatter the ashes, so nothing remains of it.*
Domingo Angola: *But we must kill them first.*
Quanimo: *In the night.*
Mingo: *By stealth.*
Jan Guinea: *Sharpen your knives, brothers.*
Quacko: *Watch carefully where they store their guns, so you can seize them.*
Simon Congo: *We shall cut their fine white throats.*
Domingo Angola: *We shall fire their guns point-blank into their surprised white faces.*
Mingo: *It is justice.*
Jan Guinea: *Then, only then, will we be free.*

Quanimo: Shall they all die?
Simon Congo: All!
Quacko: At midnight, Sunday. We shall kill them on their Sabbath.
Jan Guinea: Pray to your gods, brothers.
Domingo Angola: Do voodoo for success.
Quanimo: Go to the Burial Ground and listen to the spirits of the ancestors.
Mingo: Justice is at hand!
Simon Congo: And if the soldiers come with their muskets?
Domingo Angola: We shall kill them, too.
Jan Guinea: Our gods are stronger than theirs.
Simon Congo: Our minds are more cunning.
Mingo: Blood will run on Broadway and the Bowery.
Quacko: Fire will destroy their churches and homes.
Simon Congo: And burn their slave codes and Bibles.
Quanimo: For vengeance!
Mingo: For justice!
Jan Guinea: For freedom!

"It still doesn't prove that Grandpa was involved in the slave trade," Sal insisted. "Not absolutely and completely."

We were in the library, where I had shown her and Rick the bill of lading.

"C'mon, Sal," said Rick. "Grandpa wrote that letter about boxes of soap and the rest of it to a Captain Matthews, mentioning a Señor Martinez in Havana. This bill of lading tells us who they are, and Chris knows from his talk with Matthews that Matthews was a slaver."

"Chris said he was cagey," argued Sal. "Matthews never straight out admitted it. And how many Captain William Matthewses are there in the *City Directory*?"

"Seven," I said.

"You see? It's a common name. The Matthews mentioned in the letter may be someone else who had nothing to do with the slave trade. And how many people are there by the name of Miguel Martinez in the *Directory*?"

"Three," I said.

"Another common name! And there must be loads more in Havana. And the Martinez that Chris talked to denied that any of his family were involved in the trade."

"But Chris didn't believe him," said Rick. "And I don't either."

"Chris," Sal asked, "do you really think that Grandpa Harmony—that wonderful old man who told us marvelous stories and took us on tours of the harbor—could have engaged in something so vile?"

"I don't want to," I said, "but it sure looks like he did."

"Are you sheer convinced?"

"I suppose there's a scrap of a smidgen of a chance we've misinterpreted that letter, though I don't know what else it could mean, especially in the light of this bill of lading."

"There, Rick, you see? Even Chris isn't totally convinced. I want clear, unambiguous proof. Grandpa's signature on some document that mentions slaves, or the testimony of an eyewitness."

"All right," said Rick, "I'll give you exactly that. I had three ables lined up on the waterfront, but two of them just shipped out. I'll bring Chris and the other one together, and believe me, Chris will learn plenty."

"I want to hear it, too!"

"No, you rowdy girl, you don't. We'll have to meet this fellow on his own ground, and it won't be the Astor House bar."

"Where will it be?" I asked.

"Some dingy saloon near the waterfront. We'll have to buy him drinks."

A good Presbyterian, I wasn't too keen on visiting a saloon. "Well, all right, but don't tell Ma."

"I'll try to set it up for tomorrow."

"So as usual," said Sal, "I have to cling to the hearth and twiddle my thumbs."

Rick smiled. "Yes, sweet maid, you do. But we'll give you a full report. And Chris… "

"Yes?"

"Dress rough."

"How do, gents. And so, Mr. Chris, you're Rick's cousin and some kind of kin to Caleb Harmony, and you want to know about slavers in this city."

"Yes sir."

"Jesus, kid, don't 'sir' me. I'm Silas Webb, an able seaman who never made mate—not for long, leastwise, as I always had a muss with the skipper. So take a swig from that mug, and you'll get an earful."

"Yes, Mr. Webb, fine. Yes. I will."

I barely sipped it; it tasted sweet but foul.

"Yes, gang, this old boy's been a packet rat for over twenty years, shipped on packets, men-o'-war, whalers, East Indiamen, coastal sloops and schooners, clipper ships, and yes, you bet, slavers. I can tell you plenty."

He was fortyish or more, grizzled, with weathered features, stubble on his chin, and a sharp eye, wearing dungarees and a red shirt open at the neck. We'd joined him in a shabby waterfront saloon with a timbered ceiling and sand on the floor, and seamen all around us at the bar, talking, clinking mugs, laughing, and singing snatches of sea chanteys whose words were bodaciously gamy. There were smells of liquor, onions, pretzels, and sweat, and from the busy docks outside, tar and sawn wood and brine. I'd worn an old jacket and shirt, and a sailor's cap borrowed from Rick, in an effort to at least blend in a little. Already in his cups when we got there, Silas Webb, further inspired by the mug of rum we bought him, seemed eager to talk.

"Mr. Webb," I asked, "were there many slavers leaving from here just before the war?"

"More than ever. A dozen a month, often more, and everybody on South Street knew it. How could they not, when they was in on it? Not just the owners and masters and mates, but the riggers and caulkers and ship's carpenters, and the chandlers and provisioners, too. There was a Portuguese company on Front Street as claimed to be importing wine, and then a Spanish outfit on Pearl Street run by a Señor—get this!—Innocencio Something-or-other, and others there with names like Santos and Tejedor and Cunha, working hand-in-glove with us Yankees."

"Maybe also a Don Miguel Martinez?" I ventured.

"Him, too, the sly bastard, him and his son. Because the shipowners here needed contacts on the Guinea Coast and in the Congo, and in Havana, too, and those contacts were Spaniards or Portuguese. A real international trade!"

"And it was obvious if a ship was a slaver?" Rick asked.

"Plain as day. All those water tanks, barrels of hardtack and rice, and tons of lumber for a slave deck."

"And boxes marked 'soap'?" I suggested.

"Or 'hardware' or 'rope,' but full of chains and shackles. And the high wages offered the crew—higher than any other ships could offer.

Obvious as hell! The Custom House records might read, 'January 23, Osprey, ship's master Peck, cleared for Africa.' Or 'March 8, Amity, ship's master Rogers, outward bound for Africa.' Anyone who wanted to could see what was going on."

"How did they recruit the crews?" asked Rick.

"Runners went to the boarding houses, looked up ables who'd shipped on slavers before and kept their mouth shut. Men from anywhere and everywhere, so your shipmates might include a French Peter, Dutch Bill, Portuguese Jack, you name it. A scruffy bunch, mostly old hands with some greenies thrown in, but they knew what they was about."

"Were the captains known as well?" asked Rick.

"Of course. And they knew each other, had secret grips and passwords, so even one new to the city could make himself known pretty quick."

"Maybe a Captain William Matthews?" I put in.

"One of the shrewdest and slickest in the trade, and mean, to boot. But there was plenty of others, and the king of them all—the 'Prince of Slavers,' they called him—was Captain Gideon Lynch, who must have skippered twenty or thirty slavers over the years. Strutted around on the quarterdeck in a blue uniform with gold buttons and braid, barking orders to the mate, and a bucko type he was. I know; I shipped with him more than once."

"Did he and Matthews ever work for the Harmonys?" asked Rick.

"Many a time. Matthews was rough-cut, but on shore Lynch was a gent. But they both commanded Harmony ships."

"Which ones?" I asked.

"The schooners *Sea Eagle* and *Charity* and *Mary D.*, the brigs *Fearless* and *Lark*, and a bunch of others I disremember."

Rick and I exchanged a glance. "They were all slavers?" My heart was beating.

"Slavers this year and legit the next, so's to flummox the authorities."

"And you shipped with Captains Lynch and Matthews to Africa?" I asked.

"Not with those two, but I've known such as did."

"And Caleb Harmony knew that his vessels were being used as slavers?"

He shot us a canny glance. "Say, mates, my memory's just a bit fuzzy. Nothing focuses it like a good stiff mug of rum."

He had finished the mug we bought him, so Rick got him another. He took a swig, wiped his lips, smiled; drops of rum dribbled down his chin. Meanwhile Rick signaled to me, indicating my own mug, barely touched. Furtively, I poured half of it on the floor.

"Chris was asking," said Rick, "if Caleb Harmony knew that his ships were being used as slavers."

"Of course he knew," said Webb. "Old Caleb was no fool. He was in it with his son."

"With Jacob?" asked Rick, who looked tense.

"You bet! Any relation?"

"A cousin of some kind," said Rick. (We hadn't explained our connection.)

"Not that they was in it all the time; they had plenty of legal operations as well. For them, slaving was just a nice little sideline."

"And Mark Harmony?" I barely masked the quiver in my voice.

"The younger son?" said Webb. "He stuck pretty close to the chandlery. I'm not sure he was in it."

"But he knew they were?"

"You'd think so, but maybe he didn't ask questions. Lots of people on the waterfront didn't. Like I said, everyone was in on it one way or another. Not just the Harmonys, but the Biggses and that fellow Lynch, who ended up owning a passel of ships. And others, lots of them very high-toned gents who left the dirty work to others."

Rambunctious laughter erupted at the other end of the bar, then another burst of song.

"I like whiskey hot and strong,
Whiskey, O, Johnny, O,
I'll drink whiskey all day long,
Rise her up from down below."

Unruffled by the noise, Silas Webb spat, then guzzled.

"But wasn't this pretty risky?" Rick asked. "There were laws, after all, and British and American cruisers patrolling the African coast."

"Yes, but not enough of them. Maybe one ship in twenty got caught. There was fake owners and forged documents, and two sets of papers for a ship, so it could change its name and flag. The owner could charter a ship to someone who might charter it to someone else, so if it got caught, the owner could claim he had nothing to do with it."

"Weren't there inspections by federal marshals?" asked Rick.

"For the marshals, those inspections was a chore and a bore. They had to go through a fat lot of crates in the hold, some of them suspicious, some not. Besides, marshals could be bought off, likewise the customs men and judges. The owners and masters was always five steps ahead of the authorities. I'll wager a keg of rum that neither Caleb Harmony nor any of his kin ever put their name to a document that might link them to the trade."

My head was reeling; I forced myself to concentrate. "The schooner *Venture*, was that in the trade as well?" Again, I tried to mask the quiver in my voice.

"That's quite a story, mate, but for me to spin it, I might need another mug of rum."

Rick got him another. His speech was getting thick; I wanted to pump him all I could, before he fuzzed up completely.

"Chris was asking about the *Venture*," said Rick.

"A smart sailer, hard to overtake. Built for racing, with a long, sharp bow and a cutaway stern. Could do up to twenty knots on occasion, when men-o'-war at best could manage nine at best. With a bit of refitting, perfect for the trade. Old Caleb bought it through a dummy."

"His son Jacob bought it," said Rick, "according to Custom House records."

Webb shrugged. "Could be."

"But what became of it?" I asked.

Webb smiled. "No one knows, but I've heard lots of stories. Some say it's a slaver to this day, running between Africa and Cuba. Chartered to some dago, of course. Others say it was burned and sunk off the Cuban coast, just like so many old hulks."

"Why would it or any of them be burned?" I asked.

"To get rid of evidence, if the authorities came sniffing about. And to avoid all the trouble of having to fumigate the hold. Hell, after a slave trip, the hold would be filthy and crawling with vermin, so the crew would smoke it by sticking red-hot irons in tin pots filled with tar, or they'd sprinkle it with chloride of lime. A nasty business, and even that might not get rid of the stink. Believe me, I know. So why not just burn the ship and be done with it?"

"Even one of the finest racers afloat?"

"After a few trips that brought in several hundred thousand each, or even a half million, why not? Time to close the books, I'd say. Not that a poor slob like me ever saw chink like that. It ended up in banks in New York and Havana, and in fancy homes and shiny black carriages, and country estates and fast trotters. Some of the biggest fortunes in this city came by way of the trade. Bigger fortunes than the Harmonys'. Bigger by far." His eyes flashed, he had a vague, dreamy look. Then: "Say, blokes, how about another mug of rum? I'll tell you about shipping to the Slave Coast under Jake Harmony on the brig *Fearless*, and how I met the king of Dahomey, and fought off crocodiles, and almost ended up a slave myself."

"Another time, Silas," said Rick. "Chris and I have got to weigh anchor."

"Rick, couldn't we spare a few more minutes?" I wanted to hear about the *Fearless.*

Rick shot me a glance. "No! Gotta run."

"Thanks, Mr. Webb," I said. "We'll be in touch. Good-bye."

"All right, you little rats, run. Fat chance you'll have of pumping Silas Webb again. Screw off, mates, screw off."

We left him muttering at the bar.

"Why did you do that?" I asked Rick out on the street, as we hurried away, dodging carts and wagons in the usual jam of the waterfront.

"He was getting flaky. And that stuff about the king of Dahomey, and crocodiles, and almost becoming a slave himself—that was pure dime novel."

"Well, at least we finally got some things straight. Your pa and Caleb, and the Biggses and Matthews and Martinez, and this fellow Lynch as well, were all in the trade together."

"Maybe."

"Why maybe? The more he drank, the more we learned."

"The more he drank, the less I believed him."

"Why?" I almost yelled, projecting over the din of stevedores rolling barrels down a gangway from a ship.

"Like most storytellers, he tells what his listeners want to hear. Being Harmonys, we know all about that."

"He seemed to know the trade and how it worked. I learned plenty."

"So did I. All the general stuff he said I believe, though he probably puffed it up a bit. It's the details I don't trust. Who did what, and when they did it, and where."

"For instance?" We were away from the waterfront now; I didn't have to yell.

"He said he shipped out with Pa on the *Fearless.* But before that he said he'd never shipped to Africa on a Harmony vessel. And Pa never commanded the *Fearless.*"

"Oh. So where does that leave us?"

"In a muddle. The more we learn, the less we seem to know."

"So what do we do next?"

"Give Grandpa's papers another good hard look, keeping all these names in mind—Matthews, Martinez, the Biggses, and Gideon Lynch. Lynch I've barely heard of; he was before my time. Somehow he must fit in."

"Is he still alive?"

"Deceased, I think, but there must be heirs, and they would know a lot. Let's find them."

We'd left South Street behind and had come to Pearl, with its rows of import-export firms and wholesalers' offices and warehouses.

"Pearl Street!" I exclaimed. "Didn't he mention some Spanish and Portuguese importers with offices here?"

"Yes! A Señor Innocencio Something-or-other, and some names like Santos and Cunha. We'll look for them, too."

"In Grandpa's papers?"

"Where else? I have a hunch that there are clues there to everything we need to know. It's just a matter of spotting them."

"You make it sound like a game."

"It is! The toughest, trickiest, meanest, most maddening game I've ever played. C'mon, mate, we've got work to do! Unless that rum has befuddled you."

I made a face. "It was foul."

He laughed and dragged me off.

15

Dear Caleb,

Since the bark Arrow from Salem is departing this wretched coast tomorrow, I shall send you this letter so as to bring you to date on our enterprise. The trip over was uneventful, till we approached the Ivory Coast at Grand Bassam and felt the sultry air of this place, and the miasma from coastal marshes that so often spells death to the white man. We fired a gun to bring off the natives, who soon launched canoes and came to us, announcing, "Long time no see ship come for makee trade." We soon exchanged 20 barrels of rum and a hogshead of tobacco for a goodly amount of gold dust and prime ivory, then traded down the coast to various points, selling puncheons of rum (always in demand) and sundry other articles of the cargo.

Thinking this stretch of coast free of fever, I and two of my men rowed upriver for a palaver with King Nuba of the Maronga people, a tall, strapping fellow who received us sitting on a gold stool in front of a large tent of red and blue silk, wearing a long calico gown and a cap embroidered in gold. "No wantee war with white man," he assured us. "Wantee peace, wantee trade, wantee rum, tobacco, flints, cotton cloth, guns. Wantee sell you gold and ivory." The beads he wore around his neck, wrists, and ankles were made, so they say, from the sawed-up bones of his victims in war, and on the ground nearby was a pyramid of human skulls. We traded rum, tobacco, needles, and cutlery for gold dust, tortoise shell, gum copal, beeswax, and ivory.

Returning to the Lark, I found the third mate sunstruck and deranged, the first mate down with fever and the ague, and the rest of the men drunk. I promptly called the crew to order, but within an hour I myself felt faint and dizzy, and lost all sense of things for three days and nights, during which time I was raving crazy. Though weak, I have now recovered. But the first mate is still very low, and the third mate in a fit of delirium cut his throat from ear to ear; we gave him to the deep this morning.

Caleb, it is folly to trade on this coast. The slavers do it right: have prior arrangements with a factor on shore, race in, take on the stock, and clear away fast, before the miasma or some British cruiser can get to you. Honest merchants like us dally along this pestilential coast, exposed to its killing hot sun and fevers, and the whims of savages, and for all that our profits are less. Think on it, Caleb, think on it long and hard. Arrangements could be made with Pearl Street importers like Martinez and da Cunha, who have connections on this coast and in Havana as well.

Under Providence I shall see you in a few months' time, myself hopefully free of the shakes. Here and at home, may our joint affairs prosper. Signed at Sekondi, Gold Coast, this 14th day of April 1841. Your friend and partner, Gideon Lynch.

"There, Sal, there's your proof!" Rick brandished in triumph the old letter that he had found among Grandpa's papers. "This fellow Gideon Lynch, whom Webb called the 'Prince of Slavers,' nudged Grandpa into the trade. In this letter we catch him in the very act of doing it!"

Sal scanned the letter quickly. "It proves nothing. Lynch may have nudged Grandpa, but that doesn't mean Grandpa agreed. Maybe he told Lynch to go fly a kite."

"C'mon, Sal," said Rick. "It's as plain as the nose on your face. Chris, don't you agree?"

"Well, the letter does seem to confirm what Webb said about their being in it together, and it mentions Martinez and da Cunha as well."

"That's still not proof!" Sal insisted.

"Well, not quite," I conceded. "There's still just the slightest chance that Grandpa didn't go along with Lynch's suggestion."

"Then what about *this*?" Rick demanded, brandishing another sheet of paper. "It's obvious! I can read it at a glance!"

He passed the paper to Sal, who studied it and then passed it on to me.

Cost of vessel and stores	*$25,000*
" " 600 @ $50/head	*$30,000*
Wages of captain and crew	*$30,000*
Bribes to Spanish officials	
@ $100/head (assuming 10%	
loss at sea)	*$54,000*
Total cost	*$139,000*
Sale of 540 @ $600/head	*$324,000*
	-139,000
Net profit	*$185,000*

"Well, Sal, what do you say?" asked Rick.

"I don't understand it."

"Sal, it's as plain as the nose on your face."

"Leave my nose out of this. I don't understand it."

Rick looked expectantly at me. "Chris?"

"It's an estimate of profits for a voyage. They'll buy slaves at fifty a head and sell them at six hundred. After expenses and a loss of ten percent, or sixty slaves, on the passage, there'll be a net profit of a hundred and eighty-five thousand. Which isn't bad,

I suppose."

"A fortune!" said Rick.

"It doesn't say 'slaves,'" said Sal.

"What else could it be?" asked Rick.

"Livestock."

"At those prices, hardly. And importing livestock isn't illegal anywhere, so why the bribes to officials?"

"You found it in Grandpa's papers?" I asked.

"In the miscellaneous pile. It's probably a calculation that Grandpa did, while pondering Lynch's suggestion."

"It's not in Grandpa's handwriting!" Sal insisted. "And it's not in Pa's hand or Uncle Jake's either!"

"So what?" said Rick. "Grandpa had one of his clerks write it out. It's a cold calculation of profits, counting human beings like so many head of cattle or puncheons of rum."

"We don't know who wrote it out, or when, or why. I won't believe the worst about Grandpa, until you show me absolute proof!"

"Chris?" Rick shot me another glance.

I sighed. "Sal, it looks like Rick is right."

"You're absolutely, totally convinced?"

"Well, almost."

"But not completely?"

"Not quite, I suppose."

"There! You agree with me after all. I want an eyewitness, or Grandpa's signature on a paper that incriminates him beyond the slightest doubt."

"If I showed you such a paper," said Rick, "you'd claim it was a forgery. And if I brought you an eyewitness, you'd call him a liar."

"I wouldn't!"

"Anyway, you'll never find that paper. As Webb said, the Harmonys were much too clever to leave evidence like that around. They always kept shy of the dirty work, leaving that to dummy owners and agents, and to the captains and crews. They never saw slaves being shackled and branded, and never got a whiff of the hold. They stayed neat and clean, and raked in slathers of cash. This brownstone of yours"—(we were in the library again)—"and Pa's fancy new palace on the Avenue, were bought and furnished with money from the trade. Thanks to that trade, we grew up in clover, damn well fixed indeed. All these silks and brocades, and this fancy walnut and mahogany furniture, come from it. Caleb and Jacob Harmony were guilty of something deucedly vile, and if we won't admit it and speak out, we'll be guilty, too. Do you hear me? *We'll be guilty, too!*"

Rick's words cut me. Sal burst into tears and ran from the room.

"Grandpa, you did do it, didn't you?"

"Did what?"

"You know."

"That was so long ago, Chris, so long ago."

"Then you did do it."

"Things were different then, Chris. The mood of the times was different."

"You trafficked in human beings for money."

"I did lots of things, Chris. Things that took courage and daring."

"You and Captain Lynch went into it together. His idea, but you went along with it."

"My captains went everywhere. We brought back silks and tea from Canton, hides from Buenos Aires, sugar and cigars from Cuba, coffee from

Brazil..."

"And slaves from Africa with the help of Captain Matthews, and Señor Martinez in Havana."

"Chris, I never saw a slave ship or a slave, I swear!"

"You left all that to others."

"I never put my name to a ship's manifest or a bill of lading that mentioned slaves."

"You were much too clever for that. You and Uncle Jake."

"You've been talking to Rick. Don't listen to him. He's out to spite his father."

"And Silas Webb?"

"A drunk. He'll say anything to get a mug of rum."

"I'm so ashamed, Grandpa. Ashamed for all of us."

"Chris, boy, we had a special friendship, didn't we?"

"Yes, Grandpa, we did."

"I knew you were different. I knew you'd never go to sea."

"I couldn't, Grandpa. Just rowing around the harbor made me seasick, and climbing up rigging made me dizzy."

"I never bothered you about it. Never teased you or made fun of you."

"Never."

"You were special. Chris, the little bookworm. And how you loved my stories! To an old man, that meant a lot."

"I never thought of you as old."

"But I was, Chris. Old and feeble. All I had left were stories. The other boys were ready to get out in the world and do things on their own. No time for an old man living in the past. But you, you loved my stories."

"They were rich and wondrous. I'll never forget them."

"I love you, Chris."

"Grandpa, I love you, too."

"Forgive me, Chris. If I ever did wrong, forgive me."

"Did you do wrong, Grandpa? Can't you at least tell me*?"*

"I've got to be going, Chris."

"Please, Grandpa, say that you did it. Say it just once to me!"

"Good-bye, Chris."

"Grandpa...!"

"Good-bye."

16

Dear Graduate,

I feel quite abandoned by you. You promised to come to my Thursdays, but I haven't seen you once. Surely your research, fascinating though it must be, leaves a little time for social life. Please come. Your friend,

Louise Rivington

Sal sniffed the note, on gilt-edged satin paper. "Nice perfume. Heady, and just a bit smoky."

"I hadn't noticed."

"I'll bet."

"Men don't notice such things."

"I'll bet."

Since bursting into tears in front of Rick, Sal had brooded for a day or two, but now seemed herself again and made no reference to Grandpa or Rick. I too preferred to avoid the whole business, needing time to think.

"So, are you going?"

"I don't know. I've got a lot on my mind right now."

"That statuette she gave you—that slant-eyed temptress holding flowers and a mirror—you've put it on your bedside table."

"So what?"

"A courtesan, I'll bet. She fascinates you. And so does Mrs. Rivington."

"C'mon."

"That woman knows her way."

"I tell you, I've got a lot else on my mind. I want to read more stuff in Pa's library and check out some registrations at the Custom House."

"Fine. But are you going?"

"To Mrs. Rivington's?"

"Where else?"

"Of course."

Once again, the grandiose freestanding brownstone on the Avenue with the steep stoop and monumental entrance—even more imposing than Uncle Jake's fancy uptown residence. And once again the mulatto butler in the vestibule who, on receiving my card, ushered me into the parlor with its silk-screen landscape on the wall, blue-and-white porcelain on the mantel, and other signs of the China trade. Several gentlemen were sitting or standing about, talking quietly, among them Uncle Jake and Señor Miguel Martinez. Mrs. Rivington came to greet me, her green velvet adorned with bold jet jewels.

"Ah, here is our scholar at last! So good to see you, Mr. Chris. We have finally plucked you away from your research."

"You have indeed, Mrs. Rivington. Good afternoon." I breathed in her perfume: yes, heady and just a bit smoky.

"Let me present you to my guests. I believe you are acquainted with the eminent Mr. Jacob Harmony, are you not?" She smiled, with a hint of mischief.

"I believe I am."

"I should think so!" said Uncle Jake, giving my hand a firm, tight clasp. "I've known this young pup since he was in rompers."

"And this is Señor Martinez, one of our leading importers, who has been in this city many years. Señor Martinez, this is Mr. Christopher Harmony, who is researching a family history that should prove quite fascinating."

"I have already had the pleasure of meeting young Mr. Harmony," said Señor Martinez, smiling warmly over his neatly trimmed goatee. "He consulted me with regard to his research, but I, alas, was unable to assist him. I trust, señor, that your research is going well." His voice was soft and caressing.

"Slow but steady, señor, and not without surprises."

"Really? What kind of surprises, Mr. Harmony? Assuming that you do not mind giving us a brief, scant glimpse, so as to whet our appetites for the feast to come."

"Well, sir, old bills of lading, very informative, that turn up in the most unlikely places. And old salts on the waterfront who, if plied with a few mugs of rum, tell you in detail how things worked in the old days."

"I hope, Mr. Harmony, that you will find more reliable sources than old drunks on the waterfront."

"I search everywhere, señor. Doing research is like turning over rocks in a garden. You never know what sneaky little facts you may find lurking underneath."

"Mr. Chris," announced our hostess with a smile, "you really must find a better image than grubs under rocks in a garden. Why not say you're prospecting for gold?"

"I stand corrected, madam. Your image is far superior. Yes, I'm looking for, and sometimes finding, gold."

"Or fool's gold," said Señor Martinez. "If your sources are not sound."

"There's always that risk, señor. One learns to use one's judgment."

"Well said, Mr. Chris," said Mrs. Rivington. "Didn't I tell you, Jacob? Your nephew will go far. I anticipate with pleasure the first nuggets of his research. And his coming today makes up, just a little, for the absence of Mr. Dwight."

"Sorry about that, Louise. We'll see less of the sprout, now that he's engaged."

"Dwight is engaged?" I asked.

"Just last week, Chris," said Uncle Jake. "We were going to let you know."

"Miss Van Zandt?"

"Yes, indeed. Lovely girl."

"Mild as moonbeams, I'm sure," said Mrs. Rivington.

"We're delighted," insisted Uncle Jake. "An old Knickerbocker family. They go back to the first poltroons."

Of course he meant "patroons." From her hint of a smile I could tell that Mrs. Rivington had also caught the gaffe. Her eye met mine for an instant, then quickly looked away.

More guests were arriving. Before turning to greet them, Mrs. Rivington introduced me to some of the other gentlemen present, and waved me toward a table with urns of coffee and tea, and a buffet laden with fruits and sweets. While serving myself some coffee, I was joined by Señor Martinez.

"She is a remarkable woman, Doña Luisa, is she not?"

It took me a moment to grasp that he was referring to Mrs. Rivington. "She certainly is, señor. Have you known her long?"

"Two decades at least. Through my father, who had dealings with hers."

"Did you or your father ever meet her husband?"

"Ah, the mysterious and ever absent husband. No, I have never had the honor. She never mentions him, never."

"Her father was a big shipowner in his time, so I'm told. Heavy into the China trade, as you can tell from the furnishings here."

"Like your esteemed grandfather, he traded all over the world. Have you seen his study?"

"Yes, but I'd like to see it again."

"Come."

He led me to the study, where I was again thrilled at the sight of the prints and maps on the walls, the camphor wood and lacquerware boxes, and other mementos from the days of sail.

"Here," said Señor Martinez, "you have a shrine to the memory of Captain Lane, his many voyages, his far-flung operations."

"Captain Lane was her father?"

"Yes, Captain Geoffrey Lane. His enterprises matched those of Caleb Harmony. They knew each other, were colleagues one year and competitors the next. They had for each other an infinite respect."

"I'm surprised I haven't come across his name."

"You will, no doubt. Like your grandfather, he came from New England, became a successful ship's master here and then a shipowner, and a respected member of the Chamber of Commerce. There's a portrait of him in the parlor."

"What's this?" I had noticed a map on the wall labeled THE LEEWARD COAST.

"A map of the West Coast of Africa, I gather. Not something I know much about."

On the map I read the names Ivory Coast, Gold Coast, and Slave Coast, with settlements like Grand Bassam, Sekondi, and Whyday—names I had encountered before.

"Did Captain Lane trade in Africa?"

"Probably. He traded everywhere."

Flooding my mind were images of settlements among palm trees and mangroves, with old stone forts, and barracoons crammed with shackled slaves. I could imagine sharp-eyed factors wielding fly whisks as they scanned the horizon through a spyglass, looking for a small white dot of sail: a slave ship that, when summoned by an agreed-upon signal, would dart in, load its wretched cargo in haste, then make for the open sea.

"Señor Harmony," Señor Martinez's voice broke in softly, "do not be obsessed with black ivory. The lands you see on that map were also the source of legitimate trade. From them traders brought us ivory for our pianoforte keys, gum copal for varnishes and lacquer, and the cleanest, purest palm oil for making fine candles and soaps. The mariners involved in this trade were honest, hard-working, and brave, risking their health and their lives. To confuse them with slave traders would be shameful. We owe them respect and honor, even awe."

I felt a twinge of shame. "Señor Martinez, I cannot argue with what you say. Perhaps I am obsessed, and hasty."

"Ah, my young friend, now you are being reasonable. Yes, be cautious, do not rush to judgment, be fair. But let us return to the parlor. Doña Luisa will wonder what has become of us."

In the parlor, they were discussing the recent war between France and Germany, the siege of Paris, and the uprising there that had followed it—matters I had given little attention to, being absorbed first in my studies and then in my poking about in dark corners of my family's history.

"I'm very concerned," said Mrs. Rivington. "First that awful siege, then this insurrection. Famine and massacres in the most beautiful city in the world!"

"But France is now a republic, like us," said a frock-coated gentleman.

"That, as a freedom-loving Yankee, I applaud. The French have thrown out one emperor, but the Germans have crowned another. So it goes. France is well rid of this little Napoleon number three. It was his folly that brought all this about."

"Will you go soon to Paris, señora?" asked Señor Martinez.

"When I'm sure things have settled down. To see what, if anything, is left of my property and friends. But come, gentlemen, this subject is much too dismal. Let us speak of something else."

The conversation then ranged over railroads, Wall Street speculations, the new Tiffany's on Union Square, Delmonico's. I didn't try to keep up, just watched in wonder as she delivered shrewd opinions on every subject offered. In the course of it I gathered that she was still involved in shipping, had successful investments, and owned property in the city, upstate, and in Paris and Martinique. She was well traveled, had fluent French, some Spanish, a smattering of Portuguese.

While I watched and listened, first a ship's master named Jonathan Pell, and then a Señor Luis Santos, a Pearl Street importer who spoke flawless English, came over and congratulated me on being the grandson of Caleb Harmony. Each claimed to have had dealings with him and assured me that in every respect he deserved his reputation for probity. I thanked them and made a mental note of their names.

When I took leave, Mrs. Rivington saw me into the hall.

"We've hardly talked, Mr. Chris. I want to hear more about your research. Please come tomorrow at five for tea. It will be just the two of us. We can talk without distraction."

"I'd be glad to," I responded, though I found the thought of a tête-à-tête with her alone slightly daunting, and wondered as well if I should be attending an afternoon tea party, when most of the city's males were toiling indoors or out.

Señor Martinez was also leaving. "Young man," he said to me on the stoop, "Doña Luisa rarely invites anyone, except to her Thursday receptions. You have been granted a very special favor. Make good use of it."

Before I could ask him what he meant, he was off. On the way home it occurred to me that I had forgotten to look in the study for a print of the brig *Fearless*, which I thought I had seen there at New Year's, a ship that Rick had mentioned as a slaver. And I hadn't seen the portrait of her father in the parlor.

"Well?" said Sal. Just back from her latest enthusiasm, archery lessons in Central Park, she was waiting for me in the sitting room. She'd tossed her bow and arrows on a chair.

"Well what?"

"How's the *femme fatale*?"

"Look, she's no *femme fatale*."

"What is she then?"

"An amazing woman, prodigiously intelligent and charming. She seems to know everything and everyone."

"Ho, ho, ho."

"Now what does *that* mean?"

"You're falling in love with her."

"Are you kidding? She's old enough to be my mother."

"Not quite. Just old enough to work her wiles on a younger man and be dangerous."

"You've been reading novels again."

"Not since I took up archery."

She had me there. We'd got Ma to agree to the lessons by saying that if Sal took up archery, she'd spend less time reading silly novels.

"As for novels," said Sal, "*you* are living one."

"No, I'm pretty level-headed."

"Prove it."

"She wants me for tea tomorrow."

"Just the two of you?"

"Yes."

"Ho, ho, ho."

"She's in shipping, and her father was a prominent master and owner. Maybe I'll learn something useful."

"Maybe she will, too."

"Like what?"

"What you're up to."

"The family history? She knows about that already."

"What you're really up to."

"Meaning what?"

"The slave trade and who was involved in it."

"In that, she'd wish me well. And help me, if she could."

"I hope you're right."

She picked up her bow, aimed an imaginary arrow, pulled the bowstring back, shot. The bowstring twanged.

"By the way, Uncle Jake was there."

"I'm not surprised. They're pretty thick, those two."

"How can you tell?"

She shrugged. "I sense it." She aimed again and shot; the bowstring twanged.

"And Señor Martinez as well. The importer I talked to once."

"What's he like?"

"Very genteel, very suave."

"Elegant?"

"Braided cuffs. He gave me some advice."

"Don't take it."

"We'll see."

"Any women present?"

"None."

"Hmm."

"Why hmm?"

"You know what it means, when a lady's gentlemen callers don't bring their wives."

"I'm not sure it means anything."

"When you see her tomorrow, find out who her dressmaker is and where she gets her accessories."

"Why?"

"I like her clothes."

"How can I ask something like that? It's personal."

"Frame it as a compliment. I know women. She'll tell you."

"It would be awkward."

Another shot, a twang. She smiled, as if she'd hit a bull's eye. "Ask."

17

"Well now, Mr. Chris, here we are, just the two of us, as I promised. No babble, no distractions; *intime.*"

"Yes, *intime.*" (I could fake a few words of French.)

We were sitting in her parlor with a low table between us, and she was pouring tea. She was in a blue velvet dress with a jeweled buckle and had quickly put me at ease. Light filtered in through potted ferns hanging in a window. Blending with her perfume was a faint scent of cedar and sandalwood.

"Of course I want to hear about your research. But first another matter, if it's not too personal. You were surprised to learn of your cousin Dwight's engagement, I gather."

"I knew it was a possibility, nothing more."

"Perhaps the two branches of your family aren't close?"

"You could say that. They're doers and tellers of tall tales. Our branch, as my father put it, bear the burden of truth."

"Ah, I see. Well, let's hope that Cousin Dwight will be happy with his little moonbeam. Their union, I'm sure, will be sealed in heaven. And Miss Moonbeam's family, the Van Somethings—"

"Van Zandts."

"—Yes, the Van Zandts, are, so I'm told, a proud but threadbare clan. They could use some money."

"He'll bring them money?"

"One way or another, I'm sure of it. But enough of that. Tell me about your research. What have you been up to?"

"I've been poking about in old records, reading books in my father's library, and talking to people."

"What kind of people?"

"Ship's masters, wharf rats, importers, even a local historian."

"A historian? Who might that be?"

"Dr. Erasmus Dalrymple."

"I confess I've never heard of him."

"The title is honorary; he never went to college. He's self-educated, eccentric, keeps a lot to himself. But he knows things about this city that no one else knows. He had an old bill of lading that I got from him in exchange for a print of a clipper ship. And there are other people I've heard about but haven't found, some of them before my time."

"Name them. Maybe I can help."

"A Señor Innocencio Something-or-other, and some importers named Santos, Tejedor, and Cunha, or maybe da Cunha."

"You met Señor Luis Santos, a Pearl Street importer, yesterday."

"The Santos I'm interested in might have been his father or grandfather. Were they here at one time?"

"Possibly, but I'm not sure. I'll give you his address. The import-export business is often carried on over time by several generations. As for this Señor Innocencio, a name jumps at once to mind: Innocencio José da Cunha, a prominent Spanish merchant and ship's agent of some twenty years ago."

A twinge of excitement. "You knew him?"

"I met him once or twice through my father, who had dealings with him. Señor da Cunha was very active then, importing raw sugar and hides from Havana. Of course he retired long ago, quite wealthy, and by now is surely deceased. My father always spoke highly of him."

"I'd like to know more about your father, too. Is there a portrait of him here?"

"Come."

Rising, she led me over to a marble fireplace and, above it, a massive gilt-framed portrait in oil of a handsome clean-shaven man of another time, stocky, in a blue uniform with gold buttons and braid.

I studied it a moment in silence. "Impressive. He radiates authority."

"A born leader, very Go Ahead, very enterprising. Like your grandfather, a ship's master at twenty."

"They're from the same mold, all dash and drive. I'm sure they had many dealings."

"And probably butted heads, as well. But my father envied your grandfather his two sons. My father had no sons, only a daughter, so he raised me like a son."

"What did that involve?"

"Bowditch's *Practical Navigator*, instead of poetry. Compasses and quadrants, instead of needlework. Drawings of ships and their rigging, instead of watercolors. Tours of the waterfront, instead of excursions by carriage. And ship's manifests and bills of lading and a thousand other grubby matters of business."

"Did you mind?"

"I loved it! It freed me forever from the lady class. It gave me freedom and a life!"

She stared at the portrait, lost for a moment in thought. "Enough of him and me. I want to hear about *you.*"

"What's this?" I asked, lingering, as she started back toward the tea table.

On the wall nearby I had noticed a bit of framed embroidery: a floral border around several lines of finely stitched letters and numerals, a little house flanked by pine trees, and beneath it all, a verse.

"That? My daughter's schoolgirl sampler."

"I didn't know you had a daughter."

"I've packed her off to school."

I read the verse aloud: "On this dark Earth / Where Saints have trod / Love thy Mother / And thy God."

"There speaks New England," said my hostess, smiling wryly.

Beneath the verse were the words, *Kathleen Rivington age 13 AD 1866.* "It's quite charming and nicely done."

"But see what a hypocrite I am! I profess to scorn Dwight's intended as a little moonbeam, and here I'm raising a moonbeam of my own. But what else can I do? Kathy has no head for business whatsoever, so of course she'll end up a perfect little lady."

"What my sister Sal calls a gumdrop, a honey crisp."

"Hmm, I'll have to meet your sister. As for my gumdrop, she's at boarding school now in Switzerland, where I hope she'll make some useful contacts and get a more sophisticated education."

"Do you see her often?"

"Not often enough. She's homesick. She'll be coming back soon, to face the rigors of New York society. But enough of us, I want to hear about *you.* Where is all this research taking you?"

We were sitting again, sipping tea.

"To things I hadn't dreamed of and didn't want to find."

"Tell me. I'm on golden tenterhooks."

"To the slave trade. My family may have been involved."

She put her cup down. "Really? Are you sure?"

"No, not absolutely sure, but it seems likely."

"This changes everything. Who, precisely?"

"Caleb Harmony and Uncle Jake. Maybe not my father, we'll see."

"How do you know?"

"Old documents that suggest it, and the word of a seaman that I and my cousin plied with rum."

"Dwight?"

"No, his brother Rick, who's helping us."

"Us?"

"My sister Sal and me."

"I'd trust the documents more than a rum-soaked seaman."

"I'm being cautious. But it's coming together slowly, all of it. I'm learning more and more."

"What are you going to do?"

"Keep on, until I know the truth. All the truth."

"And then?"

"If they weren't involved, I'll say nothing. I'll just go on with the family history."

"And if they were involved?"

"I guess I'd have to say so. I couldn't hide it."

"And bring disgrace to your family?"

"It was a foul business. I've been reading up on it—old newspaper ads and published journals and the stories of runaway slaves. It's pretty awful stuff."

"You sound determined."

"I am."

"I can't believe that your grandfather, honored and respected as he was, could have been involved in the trade."

"I hope he wasn't, but the evidence is sure piling up."

"You met Jonathan Pell and Señor Santos yesterday. Talk to them; they knew him. And come by next Thursday. I'll invite the grandson of Innocencio José da Cunha; maybe he can help you, too."

"Thank you. Yes, I'd like to talk to him. Would you also know anything about the racing yacht *Venture*, or the brigs *Fearless* and *Lark*, or the schooners *Mary D., Sea Eagle,* and *Charity*?"

"No, I don't think so. Why?"

"They may have been involved. And a Captain Gideon Lynch?"

A pause. "I may have heard the name. I know nothing about him, nothing at all. Is he important?"

"On the waterfront they called him the 'Prince of Slavers.' He's disappeared, probably dead and gone."

"Mr. Chris, have you ever known any former slaves?"

"No, not a one."

"I think you should talk with some, to get more perspective. Before going on with your poking about, as you call it. Learn from them firsthand what it was like."

"I hadn't thought of that. I will."

She got up. "I'm so glad we've talked. You've opened my eyes to a lot of things. Keep on. I do wish you well."

I hadn't learned a lot, but she had given me some useful suggestions. I thanked her and started to leave. "Oh by the way, I have a request from my sister Sal. I hope you won't mind my asking."

"Ask!"

"She wants to know who your dressmaker is, and where you get your accessories."

Mrs. Rivington smiled. "Ah, now I absolutely must meet her. I'll be glad to tell her in person. We'll arrange it."

I thanked her, left.

"Well?" As usual, Sal was waiting in the sitting room.

"She's a real lady, but a lady of a different kind."

"Tell me."

I did, including the father, the daughter, and Mrs. Rivington's offer to meet her.

"You told her a lot."

"Most of it she knew already, at least in a general way."

"She didn't know about the slave trade angle."

"How could I talk with her about my research and not mention it?"

"You told her a lot."

"She wants to help."

"You told her too much."

18

REWARD—For a runaway Negro wench named Betty, the property of Jason Blake of this city, of dark complexion, about 23 years of age, many whip scars on her back, has a band of iron on each ankle and a chain around her neck fastened with a padlock. Prays a lot. Substantial reward for her return.

The right of holding slaves is clearly established by Holy Scripture, by both precept and example. Therefore it is sanctioned by God.

"Well hello there, Master Chris. What can I do for you?"

I had sought Luke out in the coach house, two blocks from Uncle Jake's mansion, where he was whistling as he polished the carriage. He was the only black person I knew.

"Good morning, Luke. I'm writing a family history and need to talk to some ex-slaves. Forgive me, but I've got to ask this. Were your parents or any of your relations slaves?"

"Lord, no, Master Chris. All my family been free for generations. We was almost never slaves."

"Do you know any ex-slaves, Luke?"

"No, and I don't want to. You see, Master Chris, the ex-slaves that come up here from the South are lazy, good-for-nothing riffraff. They talk loud, dress loud, just lounge around on the streets and get drunk. They's a scandal. We black Knickerbockers don't have no truck with them. They don't know how to polish a carriage or drive one, or how to lay silver on a table, or stoke a furnace, or anything like that. They give the rest of us a bad name. We black Knickerbockers work hard, save our money, and go to church. Some of us holler in church, and some of us pray and sing real soft, just like the white folks do. We's respectable. We was almost never slaves. Those blacks fresh off the plantation, we avoid them like the plague. They's trash!"

This shocked me. "I see, Luke. Thank you. Sorry to have bothered you. Thanks."

"That's quite all right, Master Chris. And by the way, Master Chris, about that business with the chest, when Master Dwight and I was lugging it out. I thought you wanted rid of it, honest. When you jumped on it and started yelling 'Thief!' I was dumfoundered. Never meant to do you no hurt."

"I know that, Luke. Don't fret."

"Relieved I am to hear that, Master Chris. Don't want no hitch between us. Don't want you thinking me some kind of trash, like those blacks just up from the South. Not me, no sir, not me!"

And he went on whistling and polishing the carriage.

Lesson learned: among the black residents of the city there were class differences, just like among the whites.

> ***NEGRO DOGS:*** *The undersigned, having recently acquired a pack of Negro dogs of excellent breeding, proposes to catch runaway Negroes. His charge will be three dollars per day for hunting, and fifteen dollars for catching a runaway. William Banks, High Street.*

> *The North Star is the escaped slave's friend. Trust no one, move at night, always walk north.*

> *"Friend, since thee has got out of slavery, thee has become a man. Therefore must thee take a last name, too, and think and act like a man."*

> *Blue eyes, sandy hair, may try to pass for a WHITE man. Branded on his forehead SLAVE.*

The brownstone, whose polished silver knocker I had rapped, differed in no way from the other brownstones on East Thirty-eighth Street, being a four-story residence with a high stoop and a mansard roof, looking prodigiously quiet and respectable. Yet as a good churchgoing Presbyterian I felt awkward being there, so visible, at ten o'clock in the morning. Rick's idea, of course.

The door was opened by a young black man in a tan frock coat and a white cravat.

"Good morning. I'd like to see Mr. Junius Fox."

"I am Junius Fox. What can I do for you?"

"Mr. Fox, I am Christopher Harmony, the grandson of Caleb Harmony, a prominent merchant and shipowner of some years back. I'm researching a family history that promises to become a maritime history of this city. One of my consultants suggested that I interview several black citizens, so as to get their views on how black and white citizens relate. Another consultant mentioned you as the best-known butler in the city."

He smiled. "Ah yes, the legendary guardian of the portals."

"Could you spare a few minutes of your time?"

"Certainly. Right now would be convenient, since Madame Ida and her boarders are late risers. Please come in."

He was soft-spoken, educated, and genteel. I was immediately at ease.

Junius Fox led me into a front parlor lushly furnished with crystal chandeliers, damasked sofas, floral carpeting, a pianoforte, and a large oil painting of nude cuties bathing in a lily pond. He waved me to a sofa and we sat. At the far end of the room, a black maid was plumping pillows and dusting. It tickled me to realize that I had gained ready access to the parlor of the most exclusive brothel in the city, where, in the evening, prior to any venture upstairs, gentlemen were expected to behave properly and part with gobs of cash. It was the flashiest parlor I had ever seen and all in all a bit of a tease; I was only too aware of those cuties.

"I've heard of Caleb Harmony," said Mr. Fox. "In fact, our paths crossed more than once."

"Really? Please tell me."

"My father was at one time the most sought-out barber in the city, with a distinguished white clientele. When patrons stepped down from the chair, I whisked them off with a brush and usually got a tip and a smile. In time, I got to know the regulars. Caleb Harmony was one of them. A tall, sturdy man with sharp features and a strong, bold voice. Most of the patrons I've forgotten. Not him, he stood out."

"That's helpful, Mr. Fox. Do you remember any other South Street merchants from that time?"

"There were quite a few, mixing in with the bankers and railroad men and politicians. Some Spaniards and Portuguese, occasionally an Englishman or a Frenchman. Merchants and shipowners, I think. They all knew each other."

"Do you remember any names?"

"No, it's been too long. Well, maybe one, a Captain Gideon Lynch."

A rush of excitement. "Tell me about him. This is important."

"A tall, imposing man like your grandfather, but less rough-cut, a bit more polished. Sometimes wearing a frock coat, sometimes what must have been a skipper's outfit with a cap. He and Caleb Harmony were cronies, you could tell from the way they joked around and talked."

"Do you remember anything they said?"

"Not a thing."

"Did you ever encounter a Captain Geoffrey Lane?"

He pondered a moment. "No. That name doesn't ring any bells."

"Thank you. As for black and white citizens relating, I should explain that my research has brought me to the slave trade of that time. This city was much involved."

"Indeed it was. While snipping his white patrons, Poppa heard a lot. White folks talk as if a black man has no ears. Poppa told me later that right up until the start of the war, slave ships were leaving here for Africa, to get slaves and sell them in Cuba."

"So I've learned. It astonishes me."

"'Junius,' Poppa told me, 'slavery's in this country's blood and bone.' And that was certainly true of this city. Everything depended on the cotton trade. Poppa heard the chitchat of bankers about making loans to Southern planters, and insurers who insured their crops and slaves. He snipped the planters, too, and heard them talk about how the city's hotels and restaurants made them feel right at home, and how they'd ordered pianofortes and carriages in stores, and the latest fashions for the missus. When I whisked those planters off, I usually got a pretty good tip. Young and ignorant as I was, I liked them and their tips, and I liked their Southern drawl. So with all that business coming up here, the last thing this city wanted was trouble with the South."

"But weren't there abolitionists as well?"

"Here, not many. Slavery was accepted. So it's not surprising that ships from here were taking slaves to Cuba."

I was overwhelmed. "Mr. Fox, knowing all this, it isn't easy being white in this city."

He smiled. "Mr. Harmony, knowing all this, it isn't easy being black in this city."

"Were there any ex-slaves in your family?"

"My grandfather bought his freedom in Maryland and then came North. He never talked about his days as a slave. He wanted to put all that behind him."

"Understandably. Have you ever known any other ex-slaves?"

"None. Most of the black people here are from families that have been free for generations. Not many ex-slaves come here, not since the riots of '63, when blacks were lynched in the streets. I was working in another brownstone then, and even there I didn't feel safe."

"Do you feel safe now?"

"More or less. But when I go out, I always take a good look around, to get the feel of things. The city's mood can change in an instant."

"So even black Knickerbockers can't feel safe."

"I and the other servants here aren't Knickerbockers, even though we live in a brownstone. The real black Knickerbockers wouldn't come near us. They're rich merchants who worship at St. Philip's Episcopal Church, intermarry, and keep to themselves. Very proper, very genteel. They ape the white folks who just barely tolerate them. Don't waste time on black Knickerbockers, they know nothing of the slave trade, pretend it never even existed."

"Who should I talk to?"

"The lowest of the low. Laborers, seamen, tubmen."

"Tubmen?"

"They collect the contents of the privies in tubs, take the tubs by cart to the river, and dump them out. Lovely work, as you can imagine. Only a black man would do it."

"I've never seen them."

"They work at night. You might catch them winding up their work toward dawn."

The maid, who had left the parlor minutes before, came back in with her arms full of flowers. Junius Fox stood up.

"My duties call. Madame Ida insists on having fresh flowers in the parlor daily.

I must see to it. I wish you well with your project, Mr. Harmony. Be careful."

"Why?"

I got up to leave and he saw me to the door.

"If you investigate the slave trade in this city, you'll be kicking a beehive. Be prepared to run for your life."

He closed the door. I stood there a moment on the stoop. His last remark had unsettled me. And what had I learned? Everything and nothing.

19

Burn me, you white bastards, burn Simon Congo at the stake, let me roast in torment for eight hours, as you say I will, and enjoy my screams of agony, if I utter them, and my pleas for mercy and a quick death by gunshot, which you will deny me, so as not to cut short your pleasure. Burn me till my eyes are scorched out of my head and my guts cook and shrivel. Fools, it will do you no good. My gods will still plague you, my fetishes torment you. Always you'll be wondering, When will Simon Congo rise again to slit our white throats in the night and burn our homes and churches? How can we be safe? Safe you will never be, as long as you hold us in chains and forced labor. Our hate is stronger than your chains, our cunning subtler than your cleverest schemes, our courage bolder and crueler than yours and more daring. All your slave codes and branding irons and whips and shackles cannot squelch in us the yearning you most fear: To be free! To be free! To be free!

"Excuse me, sir, I'm interviewing black people about their life in the city. It's for a book I'm doing. I'm wondering if I could ride with you and ask you some questions."

Dimly visible in the first light of dawn, he tugged his reins to halt his horse, then stared down at me from his cart. He wore an old straw hat and overalls; his cart, loaded with tubs, smelled awful.

"White boy, you be de fust person, black or white or anywheres in between, dat eber axt me to ride on dis cart. An' de fust to eber call me 'sir.'"

"Yes sir. But may I?"

"Boy, do you know what dis cart is, an' what I'm doin'?"

"Yes sir. It's a night cart and you're collecting tubs from the privies."

"An' you still want to ride wid me?"

"Yes sir."

"White boy, what are you up to?"

"I just want to ask you some questions. It needn't take long."

"Hmm. Tell you what, my partner's out sick today, 'cause he laid one on last night, so I be hustlin' dese tubs by myself. You can ride wid me, if you be willin' to lend me a hand. Is it a deal?"

"I guess so. Sure, why not?"

"All right, boy, hop on!"

I climbed up on the seat beside him. He was in his forties with fuzzy hair, slightly grizzled, and very dark-skinned. Up there, the smell from the tubs was fierce.

"Now, white boy, show me your hands."

I did; he felt them.

"Soft an' dainty like a nice little lady's. Neber worked a day in your life!"

"Well, sir, there's all kinds of work. Some kinds you don't do with your hands."

"Look at my hands, white boy."

He stuck them out; I looked.

"Now feel 'em. Go ahead, feel 'em!"

They were callused and rough.

"Dose are de hands of a laborer, a man as does real work. In my time I've hoed an' raked an' shoveled, an' carried bricks an' laid 'em, an' toted wood an' chopped it, an' hauled sacks o' coal, an' poured tar an' asphalt, an' dug ditches an' wells, an' done just about eberting de white folks let me do. Dat's man's work, an' I done it all. But you know sumpin', I'd rader be up here on dis cart, haulin' tubs o' shit, dan down dere diggin' a ditch. Funny, ain't it? Well ain't it?"

"Yes sir, very funny."

"So wid dose dainty little hands o' yours, white boy, how do I know you can help me wid dese tubs? One good heft an' mebbe you shit in your britches. Mebbe you kerplunk on your ass."

I looked him straight in the eye. "Try me!"

"All right, I will. Say, my name's Jonah." He put his hand out again. We shook.

"My name's Chris."

He chuckled. "All right, Mr. Chris, you're a rare one, ridin' wid ol' Jonah on his cart. So what are all dese questions you fixin' to ask?"

He flicked his reins; the horse started off.

"Well, Mr. Jonah, sir—"

"Just Jonah, boy, just Jonah."

"Yes sir. Yes, Jonah. First off, how long have you lived in this city?"

"Oh, a sight o' time. Fifteen years, mebbe twenty. Don't keep no count. De years just dribble by."

"Were you born up here in the North?"

"Dat I was, Mr. Chris. In Philadelphy, many miserable long years ago. Born free, at least. Born free."

"Were there any ex-slaves in your family?"

"Hold your horses, Mr. Chris. Now come de fun part, we see what you can do. Dere's one more street o' tubs to hustle. See dere, dat's de fust. So hop down an' show ol' Jonah if you can do it. Just haul it up on dis here cart."

There was a big tub sitting at the curb. I jumped down, grabbed it, tried to lift it, wincing all the time at the stink, finally got it up almost to the level of the cart, where Jonah grabbed it and hauled it up the rest of the way.

"Not bad, Mr. Chris, you learnin'. White boys pretty soft, but mebbe you shape up. No, don't hop back up on de cart wid ol' Jonah. You stay down dere wid de tubs. You be dancin' wid 'em all down de block."

Damned if there wasn't a whole bunch of tubs set out at intervals by the curb. So I hustled one of the stinking things after another, hoisting them up to Jonah, me wincing and straining all the time, and him chuckling.

"Dat's it, Mr. Chris. You learnin', you learnin' pretty good."

This went on for the whole block, my muscles getting sorer by the minute. Halfway along, I thought I'd just give out, but Jonah's chuckles, and the stares I got from early-morning passersby—shock at a white boy helping a black tubman hustle tubs onto his cart—somehow kept me going. I was determined to show Jonah and those astonished passersby that I could do it. And I did.

"All right now, Mr. Chris, we's done heftin' up de tubs. Now we takes 'em to de riber an' dumps 'em—dat's de oder fun part—an' den ol' Jonah gets hisself a snort o' rum. I an' de oder tubmen, once we's done wid de tubs an' gets paid, we's minded to raise a little hell. Not a lot, just a little. Shock de white folks to dere bones."

I got back up on the cart. "Jonah, I was asking if there were any ex-slaves in your family."

"My pa, he run away. Tried four times, finally made it. He showed me de mark on his back, where dey branded him. His mastuh wanted to sell him more dan once, couldn't do it, 'cause de buyers saw de debil in his eye." He laughed. "Yes, dey saw de debil in his eye."

"Jonah, do you know anything about the slave trade in this city? Who was involved and how it worked? The ships that sailed from here, and the men who owned them?"

"No, an' I don't want to. But I'll tell you sumpin', Mr. Chris. My pa left Philadelphy an' come here, 'cause slave catchers from de South was snatchin' black chillen right off de streets—*free* chillen, mind you—an' takin' 'em down South. An' once, when a slave catcher showed up here in New York, Pa hid me an' de oder chillen in de cellar for a week, till dat slave catcher gave up an' left de city. Dat's how bad it was back den. Dey could snatch free blacks right off de street, an' de Law 'd let 'em. Pa said, afore he'd let a slave catcher take his chillen, he'd kill eder de ones or de oder, or all of 'em, if he had to. No ways was he gonna let his chillen be snatched into slavery. Tank God it neber happened!"

This was all news to me; I sat there, speechless.

"Well now, Mr. Chris, I gives you a choice. You worked real hard, you did. You can come wid ol' Jonah an' help him dump dose tubs in de riber, or I let you off right here. 'Cause you done good, you did."

I was worn out. "I guess I'll get off here."

He tugged the reins, halted his horse.

"Dat's fine by me. Dumpin' tubs is nuttin like heftin' 'em. Well, Mr. Chris, for de two of us it's been what dey call an adventure. By way o' tanks, I gives you a tip. If you eber swim in de riber—an' lots o' white boys do—don't eber swim downstream from a tubman, 'cause he mebbe just dumped his tubs." At this, he roared with laughter.

"Thank you, Jonah. I'll sure keep that in mind."

"An' anoder ting, Mr. Chris. I know a conjure woman who gave me lots o' tips. You eber get sweet on a lady? Tell me true!"

"Well, yes, I guess I have, now and again."

"Okay, here's a tip. To make a lady get sweet on you, touch her skin wid de bone of a bullfrog. Dat's sure to do de trick."

"Thanks, Jonah. But here in the city bullfrogs are kind of scarce."

"All right, Mr. Chris, here's anoder tip de conjure woman give me. For de same result, snip a lock o' de lady's hair an' wear it in your shoe. Yes, Mr. Chris, soon she be crazy over you. Yes, she be just crazy!"

"Thanks, Jonah. I'll try it."

I got down from the cart. It was daylight now. People were walking by, and wagons were passing in the street.

"All right now, Mr. Chris, you gave me a hand wid de tubs, an ol'

Jonah gave you some tips. We's square now, don't you tink?"

"Yes, Jonah, we're square. Thanks again. Good-bye."

"Bye now, Mr. Chris. Ol' Jonah, he fixt you up good wid de wimen."

He flicked his reins and the horse started off. I watched as he jogged away toward the river. He was whistling. I liked him. I liked him a lot.

The stink was still with me. I was somewhere over near the East River in a mix of tenements and breweries. I strode off, heading west. I wanted to get home and soak my aching muscles in suds, and scrub myself free of the stink. What I wouldn't get free of was his story about slave catchers snatching black people right off the street, and his father hiding his children in a cellar for a week. Maybe I'd never get free of that.

"Mr. Harmony, my father and grandfather had extensive dealings with Caleb Harmony, and I myself, as a child, was privileged to meet him more than once. My family always spoke of him highly. Do not think for a minute that your honored grandfather could ever have compromised himself by any connection, however slight, with the despicable trade that to this day, illegally, dishonors the island of my birth. The da Cunhas, like your grandfather, have always deplored that trade and hoped to see an end to it. If you have come across any scraps of evidence that seem to implicate Caleb Harmony, I am confident that they will prove misleading or false. Please, I beg of you, do not at this late date impugn the honor of a man who is today hailed universally as a hero of the vanishing age of sail!"

So spoke Señor Innocencio José da Cunha the Third, an impeccably dressed young man whose whole manner, not to mention his jeweled stickpin and velvet collar and cuffs, conveyed the utmost in breeding and wealth. As promised, Mrs. Rivington had brought us together at her Thursday reception and then left us to chat on our own. Young Señor da Cunha was as hot in his defense of Caleb Harmony as he was in his praise of da Cunha & Company of Pearl Street, importers of raw sugar and hides from Cuba, and exporters to the island of all the Yankee machinery and manufactured thingamabobs so in demand in tropical climes.

If young Señor da Cunha's eulogy of my grandfather didn't quite overwhelm and convince me, it was because, only a few days before,

I had heard almost the exact same spiel, expressed less fervently, from ship's master Jonathan Pell, whom I had found at the Astor House bar, and from importer Señor Luis Santos, whom I had interviewed in his Pearl Street office. Everyone Mrs. Rivington directed me to revered the memory of Caleb Harmony and talked down the faintest suggestion that he could ever have done anything disreputable. If this unanimity of opinion struck me as just a bit fishy, I couldn't dismiss it completely. All these people were veterans of Pearl Street and South Street, with their nose deep in mercantile affairs.

When my conversation with Señor da Cunha Number Three came to an end, I managed to slip into the study and look for the print of the brig *Fearless*, which I thought I had seen there once. There was no such print; maybe there never had been.

When I took leave of her, Mrs. Rivington informed me and her other guests that her Thursdays would be suspended for the rest of the summer. She would soon be departing for Saratoga and other unspecified destinations. The late-summer exodus of the uppity crowd had begun.

"So she won't be back until fall?" Sal and I were in our sitting room.

"That's what she said."

"She was going to tell me about her dressmaker and where she buys her stuff."

"That'll have to wait."

"Hmm. So what have you learned from all these people she referred you to?"

"Grandpa was a paragon, a hero, and a saint."

"Well he was, though maybe not a saint."

"It all sounds too rehearsed."

"Hmm. And what have you learned from all those black people you looked up?"

"Lots."

"For instance?"

"Who the black Knickerbockers are, and tubmen and their carts, what a working man's hands feel like, how labor makes your muscles ache, how before the war this city did a roaring big business with the South, and how slave catchers grabbed free black children right off the streets and sold them into slavery."

"All very fine, but what does that have to do with Grandpa and the slave trade?"

"It all connects."

"How?"

"I don't know, but it does."

"That woman sent you on a wild goose chase."

"She didn't!"

"And you fell for it hook, line, and sinker."

"Don't mix metaphors."

"She diddled you, and you don't even realize it."

"That's not true! She's trying to help!"

Sal didn't answer, just gave me a stabbing glance of green agate. Though I wouldn't admit it, I had a sneaky suspicion she might be right.

Just then Ma brought me a note from Rick, whom I hadn't seen for several days: "Big row with the ladylove. That's finished. I'm shipping out."

So once again Sal and I were on our own.

20

With Ma still in half mourning, our family obviously wasn't going anywhere in August. Mrs. Rivington had left, and Uncle Jake and Dwight were about to, and so were all our neighbors, whose luggage was being snatched away daily by express wagons for delivery to a depot or the docks. Anyone who could leave, did, so I expected the rest of the summer to be hot, muggy, and dull. As for dull, I was wrong. It began with a note in the mail:

Dear Mr. Harmony,

I am a reporter with the New York Chronicle. Visiting South Street recently to do an article on the docks, I made the acquaintance of your cousin Rick Harmony, who told me of your joint investigation of the slave trade in this city. I have a proposal that you might find interesting. My office at the paper is hectic, so it would be better if I came to you. I hope you won't find this presumptuous. Let me know if you are interested.

Sincerely,
Rob Peterson, New York Chronicle
Printing-House Square, New York

Sal and I received him in the sitting room. He was a clean-shaven young man in his early twenties with slightly frayed cuffs and an earnest look.

"Tell me your proposal, Mr. Peterson," I said, as soon as we had all introduced ourselves.

"Shouldn't we wait for your cousin?"

"Rick just shipped out. We don't know when he'll be back."

"Oh. I see. That changes things a bit. The focus then will just be on you, Mr. Harmony."

"I'm in this, too," said Sal, who had insisted on being present.

"Well," he said, "let me explain. Your cousin told me something about your research, but I'll need to know a whole lot more. What I'm proposing is an article, maybe a column and a half, on your investigation to date. The article won't focus on the slave trade itself, since that's old stuff, not newsy. It will focus on you and your interest in it, and where that interest has led you. That's fresh and newsy, exciting. It would be an elegant follow-up to my story on the docks, which should appear in a day or two, unless some other story crowds it out. For me, it would be a welcome change from the little stories they usually give me—temperance meetings and street pavings and such. And it should help you, too, since it would make your project known and bring you more informants. So there's my proposal. What do you say?"

He struck me as diligent, sincere. Anticipating something of the sort that he proposed, Sal and I had prepared our response.

"We're interested, Mr. Peterson. What more do you need to know?"

"Everything you've been up to. Where you've gone, who you've talked to, what you've learned to date. Just talk away. I'll take notes, asking questions when necessary."

He had a stash of paper out already and sat there, pencil poised.

Sal and I had agreed beforehand on what to tell him and what to hold back. I told him a lot, but with no mention of any possible Harmony involvement, or of Grandpa's sea chest, its theft and return. Names of other people and ships I either changed or omitted. He scribbled the whole time, covering several pages with notes, and asked questions that Sal and I answered as fully as caution permitted. It all took less than an hour.

When we had finished, Rob Peterson beamed. "It's a honey of a story, what we in the trade call a scorcher. I'm sure my managing editor will go for it. Look for it on an inside page within a week. Thanks much. This should give my career a boost, and set you up as well."

He stood up, we shook hands again, and he left.

The next day we saw his article on the docks, a three-column chronicle of a daylong walk that ended only at sunset. He described the sights, sounds, and smells, made the whole scene come alive. Concluding, he promised a sequel on the waterfront's involvement in the slave trade. We had high hopes. Two days later it came.

THE SLAVE TRADE IN NEW YORK
SORDID FACTS REVEALED
A YOUNG INVESTIGATOR'S SAGA
OLD DOCUMENTS TELL THEIR TALE
MORE REVELATIONS TO COME

The story of the slave trade in this city—how it was carried on, and when and where and by whom—is a story yet to be fully told, but told it will be, and soon, if a young investigator deep in research has his way. Christopher Harmony, grandson of the esteemed Caleb Harmony of sailing days, and son and nephew of the Harmony brothers associated with a well-known ship chandlery on South Street, has made the investigation of this city's role in that ignoble commerce his project and obsession. Studied by him in detail, long-forgotten documents of another day—journals, letters, ship's manifests, Custom House entries, and bills of lading—are beginning to yield their secrets.

Young Mr. Harmony's activities are not confined to dusty archives. He has interviewed shipowners, ship's masters, importers, and common seamen (encouraging the latter's recollections with potations of rum), not to mention a colorful local historian, the legendary gatekeeper of a notorious establishment not to be named, and a Negro tubman, riding on whose night cart he greeted the first glimmerings of dawn, while giving his host a hand in hefting tubs onto the cart. His odyssey in quest of knowledge has taken him from the sumptuous brownstone parlors of the affluent to the dingiest grog shops of the waterfront. Given Mr. Harmony's energy, patience, and determination, this reporter is confident that few secrets of that nefarious trade will escape him. Anyone with relevant information can contact him through the office of the *Chronicle.* Startling revelations may result.

The article then went on to recount in detail the various phases of my research to date, with the omissions about the Harmonys that Sal and I had agreed on. It took up two full columns.

"That really is a honey of a story!" said Sal. "He sure knows how to write."

"Overblown, don't you think? He makes it sound like I spend my time plying drunks with rum. What'll Ma think?"

"We'll explain that reporters like to spin a good yarn. He piles it on a bit, but nothing that he said is really false."

"He doesn't even mention you by name."

"It's just as well. If Ma saw my name in the paper, she'd have a conniption."

"We'd better show it to her. She'll see it anyway, sooner or later."

"Okay, let's do it now."

Summoned to the sitting room, Ma read it through twice without comment. We waited a long time in silence.

"Well, I never thought the Harmonys would get their name in the paper like this. Or that a son of mine would frequent grog shops on the waterfront, or ride around the city on a night cart." (She didn't get the allusion to a "notorious establishment not to be named.")

"Just one grog shop, Ma," said Sal, "and Chris poured his grog on the floor. And almost nobody saw him riding on the cart."

"I just don't understand."

"Ma," I said, "when you're researching something, you have to poke about all over, pry into every nook and cranny."

"What'll the church ladies think?"

"Ma," said Sal, "you literally ordered us to go ahead with our research. You were confident that it would show Pa had nothing to do with the trade."

"I still believe that."

"This article will help us get the facts, facts that should prove you're right."

"Well, I just don't know."

And there we left it. She didn't scold us or tell us to stop, and that was the best we could hope for. It could have been much worse.

Two days later I began getting notes.

Dear Mr. Harmony,

Surely we don't need any more histories of the slave trade. That's over and done with. For the sake of our city's good name, your fellow citizens' peace of mind, and your own safety, give it up!—One Who Means You Well

Harmony—

If you go on with this therell be truble. Kwit wile your a head.—Rezoloot

Dear Mr. Harmony,

I applaud your effort. If you would like information that may be of vital importance, please call on me here at the Mission. I'm usually in my office weekdays between one and three. God be with you. Sincerely,

Rev. Simeon Oakes
South Street Mission, N.Y.

These notes were forwarded to us by Rob Peterson.

"Well," said Sal, "we're getting a reaction. Rezoloot sure can't spell."

"Unless he's faking it."

"I hadn't thought of that. And two of the notes without names. Do you recognize the handwriting of either?"

"No."

"Not Uncle Jake or Dwight?"

"I'd recognize their hand in an instant. Besides, they're out of town. Whoever sent these notes is in town and reacted the moment they saw the article."

"So what are you going to do?"

"Ignore the first two and go to the Mission. He knows something. We've got to find out what it is."

At 2 p.m. the following day I approached the South Street Mission, an old brick building facing the docks, with a boldly lettered sign above the entrance: SOUTH STREET MISSION, and under it, "A Haven of Peace and Sobriety." Inside I found a large hall with chairs and worn sofas, newspapers scattered on tables, Bibles and other black-bound volumes on a shelf, a big fireplace, and a battered pool table in back. On the walls were several signs: HE THAT HATH EARS, LET HIM HEAR, with THIS MEANS YOU right under it; PEACE BE TO THIS HOUSE; THE WAGES OF SIN IS DEATH;

and LOVE ONE ANOTHER, and under it, OR ELSE. Two men were playing checkers in a corner; another was slumped in a chair and snoring. Over to one side was a door marked OFFICE. I knocked.

"Come in!" boomed a voice.

I entered. A small room with several chairs, a desk a bit worn for wear, and seated behind it, a sturdy, square-shouldered man in his forties, richly sideburned, who rose to his feet at once.

"Mr. Harmony?"

"Yes. How did you know?"

"You're too well dressed for the waterfront, and too young to be applying here for shelter. The men who come here are marked by years at sea, and still more by years of rum. You have a nice, clean, healthy look. I hope you keep it."

"Thank you. You must be the Reverend Simeon Oakes."

"Who else?" he said with a grin. "Please have a seat. Hopefully it won't collapse under you. All our furniture is donated and usually about to fall apart. Why else would good Christians part with it?"

His humor had an edge; I liked it. Gingerly, I sat.

"Reverend, you know of course why I'm here. Your note promised information of vital importance."

"Exactly. But first, by way of background, let me toot myself and the Mission. I've been here just five years, trying to reclaim some of the drunks who clutter up the waterfront. Our rules are simple: no alcohol or other stimulants, no profanity, no women, no brawling, no gambling, in bed at ten every night and up at six in the morning, compulsory chapel morning and evening, and a prayer service Saturday night. We have beds for only thirty upstairs, and there's a waiting list. So the men here either shape up or get out. Once in a while one of them tries to give me a hard time. When things get physical, I assure you, I'm not the one who's flattened."

"Reverend Oakes, I think you're the right man in the right place at the right time. Not everyone survives on the waterfront."

"I thrive on it. I've never lasted long in a pulpit: too brisk, too blunt—I tread on dainty toes. But here I'm in my element. My goal, flat out, is to get them off the ardent."

"The ardent?"

"Joy water, tiger milk, panther sweat—they have a hundred names for it, but it all comes down to liquor. Next, I try to bring them close to God, and after that, I try to find them a job. If they go back to sea, they'll backslide, but they don't know anything else. So I try to find them jobs on or near the docks—with riggers or sailmakers, or in a shipyard if they have the right skills, or in a chandlery. I've got contacts, so I've had a bit of success."

"Your Mission is well spoken of."

"Thank you, but that's enough of me and it. Let's get around to you. Mr. Harmony, does the name Jared Chase mean anything to you?"

All the time he was talking, I had the feeling that I'd heard his name before, but not in connection with the Mission. Now it clicked: *Forty Years a Slaver, being the True Deathbed Confession of Jared Chase, onetime Able Seaman, Mate, and Ship's Master, as told to the Reverend Simeon Oakes of the Protestant Home Mission in New York.*

"Of course, Reverend, now I recollect. I found his confession in my father's library at home and devoured it. It's haunted me ever since."

"It's haunted me as well. The true confession of a veteran slaver who finally repented and told his tale. I found him in a shabby waterfront boarding house, age sixty, alone and penniless, dying of consumption. You know the rest—his story, remorse, and lingering death. A sad story with a sad ending, but I hope he found peace with his Maker. I got his story published on the very eve of the war, when the trade was still going like blazes here with hardly a peep from the authorities. All that, thanks be to God, has changed."

"But the story of the trade here remains to be told."

"Precisely. And that's where I can help. Jared Chase was sometimes lucid, but often feverish and out of his head. I scribbled notes as he rambled on. Later, from those notes and the fragmentary journals that he kept, I assembled the story that you read. But many of his remarks I omitted, partly because I couldn't vouch for their accuracy, and partly to avoid possible legal botherment. He cited many names of people and ships. The name 'Harmony' was among them. You'll be able to evaluate this information far better than I, so here it is!"

On the desk between us he plunked down a thick stack of foolscap scribbled over in ink, and a bunch of journals. I felt a surge of excitement.

"I'd like very much to examine your notes, but it will take time. May I study them here in your office, or anywhere else that you designate?"

"Mr. Harmony, I'm giving them to you. I have no further need of them now, nor can I, after all these years, even make out much of what I wrote. I'm also giving you the journals that he sometimes kept. You'll have to puzzle it all out on your own."

"Reverend, I'm overwhelmed. This is a prime bit of luck. I'll use these pages well."

"You'll have to decipher them first. I don't envy you the task, least of all since his comments may reflect badly on your family."

"I'm determined to find the whole truth, regardless of whom it hurts."

"So I gathered from the *Chronicle* article."

"This is the first good thing that's come of it. Otherwise I've gotten warnings and threats."

"I'm not surprised. Here at the Mission I hear lots of South Street gossip. That article has been mentioned a lot. If I ever hear anything of interest, I'll pass it along."

"Thanks. I'd appreciate it."

"And if you ever need a little help, my boys and I are available."

"Reverend, you sound like the leader of a gang."

He smiled. "Maybe I am. The boys here—those who stick—would do anything for 'the Rev.' That means a lot on the waterfront."

He stood up and handed me the notes and journals, then saw me to the entrance.

"Mr. Harmony, here at the Mission we're always pinched for funds. Please spread the word among the God-fearing Christians. We need donors."

"I'll do that, Reverend Oakes."

"And one of the men here might be able to help you. I'll talk to him tonight. You should hear from him soon."

"Thanks. You've been very helpful."

Another handclasp, firm and strong.

I came away from the Mission clutching the scribbled notes and worn-looking journals, as if someone might try to snatch them from me. Here at last, I hoped, was the key to everything, the definitive proof of Harmony involvement, or noninvolvement, in the trade.

21

. . . Schooner Friendship, Chase master, cleared NY Dec 42, owners Harmony & Biggs?—British cruiser sighted, escaped—Kabenda, Congo, factor again D. Pedro Blanco—plague of musketoes, bilious fever, stagnant air—380 prime n. branded and numbered—bore westward thou mi along equator—long calm, rain, food short—moans from hatches, smells—lost 20%—Cape Verde Islands, caught northeast trades—big meals for last 3 days, fatten up for mkt—rendezvoo 2 schooners n. coast Cuba, Migell Martines, 306 n., Martines pleased—pine flooring overboard, sprinkle hold chloride of lime—return NY, paid—no Harmony or Biggs ever seen—damn all owners keep hands clean we do dirty work...

...Mate tells him how slaver Sweet Lady, Wm Matthews master, captured off Guinea coast with slaves—M. sent NY for trial, Eldridge Street Jail—visited by mate and friends—Jacob H., Martines, J. Biggs, Lynch, da Cunha, others—parties with liquor, champagne—M. leaves jail with assistant marshal, boards steamer for Havana, never tried—influence of Caleb H.?—Jacob boasts marshals even judges can be fixed...

...Fever, blasphemies, I pray with him, calmer... mate on schooner Charity, Matthews master, hard man, tight packer despite C.H.'s orders (Caleb H.?), many deaths, fear revolt—fever: Harmony Lynch Biggs other names—calmer—reach Cuba, dodge cruisers, D. Migell—fever, mumbles...

Tuesday, 9 Sept. Befoged off Sandy Hook. Crew bored, impashent—a hard lot.

Wensday, 10 Sept. No change. News boat hailed us, got Havana news.

Thursday, 11 Sept. Fog lifted at last, took on pilot. Great surprise: Jacob H. on pilot boat, eeger to hear results of voyage, delited by results. Passed Quaranteen and Customs—no problem. Docked East River, Caleb H. on hand, informed by semafor; confered with Capt. Matthews. Home at last!—if home it be. Thanked Providence. Great dissrelish for this business, must get out.

I was hugely let down. The Reverend's frantic scrawl, recording the ramblings of a man often out of his head with fever, said much about the trade, but yielded only hints of Harmony involvement, secondhand accounts and hearsay, speculation, nothing clear and sure. Nor could I even at times tell which comments were Chase's and which the Reverend's. I could imagine Sal's reaction, her insistence that absolute proof regarding Caleb Harmony had yet to be found. And the journals proved to be no more helpful, since for every sinister interpretation, a less incriminating one could be advanced. My hopes dashed, I sank into a deep blue funk.

Another note from the Reverend:

Dear Mr. Harmony,

One of the Mission residents, Jonas Ward by name, has important information for you, but is cautious, doesn't want to see you here. Can he come by next Saturday at two?

Please let me know. Sincerely,

Rev. Simeon Oakes
South Street Mission, NY

This sounded promising. Having sent Oakes the confirmation he requested, Sal and I waited in high hopes that Saturday afternoon in the sitting room. While we waited, we noticed in the paper a report of the death of Hiram Biggs. The obituary hailed him as Caleb Harmony's junior partner and a respected shipowner and merchant of the days of sail. Lucky Hiram, he died with his honor unsmirched.

We waited and waited, but Jonas Ward never showed up. The more we hoped for, the less we got. I sank back into my deep blue funk.

Dear Chris,

We've been in camp now for weeks. No action till spring, and lots of bad news to digest. Measles went through our regiment and a third of the men never got well. I'm okay, but I did have a fling with the flux. Sickest I ever was. The doctor is a jackass so for a cure we try turpentine, castor oil, and chalk. Ugh! Needn't tell the folks.

The men cuss a lot, tell jokes I can't repeat, spend their pay on Nockum Stiff, commissary whiskey that they say tastes like lamp oil mixed with sweat. We're bored and sick of war. We're no closer to whipping the Rebs than we were two years ago. Mud, disease, rain, and fools and drunks in charge. Maybe we ought to do a deal with the South and let them go their way. Anything to end this bloody mess! I joined up all on fire to save the Union, but now I'm not so sure. Write! Write! Write!

Nathan

Rereading one of Nathan's letters didn't pull me out of my funk. And when I visited his room, all I could think of was how a fine young life had been lost.

Another note came from Reverend Oakes, promising that Jonas Ward would call, and this time, when Sal and I waited in the sitting room, Seaman Ward showed up. He was a small man in his forties, in a checked shirt and dungarees, soft-spoken, deft in his movements. I could readily imagine him moving about nimbly in rigging, furling or unfurling sails. We introduced ourselves.

"So, Mr. Ward, Reverend Oakes tells us that you can give us some useful information."

"That I can, sir. He's told me about your history. Since that story in the *Chronicle*, word of it has spread all over the waterfront. Made quite a splash, it has."

"At this point, I'm just trying to get at the facts."

"Especially about the Harmonys, I gather."

"Especially about them. Speak frankly."

"Excuse me, sir, but some matters may come up as ain't fit for a lady's ears."

Sal's eyes flashed. "Don't think of me as a lady!"

"In my sister's presence you can be as frank as you like. She's with me in this project and will take notes as you talk. We want the truth, no matter who it hurts."

"All right, sir. That takes pluck. Now here's what I propose. I'm a bit pinched for cash. If you find what I tell you useful, you'll pay me ten dollars. If very useful, twenty. And if it's of no use at all, not a penny. Isn't that fair shakes?"

I glanced at Sal, who nodded. "All right, Mr. Ward, you're on."

"Just one other thing, sir. Promise as you won't never mention my name in print. In fact, won't mention it at all. Not ever, to anyone, except of course the Rev."

"We promise, Mr. Ward. Talk on."

"Right, sir, I will." He lowered his voice and glanced about as if eavesdroppers might be lurking in our sitting room. "I been shipping out for over twenty years on about every kind of vessel you can name. What I found myself on in a given year was pretty much a matter of chance. Three times I shipped out on slavers as was connected with the Harmony name. First time, 1843, the brig *Fearless*, and a right smart ship she was, Gideon Lynch, master."

My heart skipped a beat. We were going to get some hard facts at last.

22

"Gideon Lynch," I said, "was known as the Prince of Slavers."

"Not yet," said Ward. "At that time, he was fairly new to the game. But he looked like a prince, the way he strutted on deck in his uniform. A real smart, shifty gent."

"Who else was involved?" asked Sal, who was scribbling in a notebook already.

"A Señor da Cunha of Pearl Street, an importer. I think he had connections in Africa. I signed on as an able, thinking we were going for palm oil and ivory, but once we'd cleared the land I found out different, when we started laying a slave deck. I of course was a 'greenie'; the old hands had known from the start. I had no religion then, so I shrugged and made my peace with it, especially as the pay was pretty good."

"How were the Harmonys involved?" I asked.

"Lynch and Caleb Harmony were chums and in this thing together."

"Are you sure?" asked Sal.

"As sure, miss, as I'm sitting right here in this room."

"But how did you know?" I asked. "Did Caleb Harmony ever visit the brig?"

"Never. But it was common knowledge on the waterfront. To finance the trip, Lynch needed Harmony money, and he got it, he got plenty."

His assurance convinced me; I was sweating. "What happened when you got to Africa?"

"We had to dodge some British men-o'-war on patrol, but Lynch was an old hand at that. 'They can't be everywhere,' I heard him tell the mate. 'We'll slip through, never fear.' And we did."

"Where did you go on the coast?" I asked.

"Lots of places—I can't recollect them all. The Ivory Coast, the Gold Coast, the Slave Coast. Places like Sekondi and Whydah, where Lynch or da Cunha knew the factors. Lynch had traded there before, knew the ropes. He'd keep shy of the shore, with its foul hot air that brought fevers, never stayed in close for long. He'd run in first thing in the morning, look for a signal: a flag with two triangles, one upside down on top of the other, forming a sort of six-pointed star. That meant no cruisers reported in the area, barracoons full, come in. Then he'd lie to a ways offshore, and surf boats would bring out the slaves, usually naked and in chains—I sight I won't never forget. He'd get them on board fast and be out of there by night. After three or four calls we was full up, especially as he was always a loose packer."

"What's that?" asked Sal.

"He didn't pack the slaves in tight, left them a little room to stretch in. He and Caleb were pretty decent as slavers, wanted the Negroes to have food they were used to, and plenty of water and exercise. Lynch would let a few up on deck at a time and have them dance to a drum or a banjo. That way they stayed healthy, not so many died. Yes, he and Caleb were the gents of the trade."

That there could be gents in the slave trade had never occurred to me, nor did the notion rest easy in my mind.

"What I couldn't get over, though, was how the men who brought the slaves out by boat were themselves all black, and a proud, grim bunch they were, ready with whips and clubs to whack any slave who didn't move fast. They were a sight meaner than the whites."

"So blacks too were involved in the trade?" said Sal.

"You bet! The trade couldn't have gone on without them. They captured other blacks inland, marched them in chains to the coast, and sold them to the slavers."

"Were there any problems on the way back?" I asked.

"Not as I recollect. We delivered some five hundred prime Negroes to one of the da Cunhas on the Cuban coast near Havana, ripped out the slave deck, cleaned up the hold, took on a cargo of sugar and hides, and made it back to New York. And right there on the dock was Caleb Harmony, who boarded at once and gave Lynch a big hearty hug. After that they had a long palaver in the cabin, and both came out in high glee. So that was my first voyage on a slaver."

"How can you remember all those details from so many years back?" asked Sal.

"Miss Harmony, some runs is so alike they all just blur together in your head. But my trips on a slaver were special; they stand out."

Sal was as yet maybe only halfway there, but I was totally convinced. At last a lot of hard, solid facts—damning facts—from someone sober and sane.

"Well now, folks, what do you think of my story to date? Is it worth ten bucks or not?"

"It is!" I exclaimed. "Now tell us about your second voyage on a slaver."

Once again he lowered his voice, looked about warily, and began.

"Schooner *Charity*, William Matthews, master, 1854. I was the second mate. After that first voyage I swore I'd never ship out again on a slaver, and for a long time I didn't, working instead on Harmony & Biggs vessels to Rio and Valparaiso and Guayaquil. But in those days I was a bit too fond of the ardent and had a bad habit of drinking all my earnings away. So I decided to ship out on the *Charity*, since the pay was tops."

"Was it owned by Caleb Harmony and his partner Hiram Biggs?" I asked.

"Them for sure, and probably some others, too. Maybe under their own names, but more likely through a dummy. They had me order a lot of supplies through the Harmony chandlery, including a good supply of shackles."

"Loaded in three boxes marked 'soap,'" I volunteered. My voice was trembling.

"Could be, I disremember. Anyway, I won't befog you with a lot of details. We went down to Havana to unload a legit cargo of machinery and furniture and such, and made contact with a Señor Miguel Martinez, who also had an office in New York."

"On Pearl Street," I put in. It was all coming together at last.

"Probably. Anyway, he gave us information about contacts in Africa, and got us cleared with Customs as the schooner *Esperanza*, Andreas Santos, master, and off we went under the Spanish flag."

"You had two sets of papers," I observed.

"And lots of flags to fly, depending on who we met. Matthews was still in command, with Santos ready to take over, if necessary. I think Harmony & Biggs had chartered the ship to Martinez, who may have chartered it to someone else. Caleb Harmony was getting up in the world—Chamber of Commerce and all that—so he wanted a lot of dummy owners between him and a slaver. Anyway, that's what the first mate told me."

"Who was he?" I asked.

"Jared Chase."

"Aha." Yes, it was definitely all coming together.

"In Africa it was the same game again: dodge the British patrols, scud in to take on the slaves, and scud out again. Only Matthews was a tight packer who met the Negroes on deck, stripped them of their rags, chained them in pairs, sent the women forward and the men aft, and packed them in like spoons."

"Hadn't Caleb Harmony given him orders to the contrary?" Sal asked, still scribbling.

"He sure had, miss, but Matthews ignored them. A mean, hard man, used to having his own way. Chase was pretty riled up, but helpless."

"What was the trip to Cuba like?" I asked.

"Hideous. Groans and moans from the hatches, and a stink like I'd never known. The crew wouldn't go below, so we lowered food and water in buckets, and they fought for it like crazy, gasping and shrieking and dying. Puke and shit all over them—pardon my language, miss—and lots of them chained to a corpse. Finally we had to go down and fetch out the corpses, and toss them to sharks in the sea. Those sharks followed us all the way to Cuba, knew there'd be plenty to eat. We must have lost a third of the cargo. Worst trip I ever made."

"So you delivered the survivors to Cuba?" I asked.

"To Señor Miguel Martinez, who wasn't too happy with the lot but took them anyway. Andreas Santos left us, we became the *Charity* again, took on legit cargo, and sailed back to New York under the American flag."

"How did Caleb Harmony feel about all this?" asked Sal.

"Furious, when Chase and I told him about the tight packing and all that resulted. I don't think Matthews ever worked for him again. Chase and I kept clear of Matthews after that, as he was one to hold a grudge."

A silence fell between us. Ward was lost in his memories; I was putting all the pieces of the puzzle together; and Sal, having put down her pencil, was staring in front of her, numbed.

"Your third voyage?" I finally prompted.

"Schooner *Venture*, Jonathan Biggs, master, 1859. A smart, lean ship, made for racing. I was the mate, or so I was led to believe. I didn't know it was a slaver, thought it legit. A funny business right from the start."

The *Venture*! A thrill shot through me, and trepidation, too. Now at last we'd know about Pa. Sal was worked up, too.

"What was funny about it?" I asked.

"Jacob Harmony chartered it to someone else in New York, who chartered it to Miguel Martinez in Havana, who chartered it to a Señor Innocencio José da Cunha."

"Wasn't he involved with the *Fearless*?" asked Sal.

"That was his father, miss. This was da Cunha Number Two."

"And I've met Number Three," I put in.

"Yes, there's a series of them," said Ward. "Like to go on forever. But there's more to it than that. In Havana we connected with Martinez, and I learned that Jonathan Biggs was handing the ship over to a Spaniard named Don Joaquin Tejedor. Biggs was becoming the first mate, and I was demoted to second, which I found pretty hard to swallow. The *Venture* was renamed the *La Nueva Paz*, which means something like 'New Peace,' and it was being refitted as a slaver."

"The most famous racing yacht of its day," I observed.

"And when Tejedor came on board, who did he turn out to be? None other than da Cunha Number Two, who I recognized as Andreas Santos, master of the *Esperanza* back in '54. Tejedor and Santos and da Cunha Number Two were all the same person. As a more or less respectable merchant he was da Cunha. As the master of one slaver he was Santos, and as master of another, Tejedor."

Sal put down her pencil. "I can't follow this."

"Who could, miss, who could? That's the point. With ships changing names and masters, and being fitted out first in New York and then in Havana, and having two or more sets of papers, and masters changing names, the authorities could never figure it all out. That's why, back then, no one thought it much of a risk."

"So under this name," I said, "the *Venture* became a slaver."

"That's right, sir, but not with me on board. They hadn't been square with me, so I resigned and shipped back to New York. I wasn't going to get involved in that business again."

"What became of the *Venture*?"

"All I know is rumors. As the *La Nueva Paz*, or the *Rosa*, or maybe the *Dolores* or *La Reina Isabel*, it's still plying between Africa and Cuba. Or maybe it's gone legit again. Or maybe it was burned. We'll probably never know."

Then Sal asked the big question before I got to it. "Was Mark Harmony, Jacob's younger brother and our father, involved in any way?"

"Not directly, miss, as far as I can tell, and glad I am to say it. And Caleb Harmony wasn't either. They'd made him president of the Mariners' Bank by now, so he wanted to put all that behind him. He probably didn't even know what Jacob was up to."

I still wasn't quite reassured. "Wouldn't Mark Harmony have known about it? He was Jacob's partner."

"Seems like they went their separate ways. Mark handled the chandlery—quite legit—while Jacob saw to everything else. Maybe Mark didn't want to know about it."

"But we think he'd invested in the *Venture*," said Sal.

"That's possible, miss, but maybe he didn't ask questions. Back then, lots of people didn't. It made life easier."

A small consolation. Hearing this, I didn't know if I felt better about Pa or not.

Ward got an earnest look, spoke louder. "I began to get my own life straight, when I read that book *Forty Years a Slaver.*"

"By Jared Chase," I said. "I know the book."

"That's right, sir. You see, I didn't want to end up like him. He told his story to the Rev, who got it published and made it known. So when the Rev opened the Mission, I made for it with a good wind abaft. The Rev saved me, dried me out. So when he told me about your history, I knew I ought to help. I held back at first—scared—but I got over it and here I am."

"Scared of what?" I asked.

"One way or another, half of South Street was involved in the trade. Times have changed. They don't want their name linked to it. What you're doing, writing about the Harmonys, takes pluck. But watch out. You'll make enemies."

"We won't ever mention your name, Mr. Ward."

"Thanks a lot. That'll help."

"And here's twenty-five dollars. Your story was worth that, and more. We're very grateful."

"Much obliged, Mr. Harmony. Good luck!"

"And good luck to you, Mr. Ward. You've got your life in order. We wish you the best."

"Don't worry about me, Mr. Harmony. I'll be fine, if I stick with the Rev, and I'm going to, you bet!"

Jonas Ward had a big grin when he left. I saw him to the door, but when I came back to the sitting room, Sal was just sitting there, speechless, a tear running down her face. Then, without a word, she got up and went to her room.

Sal was grieving not for Caleb Harmony, who had died some years back, but for the bully old man who told us fabulous stories and took us on tours of the harbor—a grandfather whom we had maybe concocted, and who wasn't the real Caleb Harmony at all. After the grieving would come the anger. Anger, I knew, could be a great source of energy and strength. In the months ahead we would need plenty of both.

23

A two-masted schooner with a sharp bow, a long black hull, and a cutaway stern scudding over a smooth sea, its quarterdeck paced by a tall, swarthy man with glossy black hair and a mustache and goatee, wearing a coat with braided cuffs, who fades into a massive beardless man in a blue uniform with gold buttons and braid, who announces, "The slavers do it right!" Flames dart from the hold. Leaping up on deck, Jan Guinea and Domingo Angola assail the crew with knives. "Saw de debil in his eye," someone whispers, as blacks and whites alike, ringed by fire, still fighting, jump into the shark-filled sea. The schooner burns. In the rigging high above the deck Simon Congo, licked by flames, shouts, "To be free! To be free! To be free!"

Energy Sal and I had. Having discovered in Pa's library a set of *City Directories* going back some twenty years, we skimmed through them, looking for the names Gideon Lynch, William Matthews, Miguel Martinez, Innocencio José da Cunha, Andreas Santos, and Don Joaquin Tejedor. Santos and Tejedor we never found, but all the others were there. Martinez and da Cunha appeared as Pearl Street importers, Matthews as a ship's master at various addresses, and Lynch as a shipowner and merchant at one or another address on South Street, while residing on St. Mark's Place only a block away from our brownstone. All but Lynch continued down to the present; the Lynch entries stopped in 1862, never resumed.

"He must have died," said Sal.

So far, everything was consistent with what Jonas Ward had told us.

Next, Sal went to see Rob Peterson at the *Chronicle* office on Printing House Square, hoping to consult obituaries in their morgue, while I went to the Custom House on Wall Street to check records of ownership for the brig *Fearless* and the schooners *Charity* and *Venture.* Late that afternoon we met in the sitting room.

"The *Fearless,*" I announced, "was owned by Caleb Harmony, Hiram Biggs, and Gideon Lynch in 1843, and was sold to I. J. da Cunha and some others with Spanish or Portuguese names in 1845."

"That checks, doesn't it?"

"Completely. The *Charity* was bought by Caleb Harmony and Hiram Biggs in 1853, and then sold to da Cunha & Company of Pearl Street later that same year. They in turn sold it to some others I've never heard of in 1857."

"What was da Cunha & Company?"

"A Cuban import-export firm that's still there, run by young da Cunha Number Three."

"Were there other partners besides da Cunha?"

"Silent partners. They're the '& Company.'"

"Caleb Harmony and Hiram Biggs?"

"Probably, and maybe some others as well. That's what Jonas Ward told us. And he said they chartered it to Martinez, who may have chartered it to someone else."

"Don't the Custom House records say?"

"No, they only list owners."

"How about the *Venture*?"

"No change from what Rick told us. Jonathan Biggs bought it in 1858 and that same year sold it to Jacob Harmony. He's the last owner on record."

"So we still don't know what's become of it, or even if it exists."

"No, we don't. Now what about the obituaries?"

Sal produced some notes. "Mr. Peterson couldn't have been nicer. He gave me a tour of the building, showing me the editorial offices and composing room, and the big rumbling presses in the basement—quite a sight. Then he took me to the morgue—grisly name!—and showed me the obituary file. It goes back many years."

"What did you find?"

"Nothing for da Cunha Numbers One and Two; Mr. Peterson thinks they probably died in Havana. Miguel Martinez died there, too, in 1863. There was a brief article, telling us pretty much what we know already: a prominent Pearl Street merchant with offices here and in Havana, exporting sugar, molasses, tobacco, and cigars from Cuba, dealing over many years with most of our South Street firms. Very distinguished, very reputable."

"So, like Hiram Biggs, he got out with a shining reputation. How about Gideon Lynch?"

Sal shrugged. "Nothing. Not a squib."

"The Prince of Slavers, and he doesn't merit a mention?"

"He either died elsewhere or he's still alive. There's nothing in their other files about him since 1861, and then he's simply mentioned as a well-known South Street ship's master and owner, with not even a hint of the trade."

"So he's disappeared?"

"Completely."

"Hmm. Another mystery to solve."

"But everything we've learned so far confirms what Jonas Ward told us."

"It does." I looked her straight in the eye. "For the Harmonys it's not good, is it?"

"No, it isn't. I'm still absorbing it. What do we do next?"

"Tell Ma. We've got to."

Ma took it calmly, as she always took bad news.

"I might have believed it of Jake, but not of your grandfather. You're sure, very sure?"

"Dead sure," said Sal. "We just can't deny it any longer."

"But your father wasn't involved?"

"It seems not," I said, "though he may have known about it. It's hard to believe he didn't."

"So he kept it to himself. No wonder he was so unhappy."

"There's nothing about it in his diary?" Sal asked.

"Nothing. Just sadness and shame. Now I understand why. Thank you for telling me. Harmonys and my family, the Winslows, don't run from trouble, we face it. Now, though, I want to be alone."

And she left the room. Sal and I exchanged a glance but didn't say a word.

"Pa, you knew."

"Knew what, son?"

"Everything. What Grandpa and Uncle Jake were up to."

"I tried not to know. I didn't approve."

"But you did know, didn't you?"

"Yes, I knew."

"Right from the start."

"No, not at first. They didn't tell me. They thought me too dainty, too squeamish."

"All those orders for shackles, hundreds at a time. And for water tanks

and lumber, and huge amounts of hardtack and rice."

"Yes, all those orders. That's how I found out."

"Did you try to stop them?"

"More than once. Pa said he needed the money, wouldn't be in it for long. Jake just laughed."

"They were in it for years."

"They and half of South Street. A few problems, but it was easy money. Too easy."

"Trafficking in human beings, putting shackles on them, branding them, shutting them up for weeks in the hold."

"Pa said he was different, more considerate."

"Oh yes, a real gent of the trade."

"That's what was said of him."

"And you invested in the Venture *with Uncle Jake."*

"I didn't know what he was up to."

"You didn't want *to know. You didn't ask questions."*

"I did it for my family, so we could live decently."

"There was nothing decent about it!"

"I had doubts, so finally I got out."

"Yes, after you'd made a fat lot of money. Dirty money."

"Don't judge me, Chris. I did the best I could. It wasn't easy."

"Pa, it was wrong. Not just the Venture, *all of it. Didn't you feel guilt?"*

"Every minute of my life, from the moment I figured it out."

"Pa, I'm ashamed."

"I know, son, I know."

"I'm going to make it known. It'll come out sooner or later. Better from me than someone else."

"You'll do what you have to do. But I'm sorry, Chris. Sorry for everyone, for all of South Street, for the slavers and the slaves. It blighted us all."

"Pa, it was monstrously awful. Good-bye."

"Son, do you remember the 'be-sage' and a tickle that you asked me for, when you were little?"

"Don't start in on that."

"Those were wonderful moments, just the two of us. You loved it. You'd just fall asleep."

"I'm ashamed, Pa. Ashamed of you, of us. And angry."

"Don't, Chris. That hurts."

"Good-bye."

"Chris...!"
"Good-bye!"

A note came:

Dear Mr. Harmony,

Something has occurred that I think you should know about. Please call on me at your convenience.

Sincerely, Erasmus Dalrymple

At two the next day I was rapping the brass knocker of the shabby old house on Twenty-second Street. Once again Dr. Dalrymple opened the creaking door and, shuffling in slippers, led me to his study, where we sat. All around us was the musty clutter of old books and maps and documents, an ancient pistol, a leather fireman's hat, a silver tankard with the hinged top.

"Mr. Harmony, I was quite impressed by that article in the *Chronicle.* Your commitment is commendable. I was delighted to find myself, as a 'colorful local historian'—I do assume it's me—numbered among your sources and consultants, along with shipowners, a Negro tubman, and—hee, hee!—the gatekeeper of a naughty establishment. You certainly do get around."

"Thank you, sir."

"'Old documents tell their tale,' said the caption. Yes, they certainly do. I have here—somewhere, if I can find it—- a letter from a fellow historian who claims to have shot the last grouse in Manhattan in 1831. Far uptown, of course, in a wooded area that once abounded in woodcock and rabbits and snipe. The last grouse—just imagine!"

"Dr. Dalrymple, your note mentioned something that you thought I should know about."

"What? Oh yes, of course. What was it? Ah, now I remember. You recall that old bill of lading that I gave you in exchange for a print of a clipper ship—a handsome print that now graces the wall of my bedroom."

"Yes sir, I recall very clearly."

"It came from a bunch of papers that a ship's captain had sold me some years back."

"Yes sir."

"Well, only two days ago a young man came calling who professed an interest in the city's past, though he obviously knew little about it. He asked if he could look at my collection here, which I was glad to show him, since so few young people express such an interest. He poked about here and there, and when he came upon that bunch of papers, suddenly his interest quickened. He leafed through them quickly, then offered a substantial sum for them, which I refused. He then offered double that sum, and when I still refused, offered to give me in exchange any object that he possessed or could acquire. I mentioned my interest in clipper ship prints, at which point he offered to fetch me several and let me pick the one that appealed to me most. He brought three, and one of them I absolutely had to have, so I agreed to the swap. He thanked me profusely, took his spoils, and left. After the enthusiasm for my new acquisition subsided, it occurred to me that his interest in those old papers was rather strange. Certainly he was no historian or antiquarian. So I thought I ought to tell you."

"He didn't give you his name?"

"No, and I didn't think to ask."

"Could you describe him?"

"Mid to late twenties, thickset, with a mustache."

"That could be anyone, Dr. Dalrymple. Did you notice anything else?"

"Not really."

"And where is that print?"

"On the wall there right behind you."

I turned and looked: a fine print of a clipper ship, but one like many others. Had I seen it before? I couldn't be sure.

"Mr. Harmony, you looked those papers over and didn't want any of them."

"Yes, I recall. But your visitor did. Maybe he saw something that I missed. Or maybe he just wasn't taking any chances."

"Does this have something to do with your research into the slave trade?"

"I think so. Yes, I'm sure."

"Oh dear, this is serious. I didn't realize. Someone must be scared."

"Very scared. If anyone else comes looking for old maritime documents, let me know at once."

"I will, Mr. Harmony, I will, even though I don't think I have any others. I hate the thought that I may have let go of some useful documents."

I thanked him and left.

I reported to Sal in the sitting room.

"I'll bet this results from that article in the *Chronicle*," she announced right off. "Someone wants to cover their tracks."

"Could be. Maybe that article wasn't such a good idea. It let all of South Street know what we're up to."

"What's done is done. But how did they know Dr. Dalrymple had that bunch of papers?"

"No idea. I haven't mentioned it to anyone."

"No one at all? Think."

"You. And Rick."

"Anyone else?"

"Maybe Mrs. Rivington. I don't remember."

"Aha!"

"What does that mean?"

"She told someone else."

"Who?"

"It could be anyone. Those people who come to her Thursdays. And one of them got scared."

"Look, I don't think she's involved in this."

"Maybe not. But she could have mentioned Dr. Dalrymple quite innocently to someone else who is. How did he describe the young man who came to him?"

"Mid to late twenties, thickset, a mustache."

"Dwight."

"He's in Long Branch."

"Unless he came back early."

"Look, that description fits thousands of men."

"Oh, all right. But I don't like this business. I don't like it at all."

"Okay, but don't get carried away."

And that's where we left it.

The very next day, in midmorning, I was surprised when the maid told me that a Reverend Oakes wanted to see me. I found him in the vestibule, his features warped with anxiety.

"Mr. Harmony, I've got to talk to you. It's urgent."

"Reverend Oakes, you're busy at the Mission. I could have come to you."

"No! You mustn't! Not even in broad daylight. As you value your life, keep away from the waterfront."

"Why?"

"Early this morning the harbor police found a body floating in the harbor. He was murdered."

"Who?"

"Jonas Ward."

24

I hurried Reverend Oakes into the sitting room. Ma and Sal were upstairs, so there we could be alone. His news had stunned me.

"Murdered? How? By whom? Why?"

The Reverend's normally resonant voice was muted. "They found the body early this morning, so it isn't in the papers yet. I know only what they're saying on the waterfront. He was drowned or strangled; by whom is a good question. As for why, it's obvious: he told you too much."

"Who knew that? My sister and I promised him we'd never mention his name, in print or otherwise, and we haven't."

"He wouldn't have told anyone either; he was too wary. But someone knew. Maybe they followed him here."

"I feel awful about this. In a way, Sal and I are responsible for his death."

"Then I am, too, since I sent him to you. I was worried when he didn't return to the Mission last night. Usually that means a man is backsliding, but Jonas was very steady, very strong. A model for the others. We'll miss him; may the Lord receive him. He had no family; the Mission was his home. Now he has another, a better one."

"He struck us as very honest, very decent."

"He was. One of those quiet little men, soft-voiced, whom no one ever notices. No hero, no leader, just a modest fellow who, once he got square with his Maker, went about his life quietly, meaning no harm to anyone. We'll have a service for him in a day or two, once the police release the body, and we'll take up a collection to bury him."

"I'd like to come to the service."

"Don't! Keep away from the waterfront! Whoever did him in may well have his sights on you."

"I'm that dangerous?"

"Yes! Today, no one on South Street wants to be linked to the trade. And then you come along, sticking your nose in old records, getting witnesses to talk, and promising revelations in print. You bet you're dangerous, Mr. Harmony. You've got enemies all over the waterfront, many of whom live in nice, neat red brick houses and fancy high-stoop brownstones, with parlors full of silk and brocade. One way or another, they're out to silence you."

"Well, they won't."

"You're determined to go on with your research?"

"More than ever. And if Jonas Ward was killed because of it, I owe it to him as well. No, I'm not a quitter!"

"Well spoken. Go on, but don't take needless risks. I'll help any way I can, and so will the boys at the Mission—my gang, as you call them. Jonas was well liked."

"Let me know if you see or hear anything of interest."

"Certainly. Lots of rumors come my way, some preposterous, some possibly relevant. But if the police question me, I won't mention you. The chances of their finding the murderer are slight."

"Be careful, yourself."

The Reverend Simeon Oakes stood up tall. "The Lord looks after me, but if he should ever get distracted, I'm prepared to look after myself."

I could well believe it. I thanked him, gave him something toward Jonas Ward's burial, and saw him to the door.

"Good-bye, Mr. Harmony. Be strong, be wary, be sly."

Watching him stride off down the street, I nursed a new idea: *be sly.*

MYSTERIOUS DEATH

Early this morning the harbor police recovered the body of Jonas Ward, a retired seaman now employed as a sailmaker, floating in the harbor off Governor's Island. A coroner's inquest resulted in a verdict of death by strangulation. Mr. Ward resided at the South Street Mission, where the Reverend Simeon Oakes described him as a model resident. "He is in the arms of his Maker," said Reverend Oakes, "but in this world he deserved a better fate." No arrests have as yet been made.

"What are you going to do?" asked Sal.

"Keep away from the waterfront, but go on with the research."

"What's next?"

"I've got to think. I've got to figure out *why* they got into slaving.

Especially Grandpa. I just don't understand."

"Neither do I. Maybe I should see Mr. Peterson again. He might want to do another article."

"Do we want another? Look what this one got us."

"Everyone knows what we're up to now. They're afraid of exposure. Silence helps them. More publicity might hold them back."

"All right, see what he says. But don't tell Ma about Ward. She'd have a fit."

Dear Mr. Harmony,

I tried to warn you, but you persisted, and look at the result. For God's sake, sir, desist. You're putting yourself and those close to you in harm's way.

—One Who Still Means You Well

Harmony—

Ward got it for talking too much. Your next if you doant shut up.

—Rezoloot

These notes didn't come to me through Rob Peterson at the *Chronicle*: they were addressed to me at home. All that week when I went out, I imagined someone was following me, but when I looked, there was no one. In dreams sturdy hands reached for my throat, clasped it, tightened their grip; I woke up in a sweat. Or I saw my limp body floating in water, finger marks at my throat, my face scrunched up in terror. Awake, I got hold of myself: this was the price of truth. I would keep on, I had to.

Everywhere I looked in the house, there was Grandpa. Not just his portrait in the parlor, but the silk-screen landscapes on the walls, the porcelain in the china cabinet, and the maps and prints and chess set in my bedroom. But these were mostly mementos of the China trade. From that other trade carried on furtively along the Leeward Coast of Africa, there were no spoils, no signs. But maybe the brownstone itself, with its walnut and marble and brocade, had been bought and prettied up with profits from that trade. Hadn't Sal and I been raised with tainted money, shielded from the grubby world outside? "Neber worked a day in your life." I was sick with self-disgust.

"Grandpa, Sal and I know. We know everything you did."

"I did lots of things, Chris."

"You and Gideon Lynch. And Hiram Biggs and Matthews, and Martinez and da Cunha and the rest of them. You did it for years and years."

"No, Chris, I got out. Lynch got me into it; I needed money. But I never relished it. I got out as soon as I could."

"With your hands clean. You never saw the slaves marched on board in chains, or heard their screams when they were burned by the branding iron."

"I gave orders to treat the slaves decently. When Matthews disobeyed my orders, I was furious, I got rid of him."

"Yes, you were a gent of the trade. Why did you do it? Why?"

"Everyone did it."

"Not everyone."

"Most of the men I knew. There was a demand. If I hadn't helped satisfy it, someone else would have, someone hard and mean."

"A dirty business. I'm ashamed of my name."

"Don't say that, Chris. It's a fine name, honored all over the waterfront."

"Not for long. I'm going to tell the world of our shame. We'll all be dishonored. We deserve it, for living on dirty money."

"All money is dirty, that's just how it is. Chris, I loved you. I used to tell you stories. Don't you remember—"

"To hell with your stories!"

"I've made mistakes, Chris. We all do. Someday you'll understand."

"Not this. Never."

"The young think things are simple; it's clear what's right and wrong. But things are complicated, all mixed up."

"Grandpa, it was evil."

"I'm an old man, Chris. I'm tired, worn, broken. I've outlived my time."

"Evil."

"I love you, Chris. You especially. My little bookworm, who never got tired of my stories. Say you forgive me, Chris. Say it. Please!"

"Grandpa..."

"Chris?"

"You disgust me."

In September, we saw people stepping out of shiny black carriages and mounting steep stoops, and express wagons unloading heaps of luggage, all up and down the block: the uppity crowd were back from Saratoga and Long Branch. A note from Uncle Jake informed us that he and Dwight were likewise back in town, on Sundays we once again saw them at church.

With the season about to resume, Sal and I were trying to nudge Ma out of deep mourning. Finally she added a few somber touches of purple to her black, and started attending Dorcas Society meetings again, knitting socks and mittens for missionaries. Next, we began suggesting that, come New Year's Day, she might again receive callers. She promised to think about it.

"Haloo, folks! Aunt Martha, out there on the vasty deep, gnawing at salt beef and hardtack, I've dreamed of your roasts and plum cakes, and boy, am I hungry! Cousin Sal, you look fetching, and Cousin Chris, you look pretty chipper for a scholar, but with that article—yes, I've seen it, it's all over the waterfront—did you ever whip up a gale! No fancy gifts this time, folks, I got back flat broke, but with scads of tales to tell. Hey, there's nothing like family—*this* family, I mean, my own can go to blazes. Hail the scapegrace! Am I invited to dinner? Of course! Good Christians wouldn't turn away a starving Jack Tar who needs some civilized company as well as some home-cooked vittles. So kill the fatted calf!"

He turned up again in a sailor's cap and white duck trousers, his face brick-red from the sun, his curly black hair as wild and untamed as ever. Ma untangled herself from his hugs and blather to go tell the cook to set another place for dinner. In her absence he spoke more freely.

"No ladylove to give me a snug harbor this time, this old boy's heartsick and forlorn. So I dropped anchor at the homestead and got the usual icy welcome from the Skipper and brother Dwight. Then, once I escaped to my room, didn't I hear an earful!"

"What?" Sal and I chorused.

"Tell you in a minute. But first, catch me up. What's happened?"

So we told him about Reverend Oakes, and Jonas Ward's account of his three voyages, which our research had confirmed. He'd already seen the *Chronicle* story and heard about Ward's death from friends on the waterfront, so he got a grasp of it all pretty fast. And when we showed him the notes from One Who Means You Well and Rezoloot, he announced, "Now I get it!"

"Get what?" we asked.

"The hullabaloo downstairs. The old man and Dwight were talking with someone else. Voices were raised: Pa and the visitor. You know Pa's temper; he was really on a blast. 'No one touches a Harmony but me! Do you hear? No one!' he shrieked. The visitor tried to say something, but Pa shouted him down, mouthed a few more curses, then yelled, 'Spread that around the waterfront, you bastard. If anyone dares touch or threaten a Harmony, he'll have to answer to me, and a bloody hard time he'll have of it. Now get out!' Minutes later, watching from an upstairs window, I saw the visitor leave. He was wearing a skipper's cap and jacket, but I've no idea who he was."

"What do you make of it?" asked Sal.

"Pa was off at Long Branch when all this happened. When he got back, he heard about the article, Ward's death, and the threats to Chris. He doesn't like the story, of course, but he doesn't like murder either; it gets attention, and in this business attention is the last thing he and most of South Street want. And the threats really roiled his gut."

"So he had nothing to do with all that?" I asked.

"Nothing. He came on like thunder. You can't fake rage like that."

"So where does this leave us?" asked Sal.

"Chris won't get any more threats. No one on the waterfront wants to cross Jacob Harmony. He has connections, and he's skinned his knuckles busting a lot of jaws in his time. Yes, I think Chris can walk safe."

"That's good to hear," I said. "These last few days I've been just a mite on edge."

At this point Ma came back from the kitchen and handed me a scented note that had come in the mail. I opened it, read it aloud. "Dear Christopher Harmony, I'm back in town at last and will resume my Thursdays next week. Please come. I want to hear about your adventures. —Louise Rivington."

"Rivington?" said Rick. "Isn't she the elegant one who gave you a Chinese thingamabob for graduation?"

"Yes."

Sal snatched the note from me and sniffed it. "Hmm. That same smoky perfume."

Ma registered this, said nothing.

"She has receptions on Thursdays, doesn't she?" said Rick. "Who attends them?"

"Mostly South Street and Pearl Street people, very genteel," I said. "I met Martinez Number Two there, and da Cunha Number Three."

"And Uncle Jake," said Sal. "Not exactly genteel."

"Yes, Uncle Jake, too."

"I want to meet her," said Rick. "Get her to invite me."

"Why?"

"A hunch. She invites the waterfront gentry, the very ones who have the most to lose, if you tell what you know. I want to have a look-see at them and at that portrait of her father—what's his name?"

"Geoffrey Lane."

"And I want to see his study."

"Why?" asked Sal.

"Some pieces are missing from the puzzle. We'll find them there in her brownstone. So get me invited, scholar. There's a whopping big lot at stake."

"What?" Ma and Sal and I all asked together.

"Everything!"

25

"Well, here we are again, Mr. Chris. So glad, so very glad, to see you. You're looking well. Research seems not to have impaired your health." Her voice was as musical as ever, her perfume subtly smoky.

"Good afternoon, Mrs. Rivington. Far from impairing it, research gives me energy. And determination."

"Determination?"

"To see things through to the end."

"Ah, I see. Bravo! And this young man?"

"My cousin Rick, whom you so graciously invited. Rick, may I present you to Mrs. Louise Rivington. Mrs. Rivington, this is Rick Harmony, my uncle Jacob's younger son."

"Good afternoon, Mrs. Rivington. I'm delighted to meet you."

"And I am delighted you came. Harmonys are always welcome here."

Rick had shed his sailor's togs and turned up in a frock coat and cravat, looking very much the gentleman.

"And welcome back, sir," she added. "You've been recently at sea."

"I have, ma'am. How can you tell?"

"Those handsome features bronzed by the sun. And the firm, rough clasp of your hand, a hand that has holystoned decks, hauled cordage, tied knots."

"Yes, ma'am, I confess that recently I was giving my hand to all those things and more."

"Gentlemen," she said, addressing the other guests, "may I have your attention for a moment."

The guests stopped their conversation, turned to her. Among them were Martinez Number Two, da Cunha Number Three, and Jonathan Biggs, who had given me the coolest of nods, no doubt recalling our previous conversation, when he denied any knowledge of the yacht *Venture* after selling it to Jacob Harmony.

"Gentlemen," said Mrs. Rivington, "joining us today is Mr. Rick

Harmony, an able seaman who has also, I am sure, served on occasion as ship's master or mate. We who build and own ships, and load them with cargo for distant ports, must remember that all our endeavors depend on those who man them. In their presence I am always humbled and just a bit awed. Thank you, Mr. Rick."

Applause and cries of "Hear, hear!" greeted her speech. In Rick's shoes I would have blushed to the bone, but he grinned broadly and seemed to take it all as his due. Having their attention, he launched into the story he had regaled us with at dinner: how, in a storm on his last voyage to Havana, a huge waterspout had swept over the deck of his ship, terrifying even the most seasoned of the crew, until, in less than a minute, it passed on and receded in the distance. A born storyteller, he held them to the end.

"There you are, gentlemen," said Mrs. Rivington. "See what perils sailors expose themselves to, while serving us and our ships!"

"So the sprout's been telling stories, has he?" came a booming voice, as Uncle Jake strode in, all spruced up in broadcloth and patent leathers. "He gets that from his old man, who's seen a thing or two himself in his time. Good afternoon, Louise. Welcome back!"

He gave her a quick kiss on the cheek.

"Yes," he continued, "the sprout's been sailing free, not that his skipper has any idea where. He comes and goes as he pleases, raises hell or whatever, then comes home when in need of a bunk."

Rick grinned. "He comes home when his bowels ache for the warmth of his family, a tranquil hearth, and the loving gaze of his pa."

Rick's remark provoked smiles all around.

"See how the Harmonys take over!" said Mrs. Rivington. "I really do protest! Though I make an exception for Mr. Chris, who like a good historian hugs the sidelines and observes. Gentlemen, while resuming your brilliant conversation—what other kind do these occasions inspire?—please partake of coffee, tea, or wine. Those of you who crave rum or whiskey, so esteemed by mariners, will be sadly disappointed. As you know, my Thursdays breathe decorum. A fine wine is as far as I go."

At this, the gathering broke up again into small groups, each engaged in its own conversation. While Uncle Jake conversed with our hostess, Rick addressed Martinez and da Cunha in fluent Spanish, and I found myself talking to Monsieur Lefèvre, a Frenchman whom I had never seen before. He had a neat little mustache, graceful gestures, excellent English, and a knowing manner.

"A charming woman, your Mrs. Rivington." He pronounced it "Meeses Reeveengton." "It is a privilege to know her."

"Monsieur, have you known her long?" "Monsieur" was about the extent of my French.

"Since the war. Not our war—yours. Madame was there to ride out the storm, so to speak. Now she is back here, and I look after her property in Paris."

"That must have been quite a job, monsieur, given the recent siege and uprising."

"Ah, sir, I was not in Paris during those unfortunate events. I watched them with great concern from my country house in the south of France."

A curious way, I thought, to look after Madame's property in Paris.

"Stirring events, even so. And now you have a republic."

"Our third. I am of course a fervent republican. A year ago I was a fervent supporter of the Empire. And a year from now, perhaps, if they bring back our dear old, tired old Bourbons—the dynasty, not the whiskey—I shall be a fervent monarchist. So it goes in *la belle France.*"

"You have more options than we do. We're a republic, and that's that. Did you by any chance know her husband?"

"The ever absent Mr. Rivington? No, I have not had the honor, nor has anyone else that I know. But I did meet her father, Captain Lane. A formidable presence, as that portrait on the wall indicates. He helped her on her way."

"Really? How?"

"Madame is what we call an *arriviste*, albeit a subtle and charming one. She has money and wants to get ahead socially. Captain Lane was a sterling example of the New Man, the American, the artist of Go Ahead: self-made, solid, a real doer, without fuss or frills. In Paris he had success. Hostesses welcomed him, even with his minimal French, and his daughter was carried along, translating for him when necessary—her French is excellent—and generally smoothing his way. They could have gone far, had they not returned here after the war."

"He died not long ago, I gather?"

"In '68, I believe. For her, a great loss. You have seen his study here, I am sure—a shrine to his memory. Now she makes her way alone. In business, fine. But socially, as you can tell from this gathering—shipowners, merchants, and such, but alas, no ladies—her progress has been limited. Granted, I do not know how such things work in New York, but surely these are not the most select circles, the summit of your society."

"Hardly. We're very middle class, very bourgeois."

"As am I, Mr. Harmony, and happily so. But Madame aspires to more for the sake of her daughter."

"At school in Switzerland, I believe."

"Not at all. She's right here in this city, this house. Not two weeks ago Madame brought her back from Europe."

"I had no idea."

"A charming young lady, but without her mother's flair. Madame, of course, wants to marry her off, as respectably as possible. It should work out; Miss Kathleen will have a dowry. A very generous dowry."

"We won't see her today, I gather."

"Certainly not. Madame keeps her in semi-seclusion, is very careful about whom the girl meets. Beware of invitations to tea, Mr. Harmony. You are young, respectable, and certainly not impoverished. If Madame cannot scale the summits, she will settle for the foothills, and that might just be you."

"The girl will have something to say about it, I should think."

"I doubt it. Not for nothing did Madame have her educated in Europe. She wanted a docile daughter and she got one. But I am indiscreet. You will purge from your mind everything that I have said. Madame is a friend, and I admire her immensely. Not for anything would I want to ruffle her feathers."

"Monsieur, I promise that her feathers will remain unruffled. I shan't say a word."

"Spoken like a gentleman. And if you do indeed get an invitation to tea, think twice before declining it. The girl is charming. You could do worse, much worse."

So ended our conversation. He was soon conversing with our hostess in rapid French.

Rick approached, winked. "She's giving me the treatment."

"What treatment?"

"The full blast of charm. Now take me to the study."

In the study, he looked long and hard at the charts and prints, the ship models, the nautical instruments, the skipper's cap hanging on a peg. He had already seen the portrait in the parlor. The map of the Leeward Coast, showing settlements along the Gold, the Ivory, and the Slave Coast, had been removed, replaced by a chart of the South China Sea.

Rick finally spoke. "Yes, Captain Geoffrey Lane was of the same stamp as Caleb Harmony. They must have known each other. How could they not, both of them being big bugs on South Street for years? Yet Lane's name is hardly ever mentioned. How come?"

On that I couldn't help. I was baffled, too.

"Ah, Señor Chris, once again you visit the shrine. As well you might, it's impressive." Señor Martinez's soft voice reached us as he entered the room, trimmed and slick as ever, with braided cuffs and a whiff of cologne. "I told Señor Rick of it earlier, of course he has come to behold it. And you, Señor Chris, are you still prospecting for gold?"

"Señor Martinez, I've switched back to my original image. I'm turning over rocks and finding sneaky little creatures that scurry to avoid the light."

"I wish you well in your buggy endeavors, as do we all."

Young da Cunha then joined us, but before he could launch into another eulogy of his honored father and grandfather, Rick pulled me away.

"Let's up anchor," he said. "I've learned all I'm going to learn here, and believe me, I've learned plenty."

We exchanged a few more words with our hostess, then bade her and her guests good-bye and set a course for home.

"You're invited for tea tomorrow at four," I informed Sal, who, just back again from an archery lesson, was waiting for a report in the sitting room. "You should learn all you want to know about her wardrobe."

"High time! So what did you two learn?"

"Yes, Chris," said Rick, "what did you find out from gabbing with that Frenchman?"

I gave them a brief report, including the daughter's arrival in New York.

"So," said Rick, "Mrs. Rivington and her father were in Paris for the duration of the war."

"That's what he said."

"I wonder why. There was money to be made in New York. The Skipper raked in plenty, and so did your pa, too, by supplying the Brooklyn Navy Yard and chartering ships to the government. But

Geoffrey Lane, a real Go Ahead type, chose not to join in the fun. Strange."

"Does it matter where they were, and why?" Sal asked.

"It matters a lot."

"What did you get out of Martinez and da Cunha, while rattling away in Spanish?" I asked.

"Young da Cunha is an innocent, knows nothing. Martinez is a liar, knows everything. He's the one to watch out for. One of the ones."

"Anything else?" asked Sal.

"That house reeks of money, big money. Lane did all right, and she's doing all right, too. And wasn't Pa at home there? Maybe too much at home."

"What does that mean?" Sal asked.

"I'm not sure, but it does mean something."

"Rick," I said, "you told us you'd find the missing pieces of the puzzle in her brownstone. Did you?"

"Almost. Let me check a few facts here, then elsewhere, and I'll get back to you tomorrow. You'll be aghast, agape, and agog."

At his insistence, I led him to Pa's library, where he consulted several years of the *City Directory* and then dashed off, answering our queries with the shouted promise, "Tomorrow!" Sal and I exchanged baffled glances, shrugged.

"So the gumdrop's here in New York," she said, "and no one's seen her to date."

"Not that I know of. She's sure not on display."

"Mystery on top of mystery."

"Maybe you'll see her at tea tomorrow."

"In time, maybe you will, too. Maybe she's a *fille fatale*."

The following afternoon I was the one waiting for reports in the sitting room. Sal arrived first.

"So?"

"She's crackajack, she's prime."

"Mrs. Rivington?"

"Poised, generous, and charming. I've never known a woman like her."

"No *femme fatale*?"

"Anything but. I was wrong."

"So you've unlocked the secrets of her wardrobe?"

"Better still, tomorrow she's taking me herself to her dressmaker."

"Ho, ho, ho."

"And she's going to teach me to shoot."

"Shoot what?"

"A Colt revolver. I told her I'd taken up archery. She thinks I should learn to shoot. She knows a shooting gallery that welcomes ladies. We'll go once a week, maybe twice."

"Ho, ho, ho."

"Meaning what?"

"She's giving you the treatment."

"She's aces, she's *ravissante.*"

"And the gumdrop?"

"She served us tea. Well mannered, quiet, attractive."

"But not aces, not crackajack?"

"A gumdrop with a difference. She has that Continental polish."

"Whatever that is."

Sal shrugged. "You sense it. She's really quite charming. The opposite of her mother, but charming."

I had a lot more questions to ask, but at this point Rick burst in.

"I've got it! It all fits!"

"Tell us!" Sal and I demanded.

He sat down, out of breath. We waited.

"First, the *City Directory.* Entries for Geoffrey Lane and Louise Rivington from 1866 on, but nothing for either of them earlier. They're on St. Mark's Place at the same address. He disappears after '68—"

"Deceased," said Sal.

"—And she moves to the mansion on the Fifth Avenue. But before '66 it's as if they didn't exist."

"They were in Paris during the war," said Sal.

"Yes, but how about before that? Next, the obits at the *Chronicle.* Rob and I searched thoroughly. Nothing for a Mr. Rivington, and in '68 a squib for Geoffrey Lane. Listen!" He produced some notes, read: 'Geoffrey Lane, shipowner and ship's master, well known on South Street, long a resident of this city. Survived by one daughter.' That's all—a mere three lines. Yet we know from a glance at his study that he was active for years in the China trade and all over the world, and amassed a fortune. Grandpa got three columns; he barely gets three lines!"

"What are you driving at?" I asked.

"It's as if most of his career had been wiped out. And now, the Custom House records. Mrs. Rivington told Chris that she was part owner of the clipper ship *Falcon* back in '51. So who were the owners then? A bunch of people, including Jacob Harmony, Gideon Lynch, and Louise Lynch. Not Lane or Rivington—Lynch. Get it? Gideon Lynch and Geoffrey Lane are the same person. Mrs. Rivington is the daughter of the Prince of Slavers. She's in this up to her ears!"

26

"What do you mean?" asked Sal.

"She got into it through her father. She was in it with Grandpa and Pa, and the Biggses and William Matthews, and one or another Martinez and da Cunha, and others we haven't even heard of. That's where her money comes from. She's as guilty as the rest of them. Leaving the dirty business to others—she'd never set her dainty little foot on a slave ship, or offend her genteel nostrils with the stink—but guilty even so!"

"I don't believe it!" said Sal. "Her father, yes. But she didn't know, any more than we knew, or maybe even Pa. I don't believe she was a slaver, even at a safe remove. She's too charming, too refined."

"Chris," said Rick, "what's your opinion?"

"It's beginning to make sense. The moment I first mentioned Gideon Lynch, the Prince of Slavers, to her, she changed the subject and urged me to talk to some ex-slaves. Interesting, but a sidetrack. It got me off course, away from her and her father. She said she'd help me, but everyone she referred me to assured me that Caleb Harmony was above reproach; they praised him to the skies. And in her father's study I'm pretty sure I saw a print of the brig *Fearless*, a slaver, and for sure, a map of the Leeward Coast, where slavers got their slaves. But when she learned what I was up to, they both disappeared. And she herself told me her father destroyed all his papers."

"Or maybe she destroyed them herself," said Rick. "And when he left the city in '62, she went with him. She was just as scared as he was."

"Scared of what?" I asked.

"The Lincoln administration had tried and convicted a slaver, a Captain Gordon out of Portland, Maine, who'd been caught with a load of slaves off Africa. Slaving had been a capital crime for forty years, but for the first time someone was convicted and sentenced to death. His lovely young wife and little boy came from Portland to be with him, arousing much sympathy. He claimed he'd never harmed anyone. Thousands of New Yorkers—your pa, my pa, Grandpa Harmony, everyone—signed petitions begging for mercy. A big to-do."

"So what happened?" asked Sal.

"In '62, right here in the Tombs, with lots of people watching, he was hanged."

The man's crime was horrible, but the finality of his death overwhelmed me. "Did that end the trade?" I asked.

"Did it ever! Fearing arrest, lots of people fled the city. So when Gideon Lynch went to Paris and became Geoffrey Lane, his daughter went with him, and for good cause. Over there they hoped they could ditch their past and come back pure as the morning dew. Look, there's a letter to Grandpa that we never figured out, just the first page, no date, no signature. It's here in the desk, let me find it."

As Sal and I watched, puzzled, he went through a file in the desk, pulled out a sheet of paper.

"Listen! 'Dear Caleb, you old dog,' etc., etc. 'If you can holystone yourself, so can I. Gideon of old I shall no longer be'—Get it? Gideon Lynch! 'I shall put on the sheen of Virtue, and tread its narrow Lane.' 'Lane' with a capital L: Geoffrey Lane! And then: 'I shall strut not a prince, but a king.' The Prince of Slavers—see? Quite a way he had with words, and quite a sense of humor!"

I looked at the letter, which had always baffled us. "Yes, now it does make sense."

"So they sat out the war in Paris and then, when there weren't any more trials or executions, they came back."

"But your pa didn't flee," I said. "And Grandpa Harmony didn't either. Why not?"

"They'd been careful; they weren't known as the Prince of Slavers. Grandpa was respectable—president of the Mariners' Bank and member of the Chamber of Commerce—and Pa waved the flag during the war and snagged a lot of government contracts. And it soon became clear that one execution was enough, the government had made its point."

"But if Lynch was known all over South Street as the Prince of Slavers," said Sal, "how could he get away with changing his name? Wouldn't people know who he was?"

"A lot of the old timers were gone by then, and the younger ones didn't much care: let bygones be bygones. And most of those who did know, like my pa and Grandpa and the Biggses, weren't going to make any trouble. They wanted to put all that behind them."

"And Mr. Rivington?" I asked.

"Still a mystery. The one thing we haven't figured out."

"I'm still not convinced," said Sal. "Not about her."

"She's working hand in glove with the others," Rick insisted. "I'll bet that, right from the start, the moment she heard about Chris's research, they had their heads together. She and Pa and the rest of them. Whatever Pa knew, she knew, and whatever she knew, Pa knew. And we, poor lubbers, weren't aware of it. They've been fighting us every step of the way."

"Look," said Sal, "she may never have been in the trade. She may be trying to protect her father's reputation, for his sake, her own, and her daughter's. That would only be human. Chris, don't you agree?"

"At this point I don't know what to think. What Rick says makes good sense, but yes, there's a chance she's only trying to save the family name."

"Time will tell," said Rick.

"But what do we do right now?" I asked.

"I know what I'm going to do," said Sal. "I'm going with her to her dressmaker tomorrow, and with her to a shooting gallery as often as she'll take me. I won't give any of that up."

"She's using you," said Rick.

Sal shrugged. "I'm becoming the daughter she wishes she had, while being friends with the daughter she does have. If she's using me, I'm using her just as much."

"So what will *you* do, Rick?" I asked.

"I'm going to throw it all at the Skipper, tell him everything we know. I've been waiting all my life for a chance like this. I want to see him squirm."

"As for me," I said, "I'll ask Rob Peterson if he wants another article for the *Chronicle.*"

"Good idea!" said Rick. "I'll mention that as well to the Skipper. He won't just squirm, he'll sweat."

"All right," said Sal. "But I think you two should keep on seeing her."

"Rick," I explained. "She's charmed Sal out of her head. Sal thinks she's the *nec plus ultra.*"

"She's tops," said Sal. "Give her a chance. See if I'm not right."

"Okay," I said. "But we'll do it with our eyes wide open."

"Agreed," said Rick. "That's our course for now. You two make nice with her, and I'll unhinge the Skipper. Ahoy, mates, we've got a smart wind abaft. Great fun! This should be a shindy."

A shindy indeed. We were deep into a wild, wild story, one that promised to be far wilder—and darker and more sinister—than any of Grandpa Harmony's tales, or any of the dime novels I had devoured as a kid.

(An assembly of African warriors and chieftains in loin cloths and robes of many colors.)

<u>All</u>: The King! The King! The King!

(Drums, rattles, horns. Resplendent in a red and gold silk robe with an embroidered cap, and bright gold rings dangling from his ears, King Africa enters, his eyes flashing, his shining teeth sharpened into fangs, rings on his fingers, a fly whisk in one hand. All bow; he sits on a stool of gold.)

<u>King Africa</u> (flicking the fly whisk back and forth): Bring in the prisoner!

(Captain Patriot is brought in, shackled, his head in an iron yoke, carrying an iron ball chained to his feet. He stands tall and manly amid hisses, grunts, shrieks. Some clutch their spears, some spit. A gesture from the King brings silence.)

<u>King Africa</u>: Your name, wretch.

<u>Captain Patriot</u>: Captain Patriot.

<u>King Africa</u>: Your nationality?

<u>Captain Patriot</u>: Whole-souled, true-blue citizen of the Land of the Free and Home of the Brave.

<u>King Africa</u>: Your trade or occupation?

<u>Captain Patriot</u>: Ship's master, champion of justice, and scourge of malefactors.

<u>King Africa</u>: Indeed. And what, as such, have you accomplished?

<u>Captain Patriot</u>: I have rescued Christian ladies from the lust of pashas. I have labored heroically to purge the seas of pirates. I engaged those fell marauders, the Crimson Avenger and Dead Notch the Destroyer, in personal combat and slew both. In the aptly named Straits of Death I—

<u>King Africa</u>: Enough! Did you ever participate in the evil trade that victimized my people?

<u>Captain Patriot</u>: Never!

King Africa: *What did you do to stop it?*

Captain Patriot: *I denounced it at every opportunity and pursued suspected slavers whenever I encountered them at sea.*

King Africa: *How many did you overtake and board?*

Captain Patriot: *None. They were too fast; they eluded me.*

(Hoots of derision. The King gestures for silence.)

King Africa: *Did you interfere with slave catchers?*

Captain Patriot: *No. I was at sea.*

King Africa: *Did you free any slaves?*

Captain Patriot: *No. Being at sea, how could I?*

King Africa: *Do you hear, warriors and chieftains? He did nothing!*

(Drums, rattles, horns, cries of outrage. At a gesture from the King, silence.)

King Africa: *To hate slavery but do nothing to end it is a crime. It gives an edge to the heart. What say you, Juror no. 1?*

King of Ashanti: *Guilty!*

King Africa: *Juror no. 2?*

King of Togo: *Guilty!*

King Africa: *Juror no. 3?*

King of Dahomey: *Guilty!*

King Africa: *Jurors 4, 5, 6?*

Quanimo, Mingo, Quacko: *Guilty!*

King Africa: *7, 8, 9?*

Simon Congo, Domingo Angola, Jan Guinea: *Guilty!*

King Africa: *10, 11, 12?*

Luke the Coachman, Junius Fox, Jonah the Cartman: *Guilty!*

King Africa: *Prisoner, you are sentenced to death. We won't torture you or burn you alive, or foul our mouths by eating you. Following the customs of your country, the so-called land of freedom, you shall be hanged by the neck until dead.*

Captain Patriot: *I appeal!*

King Africa: *From this court, no appeal!*

Captain Patriot: *I swear to you, by my God in heaven, and all your gods in the forest and the veldt, I am innocent! There is no evil in my heart. Do not answer injustice with injustice. I appeal to your compassion, your humanity. Spare a foursquare Go Ahead American who intends you no ill and never has—a man whose deeds, recorded in a hundred dime novels, though I never sought fame, have inspired the youth of the nation. In the name of true justice, spare me!*

King Africa: Take him!

(The guards seize Captain Patriot, who with great force shakes them off, then speaks with icy calm.)

Captain Patriot: There is no need. Show me the way.

(At a gesture from the King, the guards stand back, then point the way with their spears. Captain Patriot exits with dignity, followed by the guards. Silence; the King and the others listen. The King flicks his fly whisk back and forth. Then, from a distance, a muffled gasp. Drums, rattles, horns, cries of joy. The King gestures for silence, rises from the stool of gold; all bow. He leaves. Pandemonium: grunts, shrieks, cheers, stomping of the feet, clicks and whistles, wild dancing.)

All: Justice! Justice! Justice!

Sal came back radiant from her outing with Mrs. Rivington. She informed me that dresses in the finest fabrics had been ordered at the dressmaker's, and the most optimal accessories acquired. In addition, she modeled a pillbox hat perched on her forehead.

"It's called a casquette. It's egregiously chic. She paid for it."

"Mrs. Rivington paid for your hat?"

"I protested, she insisted. Boy, does she have money! Not that she's forgotten about you. You'll be invited again for tea."

"To meet the gumdrop? The honey crisp?"

"Miss Rivington is charming. And tomorrow I'm going with her to the shooting gallery."

"With the honey crisp?"

"No, with *Mrs.* Rivington! Kathleen won't be joining us. She's much too gentle, too domestic."

"As you are not."

A smile. "That's right—as I am not."

Rick burst in, exuberant.

"I just had it out with the Skipper! I threw it all at him, didn't leave anything out. This was in his office, the door shut, just the two of us."

"How did he take it?" I asked.

"He just sat there, glaring. Never admitted a thing."

"He didn't deny it?" asked Sal.

"He knew he'd be wasting his time. The Skipper is one cool character, I'll have to grant him that."

"He didn't sweat or squirm?" I asked.

"Not visibly. But he kept fingering that gold penknife, like he always does when he's nervous. Gave it quite a workout, especially when I told him that Rob Peterson at the *Chronicle* is eager to do another article."

"He still said nothing?"

"Not a word. He was breathing heavy now, fists clenched, staring through slit eyes. I've never seen him so wound up, so tense. I'm lucky he didn't bash me."

"So that's how you left it?" asked Sal.

"No, right off the top of my head, I made him an offer. He won't be named in the article, if he makes a full confession and apology, first in church, then in print."

"Apology to whom?" I asked.

"To all the Africans he abused. To his family, the city, the nation. To everyone."

"What did he say?"

"He said he'd think about it. And that was the end of our palaver."

"So what do we do now?"

"Wait. He'll chew it over, maybe consult Dwight or some cronies."

"Does Dwight know about all this?" asked Sal.

"Maybe, maybe not. I can't tell. Well, there's the news. Now if you'll excuse me, I'm going off to carouse. For the first time in my life, I've got the Skipper at the mean end of a lash. It feels roaringly good."

And off he went. Sal and I pondered a bit and then told Ma.

Ma frowned. "Rick wants his father to confess and apologize in public? Jake will never do that, too proud. The Harmonys are great doers. They build, they amass things, they conquer. They're Go Ahead, they make this country run. But they have no humility. They never doubt themselves, never admit they're wrong. Never."

"Pa?" I put in.

"To himself, in secret, yes. Finally, after years and years, if you read between the lines in his diary. The slave trade, the *Venture.* But even for him it wasn't easy. Jacob will never do it, never. He'd die first."

27

"So you are Mr. Christopher Harmony. I am so glad to meet you. Maman has mentioned you often. You are a writer, I believe. For me, this is an event. I have never before met a writer."

"Mademoiselle, I have yet to put pen to paper. I'm only researching, and that can take a very long time."

She smiled. "Well, I have never met a researcher either. You must tell me about your researches."

"Research," said Mrs. Rivington. "In English we don't use the plural."

"Oh, of course: research. You must forgive me, Mr. Harmony. English is my native tongue, but I have studied abroad so long, I make silly mistakes. My English is full of—what is the word, maman?"

"Gallicisms."

"Yes, gallicisms. I make my English sound like French. I say 'changement' for 'change,' and 'sympathetic' for 'likable' or 'pleasant.' You see what a mess I make of your tongue—I mean your language—which is mine as well."

"Miss Rivington, your English is charming. I wouldn't have you alter it a bit."

Charming it was, though slightly quaint, as if she'd learned it in school.

"You are most kind, Mr. Harmony, very patient and very discreet. With you I shall be less self-conscious, less afraid of making gaffes. You do say 'gaffes,' do you not?"

"Yes, mademoiselle, we do. And we make them all the time."

Clothed in a cloud of white muslin with not a speck of jewelry in sight, Kathleen Rivington was soft-voiced, poised, and exceedingly courteous and refined. Meeting her over the tea table in Mrs. Rivington's parlor, with her mother in attendance, I was vastly charmed. We were all three munching sugary wafers and dainty little cakes, while sipping hot mint tea.

"So, mademoiselle, after many years abroad, you have returned to your native land."

"Yes, Mr. Harmony, I have indeed, just a month ago. Maman thinks I should get to know this country better and become American again."

"Bravo! I heartily approve. What do you think of New York?"

"Very big, very noisy, very exciting. Less elegant than Paris—Paris before the war, that is—but much more, oh what is the word?" She thought a moment. "Intense."

"I wouldn't have thought of that word. Yes, we are intense."

"And very—you do use the phrase, I believe—very Go Ahead."

"Yes, very. I see it in my own family, ship's masters and shipowners sending ships all over the world. That's why I'm researching a family history."

"Tell me! I want to know all about it."

"I've looked at musty old documents and talked with people who knew my late grandfather, a hero of the age of sail. But I'm not too happy with some of the things I've discovered."

"Oh? Why not?"

"It seems that certain members of my family were involved in the slave trade. They brought slaves from Africa to Cuba."

Her eyes grew wide with wonder. "Really? But was that not illegal?"

"Very, but they got round the law, they and all their cronies. Lots of people were in on it, seemingly respectable people."

"But that is terrible! How could such persons be considered respectable?"

"They let others do the dirty work, kept at a safe remove. Then, having made their money, they quit the trade and pretended they'd had nothing to do with it. Some of them even changed their name."

"What a strange world we live in! And an evil one, it seems."

"Yes, mademoiselle, it is. I've shucked off a lot of illusions."

"And you are going to write about this, even with your own family involved?"

"Yes, mademoiselle, I have to. The truth has got to be told."

"I admire you, Mr. Harmony. That takes—what is the word?—pluck."

"Thank you, mademoiselle. But first there'll be an article in a newspaper, telling about the results of my research."

"Soon?"

"Very soon."

"I will read it. How exciting! Just think, maman, Mr. Harmony and his research will be mentioned in the paper."

Mrs. Rivington had witnessed our conversation without betraying a hint of emotion; not once had her poise been dented. "Be sly," the Reverend Oakes had advised me, so I was being sly. Now, Mrs. Rivington looked directly at me.

"This article, Mr. Chris—in the *Chronicle* again, I assume—will it mention names?"

"Yes, Mrs. Rivington, lots." (With due care, so as to avoid charges of libel, but why go into that?)

"Is that wise, at this point?"

"Nothing about it is wise. But those involved in the trade should be exposed. They shouldn't be protected."

"Admirable!" exclaimed Kathleen Rivington. "At school they taught us that, come what may, it is always best to tell the truth."

Mrs. Rivington smiled. "The world, my dear, is a bit more complicated. The truth can be tangled, ambiguous, elusive. Out of season, it can even do a great deal of harm. And often those who tell it come to grief."

"But surely Mr. Harmony must do what he thinks right."

"Of course, my dear. We must all of us do so, and shall. But come, you two, this subject is much too grim for a tea. Kathleen, tell Mr. Christopher about the outing we've planned."

"Oh yes. An excursion by carriage to the Central Park. Two carriages, in fact. No gentlemen, just maman, me, and my friends. Your sister has been so kind. I know no one here, so she is introducing me to all her friends: Miss Moffat, Miss Throgmorton, Miss Moore, and many others. They are all so friendly, so welcoming. We will have such a jolly time together. And I am dying to see the Park. They say it is every bit as beautiful as the Bois de Boulogne in Paris."

What was Sal up to? What was Mrs. Rivington up to? These girls were Sal's friends and mine from our dancing class, some of them daughters of Ma's friends at church.

"The Park is a bang-up delight," I assured her. "I would love to take you both there sometime myself."

"'Bang-up': I love your American English—so vivid, so alive! And the Park would be great fun. Do not be offended that we do not invite you for our promenade. No gentlemen, on this occasion. We will invite you another time, will we not, maman?"

"Of course. There'll be a ball in December."

"Oh yes, Mr. Harmony, we are giving a ball in December. There is a big ballroom upstairs that cries out to be used. I do look forward to it. You of course will be invited. And Sal, too, dearest Sal."

"We'll be delighted to come." If your mother is still speaking to me, I might have added.

Our patter continued for an hour: my compliments on her sampler framed on the wall ("Oh, *that!* It is nothing, just a schoolgirl exercise."); my descriptions of Broadway, the harbor, and the waterfront ("I must see it all!"); her further impressions of New York.

When I rose to leave, Mrs. Rivington had her daughter clear away the tea things, so she herself could see me to the door. She stopped in front of it; our eyes met.

"You have gone very fast," I said.

She smiled. "I have to, don't you think?"

She opened the door and I left.

I had lots of things to ask Sal, but before I could see her, Cousin Dwight came calling, which, during business hours, was strange. We talked alone in the sitting room. He looked all wrought up; his waxed mustache quivered as he spoke.

"I didn't know, Chris. I swear I didn't know!"

"Know what?"

"The trade! Anything, everything about it! I was a child back then, like you, like Rick. We didn't any of us know."

"Has Uncle Jake told you about it? About him and Grandpa?"

"Not really. Blunt as he is, he can be cagey. He said you and Sal have got a lot of information—alleged information—about Harmony involvement in the trade and are threatening to have it published in the paper. Are you?"

"Yes."

"Pa was involved for sure?"

"Yes. And Grandpa, too. And a lot of other people as well. Awkward, isn't it?"

"Awkward? It's a disaster! Susanna and I are engaged, but her parents are still holding off; no date has been set for the wedding. If word of this gets out, there won't be a wedding. The Van Zandts are old Knickerbockers, and shun even a hint of scandal."

"She loves you, doesn't she?"

"Of course."

"Then elope."

"Impossible. She'd never marry against the wishes of her parents."

"I see. A dutiful daughter."

"That's the way they raise them. Chris, are you absolutely sure about all this?"

"Absolutely."

"Based on what?"

"Old documents, and the testimony of seamen who shipped out on Harmony vessels."

"Oh God, how could Pa and Grandpa Harmony do this? Look what it does to us!"

"I know. Sal and I and Rick are all of us pretty shook up."

"But you aren't about to marry into Old Money. If you knew how I've longed for this, and planned for it and schemed. It's a step up for me, for all of us. Maybe someday you and Sal will want to step up, too."

"Dwight, I have to do it. Truth will out. It can't be swept under the rug forever."

"Why not? What's done is done. It was wrong, but it's finished now, it's buried in the past. Leave it there. Why bring it up now? Who cares?"

"*I* care. It was a dirty business. Those who made money from it ought to be exposed."

"No matter who gets hurt?"

"No matter who."

"Even you?"

"Even me."

"That's blind, that's selfish. You're not just hurting Pa, you're hurting me and anyone bearing the Harmony name. You're… you're destroying us!"

"Did Uncle Jake send you here?"

"No! I've come on my own!"

"Dwight, I can't help it. It has to be done."

"Chris, for God's sake, don't!"

"I have to!"

"Don't!"

We were on our feet now, face to face. He stared at me, heavyset, fists clenched, his features wild with rage. And hate: the same hate I'd seen once before, when I stopped him from stealing the chest. He was about to pummel me; I would dodge as best I could, using my boxing to fend off his blows, and maybe even plant one smack in his face. But against his massive frame I felt small.

With effort, he choked back his rage. "You puny little bastard," he murmured, spun about, and stalked out of the room and the house.

He hadn't pummeled me; he'd try something else.

Minutes later Sal came in.

"You're introducing Kathleen Rivington to all your friends. Why?"

"She doesn't know anyone here. Why not?"

"You hardly know her."

"We get on."

"I gather there's going to be a ball in December."

"A big one—great fun. I've seen their ballroom; it's stupendously huge and magnificent."

"What's this all about?"

"Mrs. Rivington wants her daughter to have some society. Our friends find Kathleen charming. They'll mention her to their mamas, who will also find her charming. And they'll find her maman charming as well. Especially if maman gives the smash ball of the season, one that all the young ladies will be dying to attend."

"So that's it: you're selling Mrs. Rivington to the mamas."

"Of course. A respectable ball has to be chaperoned. Get the girls, and you'll get the mamas, and then you'll get the papas, too. *Voilà!*"

"And the daughter of the Prince of Slavers will be accepted by society."

"Exactly."

"Why are you doing this?"

"I like them both, mother and daughter."

"The mother was up to her ears in the trade."

"I'm giving her the benefit of a doubt."

"What about Rob Peterson's article for the *Chronicle*?"

"That can wait till after New Year's. By then, we may know for sure about Mrs. Rivington. Maybe she needn't be mentioned at all. Meanwhile we can kick up our heels."

"Whose side are you on?"

"Everyone's. Whose side are *you* on?"

"I'm on the side of Truth, with a capital T."

"Oho! And how do you like Kathleen Rivington? Has she affected in any way your devotion to capital-T Truth?"

"Kathleen is, as you say, charming. A gumdrop, but prodigiously charming."

"Nothing more?"

"Not really."

"Look, I expect you to fall for either the mother or the daughter, or both."

"The mother was probably a slaver. The daughter is sugary and sweet, nothing more."

"Okay."

"Nothing more."

"Okay."

For days to come, my dreams and fantasies were haunted by a cloud of white muslin, and a soft musical voice that said "tongue" for "language" and used expressions that were deliciously quaint.

28

The next few weeks were giddy with fun. Sal modeled for Rick and me several smart outfits that she had ordered from Mrs. Rivington's *couturière*, then went on the excursion to the Park with the Rivingtons and six other *demoiselles* in two carriages that she described as "monstrously chic." The outing, she reported afterward, was *"inoubliable,"* meaning "unforgettable." (Miss Rivington was helping her work up her French.)

Meanwhile, not a word from Dwight.

On a deep lawn behind the Rivington residence, one fine autumn afternoon, I and several other young gentlemen—including, to my surprise, Señor Innocencio José da Cunha the Third—joined the young ladies in a spirited game of croquet. Under the watchful eye of maman, we drove brightly colored balls through wickets—or at least tried to—amid a chorus of squeals and exclamations and giggles, and some prodigiously genteel disputes. Throughout the game Sal was getting attention from Dan Hunter, my sparring partner of yore, now fancy-free, whose manly charms, I hoped, just might grab her fancy. As for me, given the opportunity to drive Miss Rivington's ball deep into the ornamental shrubs, I gave it only the gentlest of taps, sending it but a scant few feet toward the shrubs—an act of gallantry that Sal denounced as craven. Later, when the players were rewarded with a sumptuous spread of snacks in a back parlor bathed in sunlight, Miss Rivington showed her gratitude, when her mother's back was turned, by popping ginger snaps of her own making into my mouth, while I brushed her dainty fingers with my lips, eliciting smiles from us both. Yes, Miss Rivington was adapting to American ways.

Meanwhile, not a word from Uncle Jake.

Next, Sal reported with great enthusiasm several outings to a shooting gallery with Mrs. Rivington, describing her improving skill with a pearl-handled Colt revolver as one of the most optimal experiences of her life.

"She's using you," said Rick.

"Maybe, but I'm getting to be a pretty good shot."

A few days later Rick informed us that further research on Pearl Street and the waterfront had revealed that the "someone else in New York" to whom, according to Jonas Ward, Uncle Jake had chartered the *Venture* in 1859, and who had then chartered it in turn to Señor Miguel Martinez of Havana, was none other than Louise Lynch. So Mrs. Rivington had been a part of that baffling maze of operators involved in transforming an elite racing yacht into a mysterious and elusive slave ship. Or had she?

"It doesn't mean a thing!" insisted Sal. "She may not have known what the others were up to."

Rick scoffed; I was inclined to agree with Sal.

Said Rick, "She's using you both."

One fine late October afternoon I rented a rig and took Ma, dressed soberly, and Sal, togged out in the height of fashion, on an outing in the Park. This was Ma's first promenade in a year and a half, and one more step in our discreet campaign to nudge her out of mourning and into receiving callers on New Year's Day. The Drive in the Park was jammed. Parasoled ladies and their top-hatted beaus rode in shiny black equipages with jingly silver-mounted harnesses, attended by flunkeys in livery: a splendacious parade of the uppity. Ma wasn't sure that a respectable churchgoing Presbyterian lady should be seen in such "flash" company, until we passed several members of the First Church congregation who, upon recognizing her, nodded graciously without a trace of embarrassment.

Suddenly Sal remarked, "Well, well, look who's coming: Papa Bear, Mama Bear, and Baby Bear!"

Passing us in the opposite direction was an open carriage where Sal and I recognized Mrs. Rivington and her daughter, with Uncle Jake at the reins. He was directing their attention to something in the Park, so they never saw us. In an instant they were gone.

"Well," said Ma, "we always knew that Jake was a friend of that woman. It was her daughter with them, I assume."

Ma thought nothing more about it, but Sal and I traded a startled glance. Sal's remark—a casual joke, nothing more—had prompted in the two of us, simultaneously, the same revelation: Uncle Jake was Kathleen's father! We said nothing then, but later, by ourselves, shared our discovery. There was no Mr. Rivington and never had been; he was simply a sham to mask the poor girl's illegitimacy, of which she herself was totally unaware. Armed only with an intuition, we were dead sure we were right. When we informed Rick, he agreed.

"Of course! That explains everything! They're in this thing together, they're allies. Don't trust them, either one!"

For Sal and me, a dilemma. Did we dare be friends with Mrs. Rivington? Was she, as Rick insisted, merely using us? While promising to keep his suspicions in mind, we decided to go on as if nothing had happened, partly because we liked Kathleen and wanted her to make friends in New York, and partly because we wanted to see what the mother was up to. Besides, why miss out on the biggest ball, the smash of the season? But the three of us agreed that, if at all possible, we would never reveal to Kathleen, who thought him long since dead, that she had a living father.

"Still," said Rick, "a risky game. Watch out!"

That game continued. Sal accompanied the mother and daughter on a tour of the most exclusive shops in the city and came back with a mantle of black taffeta: "If that woman wants to give you something, just try saying no!" The mantle was, as she put it, *"ravissant."* In exchange, when Mrs. Rivington consulted her about the guest list for the ball, Sal explained that, to propel her daughter into polite society, she must at all costs avoid the taint of Shoddy, those free-spending parvenus—war contractors, gold speculators, patent medicine kings, and grubby projectors of grandiose railroads—who were crawling all over the city like vermin. For one whole afternoon Sal monitored the tentative guest list, striking out some names and adding others, until she pronounced it impeccable. For this, Mrs. Rivington was, as Sal put it, "just monstrously, egregiously grateful."

"Look, you two," said Rick, when informed of these latest developments, "we've got to have a talk with Rob Peterson. He's dying to do another article, this time naming names, and his managing editor is all fired up at the thought of it. They see a tie-in with the unsolved murder of Jonas Ward. We can't let Rob down!"

A four-way conference resulted in our sitting room, with the three of us explaining to Rob Peterson the results of our research, including details about the slaving voyages of the *Fearless*, the *Charity*, and the *Venture*, as reported by Jonas Ward and confirmed by our own snooping about. Rob scribbled notes as we talked.

"This is hot—a scorcher! My editor will really go for it. But to avoid libel, he'll want solid, detailed proof. Show me what you've got!"

We produced letters, journal entries, and ships' papers documenting the involvement of Harmonys and Biggses, William Matthews, the Martinez and da Cunha families, and Gideon Lynch. In accordance with a condition imposed by Sal and myself, we made no mention of Geoffrey Lane or Mrs. Rivington. To these documents we added Sal's notes on Jonas Ward's testimony.

"Capital! Just what my editor will want! Can I borrow this stuff to write the article? When not using it, I'll keep it in our safe, which has a combination lock known only to a few trusted members of the staff."

We agreed, but stipulated that the article must not appear until after New Year's, at which time we would further update him. At this he looked a bit dashed, having counted on a "hot" new story before or during the holidays.

"How about the most ultimate, most bang-up ball of the season?" proposed Sal, who described Mrs. Rivington's plans in glowing terms. "A scorcher of a story, don't you think?"

"No," said Rob. "Just a honey. I'll talk to my editor. He's a tough old bird, but I think I can bring him around."

"Fine!" said Sal. "I'll get you an invitation."

"She won't mind having a journalist on hand?"

"She'd pay for the publicity. Besides, she's inviting oodles of girls, so she needs more young males to balance things out. I hope you can dance."

So Rob Peterson was recruited for the ball, and was promised another invitation to the hostess's New Year's Day reception, so he could report on that as well. When, all keyed up, he left with the relevant documents, Rick accompanied him all the way to Printing House Square and saw the documents deposited in the *Chronicle*'s big steel safe.

One week later, Ma received an engraved invitation to the Harmonys to attend Mrs. Louise Rivington's ball in honor of her daughter Kathleen—an invitation, Sal and I assured her, that was now being clutched at by the most respectable matrons in the city, including a fair number of her more liberal-minded First Church friends. (Presbyterians of our acquaintance were evenly divided between those who shunned dancing as a gateway to hell, and those who viewed it as a harmless entertainment.) Having heard us out, Ma smiled but declined to attend, adding that we were free to go.

By way of compensation, Ma then announced that, yes, she would receive callers on New Year's Day, albeit in a toned-down, decorous way. Sal was thrilled, since Ma's failure to do so a year before had condemned her daughter to a day of reading silly novels by the hearth. Sal at once sprang into action, planning refreshments with Ma and undertaking to order invitations. For the first time in months, I heard Sal singing in the house, where the soupy gloom caused by Pa's death seemed to be lifting at last. The approaching holidays promised to be jolly.

Just then a note came from Rick:

Dear Aunt Martha, Sal, and Chris,

I'm shipping out. Just got an offer too good to turn down—ship's master of a brig to New Orleans and maybe the Caribbean. Good pay, too. So huzza and hip, hip, hooray! And Merry Christmas and Happy New Year to all! Won't be gone long. Keep at the project. See you next year!

—Rick

"Well," said Ma, "he's done it again. But at least he's moving up. I wish him Godspeed."

"Something fishy here," said Sal. "Too sudden, too good to be true."

"Meaning what?" I asked.

"Uncle Jake's doing. He's pulled some strings on the waterfront."

"Why?"

"To get Rick out of the way."

"That would be like Jake, wouldn't it?" said Ma. "Sometimes blunt, sometimes slick and sly."

Later, Sal spoke to me out of Ma's hearing.

"I'm worried."

"Why?"

"You and I may be next."

29

It was a clear, starry night. Street lamps cast their glow on fresh white drifts of snow. When Sal and I got out of our cab and approached the brownstone, we found its windows ablaze with gaslight, and a jam of carriages in front, where a carpet sheltered by an awning ran from the curb up the stoop to the monumental entrance. Guests were flocking up the stoop, but before we joined them, Sal pointed out several closed carriages passing by, their occupants peering jealously at these indications of a flash affair to which they hadn't been invited.

"That's proof already," said Sal. "It's a success!"

In his article on the coming season, Rob Peterson had done his work well.

In the vestibule the mulatto butler greeted the guests courteously and received their invitations. Having deposited our wraps in a cloakroom, we proceeded to the front parlor, where Mrs. Rivington and her daughter were welcoming guests amid a sumptuous floral display and the murmur of genteel conversation. I was sporting my best black frock coat and a ruffled shirt adorned with a diamond tiepin inherited from Pa. Sal wore a low-cut gown of white lace and tulle, with a gardenia in her hair. The two of us, I thought, were about as swank as Presbyterians dared to be.

"Miss Sal Harmony and Mr. Chris!" came the hostess's silvery voice. "How good to see you, and how radiant you look!"

Radiant herself in green silk and a turquoise brooch set with pearls, she shook hands briskly with me and exchanged kisses on the cheek with Sal. Kathleen, in gauzy white, likewise greeted us warmly, giving me a slightly firmer clasp, then advised us that for eight dances the gentlemen must request the honor from the ladies in advance, those so honored inscribing their names in the ladies' dance cards. Other dances would be "open," and one a surprise.

"Miss Kathleen," I said, "may I be so presumptuous as to request the honor of the first and last dance?"

"Mr. Chris," she replied with a smile, "all my dances but two are taken." She showed me her dance card, with the first and last dances still blank, then whispered, "I saved those two for you."

Heart thumping, I could barely scrawl my name in the card. While doing so, I noticed that young da Cunha had claimed the second dance, and Sir Somebody-or-other the third. How this "Sir" got in I couldn't imagine, since Sal had warned Mrs. Rivington against the fake marquesses and broken-down counts who often slipped into fancy balls. Worse still, I had to acknowledge that the title, whatever it was, might be dead to rights sound and authentic.

As our hostesses greeted other new arrivals, Sal and I went on into the parlor, which was fancied up with holly boughs and candles, and a huge Christmas tree hung with ornaments and candy canes. There we nodded to young ladies of our acquaintance and to their brothers and parents, the presence in force of the mamas guaranteeing chaperones and decorum galore. Yes, our hostess knew her way and, with Sal's help, had gone very far.

Sal sat in an armchair placing her in view, with the desired result: several young men, Dan Hunter among them, flocked to inscribe their name in her card. Rob Peterson surfaced, looking slightly uncomfortable in his frock coat and cravat, and was granted dance number two.

"Are you taking notes?" I whispered.

"Mentally," he confirmed. "No notepad or pencil: too gross. I'm trying to blend in."

"You've succeeded."

"Thanks. Fanciest affair I've ever attended. Very flash."

Faint strains of music from the third-floor ballroom told me that the orchestra was tuning up, so I hurried off to claim more dances. When the guests began drifting upstairs, Sal and I joined them.

The ballroom was indeed, as Sal had put it, stupendously huge and magnificent, lit with crystal chandeliers and splashed with more bouquets of flowers giving off a whiffy freshness, and sprigs of mistletoe and holly. The small string orchestra was still tuning up on a platform at one end, and chairs lined the walls so the older element could look on at their ease. All around us we sensed a mood of anticipation, of being part of a very optimal event. When the Rivingtons arrived, couples began lining up for the first dance, a polonaise. Now I understood why Sal had rehearsed me repeatedly at home, echoing the words of our dancing teacher of some years back: "Head high! Be stately and grand!" As Kathleen's partner, I would join her in leading the procession. Searching for her among the jabbering throng, I was greeted with a smile. With all eyes on us, we stood side by side facing forward and, hands clasped, stretched each an arm out straight ahead, positioned for the dance. Kathleen smiled at her mother, who nodded to the maestro, who raised his baton. A sudden silence fell, then the orchestra began a majestic piece in triple time, and off we went.

I had never danced with Kathleen, but the moment we began, I knew I had the perfect partner, one who needed no reminder to hold her head high and be stately and grand. As we promenaded to the music, at intervals bowing first to the onlookers and then to each other, an audible "Ah!" came from those watching. Round the room we strutted three times with the other couples following behind. Then, at a given moment, we stopped, facing each other, and with the other dancers held our arms up to form an arch, under which the last of the procession passed, and then the dancers near us, till we were the only ones left, at which point we turned and promenaded off in opposite directions until, coming full circle, we met again, thus ending the dance. By now we and the other dancers were breathless, all frothed up and giddy; Mrs. Rivington beamed approval. As leaders of the polonaise, Kathleen and I had made a hit!

I escorted Kathleen back to a seat on the sidelines, where her mother sat enthroned, wielding a black lace fan. When I thanked Kathleen and kissed her hand with what I hoped was Continental flair, she answered with a squeeze. Sitting nearby, Sal watched with a hint of a smirk. She had danced the polonaise with Walt Simpson, a boy from dancing class whom I loved to dismiss as an oaf, and would now pair off with Rob Peterson for the next dance, a quadrille. Rob had had no trouble finding partners, since Sal had talked him up to her friends as a "dashing young reporter of great promise." When he came to claim her, he looked more at ease, having managed the polonaise quite well. My partner was now Miss Ruth Ann ("Twinkletoes" or "Toothy Ruthie") Moore, with whom I skipped and romped through the square dance with (another new word) aplomb.

Various round and square dances followed, then a waltz where I and Miss Sarah Throgwhistle whirled rapturously in a circle of dancers, while Sal yielded to the lumbering grace of Gus Miller, whom I still called Gorilla Gus. In the intervals between dances I noticed Peter Biggs, who nodded but kept his distance, doubtless recalling Rick's fierce interrogation of his grandfather; conspicuous by their absence were Dwight and Uncle Jake. At one point I saw Sal chatting with young Señor da Cunha, who, it now occurred to me, was cuttingly handsome in a Latin sort of way. Noticing me, Sal winked, which might've meant "I'm in the enemy's camp," or "I kind of like him," or "What fools these mortals be!"

An adjoining supper room was opened at ten; servants bustled, people flocked. In the crowd that was munching and babbling, Señor da Cunha sought me out.

"Mr. Harmony, we should be friends. Your family and mine are illustrious. Ancestors of mine, both Portuguese and Spanish, sailed with the Armada against England. Ancestors of yours may well have fought the Armada under Drake. What does it matter, if they fought on opposite sides, as long as they had valor? We should both be proud!"

Though totally unaware of any ancestor who had fought under Drake, I agreed.

"We have no titles, you and I," he continued. "But our forebears behaved with courage and dignity, which is probably more than can be said of the family of that fop over there."

He directed my gaze to where Sir Somebody-or-other, a young Englishman who had appeared out of nowhere, was now entertaining a throng of bedazzled damsels. "I'm frightfully eager, don't you know," he was saying, "to have a crack at a buffalo." To my American eye, he did indeed have the look of a fop.

"I don't know the gentleman," I confessed. "I don't even know his name."

"Sir Robert Chippendale, or Farthingale, or Nightingale, or whatever. Some kind of minor marquess, or the son of one, who's never worked a day in his life. But he has a title, so the girls flock. Let us show him, you and I, by our grace and wit and verve, what a true *caballero* should be."

"Ah yes," I said importantly, "*un hombre muy decente y refinado.,*" echoing, in my faulty Spanish, a pronouncement of Don Miguel Martinez of the braided cuffs.

Young da Cunha glowed. "Well said, señor. We are indeed of a mind. We tolerate no fops!"

Just then, from the admiring group around Sir Robert, there came a burst of feminine laughter, capped by his piercing voice: "My dears, I just thought it rippingly funny!" No question, the fop was a hit.

Talking to a crowd of elders nearby was our hostess, whose poise and savoir-faire (yet another new word) amazed me. Tonight, no mention of stock speculations or gold, or clipper ships and the sea. Instead, she talked of Emerson's essays, the sublimity of the Alps, the latest regatta, the inexhaustible delights of the Central Park. Where she herself had little knowledge and no opinion, she elicited them from others; the conversation flowed. Seconding her was her daughter, totally at ease in the midst of her elders, never obtruding herself, but ever ready, if appealed to, to provide an elegant comment or fine touch of wit. The two of them were a marvel.

Next, our hostess announced the promised surprise: a daring innovation, a turnabout, where each young lady must ask a young gentleman for the honor of the dance. As a murmur ran through the crowd, numerous young gentlemen made themselves conspicuous, while a few others fled in dismay. Seeing Kathleen Rivington coming my way, I flashed a gracious smile, then watched in chagrin as she sailed right past me to honor young da Cunha with her choice. Miffed, I had to mask my feelings as the orchestra struck up a polka, and Miss Constance Moffat ("little Miss Muffet"), beating out two other damsels by seconds, claimed me for the dance. Sal had chosen Dan Hunter.

As we went prancing around the room, my eye was fixed on Kathleen and da Cunha Number Three, who were dancing up a storm. Two innocents, I thought, whose family pride and peace of mind would be shattered, the moment the results of my research appeared in print. After the dance, these thoughts continued to bedevil me. How many young people present—Peter Biggs, for instance—were likewise vulnerable, being unaware of their families' sins? How many of them, like Sal and me, had been raised on dirty money and now lived in proud houses bought and furnished with proceeds from the trade? Did I have the right to strip these happy young dancers of their innocence and burden them with shame for the misdeeds of others? For the first time, I had doubts.

By now the papas had thinned out, retreating to a back parlor downstairs where they could smoke, but the mamas remained, a few of them drowsing in armchairs, but most of them fiercely vigilant. The next several dances I went through in a funk, plagued by my new doubts. But when the last dance, a waltz, was announced, I focused my thoughts and went to find Kathleen.

"Mademoiselle," I said, "I'm going to waltz you as you've never been waltzed in your life!"

"Monsieur," she responded quite seriously, "I entrust myself to you and will endeavor to meet your challenge."

Mrs. Rivington, I noticed, was watching us discreetly from a distance. She had, in fact, been observing us all evening. To discover a daughter's inclinations, if any, what better way than to expose her to the attentions of a slew of young men at a ball?

When the music began, other dancers held back, leaving the floor to Kathleen and myself. As we whirled about, from the crowd there came another soft cry of "Ah!" Then, one by one, other couples joined in, and we all went whirling together in a huge circle round the hall. Kathleen was as smooth and graceful in the waltz as she had been stately in the polonaise. Blurred impressions of mamas, flowers, chandeliers, and other dancers flashed past us at intervals, as we spun round and round, till finally there seemed to be only the two of us, ever sure, ever mindlessly happy, in a world that was all music and dance. When at last the music stopped, we whirled for one last time, then stood there facing each other, dazed, unaware of others around us. Then, after a moment or two, we realized that everyone was watching us with an indulgent smile. Delivering her to the sidelines, I thanked her and again kissed her hand.

The ball was over; guests were starting to leave. Sal joined me and we thanked Mrs. Rivington and said good night. Kathleen and I clasped hands a moment, looked longingly, then parted without a word.

"Well, weren't *you* the couple!" said Sal, as we went down the stairs.

"Who?"

"You and Kathleen. First the polonaise and then that waltz. Everyone was watching."

"Everyone was watching everyone."

"That's what you think. You're a couple; you might as well get engaged."

"You're crazy! We haven't even thought of it."

"Well, everyone else has. The two of you had better catch up."

We got our wraps, said good-bye to friends around us, and started down the stoop. It was snowing lightly; the flakes seemed to be whirling in a waltz. Young da Cunha had offered us a ride in his carriage, but was nowhere to be seen in the line of carriages waiting at the curb. "Maybe that's it," said Sal, indicating a rig at some distance down the street. As the two of us trudged in that direction through the snow, in my head I still heard the music, felt as if I were turning round and round in a waltz that had no end.

Suddenly a hand was clamped over my mouth, and my arms were pinned to my sides. As I tried to wrench free and shout, producing little more than a grunt, I saw Sal pushed down in the snow, and felt myself dragged to the curb and lifted by sturdy arms into a vehicle. Doors shut, and with someone strong on either side of me still gagging my mouth and pinning my arms, the vehicle lurched forward and started down the street.

"This will keep him quiet," said a voice.

A cloth reeking of fumes was pressed to my nose. As I squirmed futilely, the fumes penetrated my nostrils. I felt my brain go blank and my body limp, and passed out.

30

K*athleen Rivington and I, whirling rapturously in a waltz over the deck of the* Venture, *with moans and groans mounting from below. Croquet: with a mischievous smile she knocks my ball deep into the ornamental shrubs, where an escaped slave with an iron yoke round his neck, his back ridged with pus-oozing wounds, leaps up and seizes me, and Noah Harmony, yellow-skinned, his face smeared with bloody black vomit, jabs his skinny finger: "Why do you disturb us? Why?" Then the two of them fuse into Jonas Ward, his small body adrift in the harbor, his features a ghastly white, bloated, eyes open, mouth agape. "Kwit wile your a head," whispers Rezoloot. Resplendent in red and gold silk, King Africa prods with his fly whisk the hanged, lifeless body of Captain Patriot dangling from a palm tree, while to a chorus of grunts, shrieks, clicks, and cheers Jacob Harmony and Mrs. Rivington, heads high, dance the polonaise.*

"Who is he?" came a voice.

"None of your business. Just let me know when he comes to. And don't rough him up: strict orders."

To die here is doom and desolation. You puny little bastard. With a bit of discipline, will make a very good drudge. Justice! No one touches a Harmony but me.

I opened my eyes: a cabin with bunks, a lamp swaying slightly, a pair of eyes watching from a corner. Smells of tobacco, tar, some kind of oil, and paint. Creaking masts, gentle motion: a ship. At sea. I was lying on a bunk in my underwear; it was cold, I shivered.

A face appeared, bronzed, stubbled. "Well, well, little matey, coming round at last, are you? High time. Welcome aboard."

"Where am I?"

"Brig *Dolphin*, cleared for Africa. For Zanzibar, to be exact. And maybe points east."

"No…"

"Yes, little matey, yes. For Zanzibar."

"I don't…"

"Don't want to go to Zanzibar? Now matey, why did you sneak aboard?"

"I didn't."

"Oh yes you did. Granted, you had a little help. But the old man considers you a stowaway and will treat you accordingly."

"Why…?"

"Why anything, little matey? Don't worry, you'll get your sea legs in a day or two, all the greenies do. You'll be swabbing the deck with the best of 'em, and climbing up the rigging, too. The old man will make a first-rate able seaman of you, or know the reason why. For a start, put these togs on. Got 'em from the slop chest; they may fit."

He tossed some clothes at me, dungarees, a red wool shirt. Groggily, I sat up, put them on; they felt rough. My mind was slowly focusing: I'd been shanghaied, was on a brig at sea. Zanzibar: on the east coast of Africa—a voyage of weeks, of months. No! Things like this didn't happen! A bad dime novel, unreal.

I sank back on the bunk, shut my eyes. The fumes they had used to drug me still burned my nostrils, numbed my mind.

Papa Bear, Mama Bear, Baby Bear. Un hombre muy decente y refinado. Be strong, be wary, be sly. Inoubliable! Be sly.

"Hit the deck, little matey! The old man wants to see you."

The bronze face was back, prodding me in the ribs. Still groggy, I sat up, put my feet down, managed to stand up. I took a step, wobbled, took another.

"Your boots, little matey, put them on!"

Beside the bunk were a pair of sea boots. I put them on; they were too big but more or less fit. I also donned a cap and jacket that he handed me, then followed him up some stairs to the deck. When I stepped out, a blast of cold air slapped my face; it cleared my mind, focused me.

As he led me forward, I looked around, got my bearings. We'd been in the forecastle, the crew's quarters, and were now going aft to the quarterdeck. It was morning; seamen were swabbing the deck. We had dropped the pilot, whose boat was far astern. Off to starboard was a long, thin strip of sand, gleaming like polished silver in the sun, with a lighthouse at the tip: Sandy Hook! We were in the Outer Bay, then, not quite yet at sea: there was still time to escape! But how? There were small boats around us—pilot boats, fishing craft, and news boats out to get the news from incoming vessels—but none of them was close.

Waiting for me on the quarterdeck was a stocky man in a skipper's cap with iron-gray hair. He was looking to port with a spyglass, so he didn't see us approach.

"Here he is, sir," the bronze face announced.

The man pocketed his spyglass, turned toward us, grinned. "Welcome aboard, greenie. We're going to put you to good use."

I knew him at once: William Matthews, onetime master of the schooner *Charity*, the tight-packing slaver who ignored Caleb Harmony's instructions and lost so many slaves at sea. When I'd interviewed him, he'd offered to break my jaw.

"Yes, greenie, whoever you are, we're going to see what stuff is in you."

Still a bit wobbly, I made a great effort to gather my wits. "You know who I am, Captain Matthews, and I know who you are. What do you think you're going to do?"

He waved the bronze face away. "Put a stowaway to work."

"I'm not a stowaway and you know it. I demand to be released and sent ashore."

"Listen to the little lubber talk! Demands to be sent ashore, does he? I'll have to put his tender little limbs in irons. Which would be a black shame, since I've been told to look after him—no rough stuff, just a few months, maybe a year or two, of good hard work at sea."

"Told by whom?"

"Them as has your true interest at heart. As a Harmony, Mr. Chris, you should have gone to sea long since. We're going to take care of that, so's to keep up the Harmony tradition. Which is fair shakes, don't you think?"

Looking astern past the captain, I spied a small craft—a schooner, maybe a pilot boat—that was fast approaching, as if trying to overtake the brig. I felt a flash of hope. *Keep talking,* I thought. *Keep talking.*

"Let's talk about you, not me, Captain Matthews. If you know something about me, I know a lot about you. Like how Caleb Harmony wrote you as master of the schooner *Charity*, carrying boxes labeled 'hats' and 'soap,' urging comfort for the so-called passengers, and how you crunched them in and lost a third on the voyage, which made Señor Miguel Martinez in Havana very unhappy."

He looked taken aback. "My, my, don't we know a lot!"

"I know plenty more. The schooner *Sweet Lady*, William Matthews, master, captured off the Guinea coast with slaves. You were in

Eldridge Street Jail, where Jacob Harmony and others visited you—wild parties with liquor and champagne."

"I've never been convicted of a thing!"

"Of course not—the authorities were bribed! You left jail with a marshal and caught a steamer to Havana, where you got right back in the trade."

"Irrelevant, you lubber. Besides, you have no proof of anything."

"I have Martinez's bill of lading acknowledging receipt of over five hundred slaves from you, schooner *Charity*, dated Havana, 1854."

He eyed me meanly. "All the more reason, you snooping little bastard, to get you out of the way."

"Groans and shrieks from below, the stink so bad the crew wouldn't go down there, lowered food and water in buckets."

"Says who?"

"Jonas Ward, seaman."

"Dead and gone."

"And Jared Chase, your mate."

"Dead and gone."

"I have notes on the testimony of both. Very detailed, very graphic."

"Hearsay: irrelevant. And today, who cares?"

The small craft was drawing near; several people were standing on deck. *Keep talking!*

"When Caleb Harmony learned of it, he was furious. You never worked for him again."

"Harmony did me dirt. Another good reason to work his grandson over a bit on a cruise."

"You can't work me over too hard. Remember Jacob Harmony's warning: 'No one touches a Harmony but me!'"

A wild shot; it struck home. Matthews scowled.

"You little punk, you'll pay!"

"Jacob Harmony knows everything that happens on South Street, and on the ships that dock there. Whatever you do to me, he'll hear about. And if he doesn't like it, he'll come for you, and you won't stand a chance. He'll swab the deck with you, because for all your blab and swagger, you aren't the man that he is, not by half!"

Through a curious logic, Uncle Jake was becoming my protector.

Matthews's face was screwed up tight with rage. "You'll pay, you puny little lubber, you'll pay!"

The small craft had pulled alongside. "Ahoy, *Dolphin*!" cried a voice.

The bronze face came running. "Sir, there's a federal marshal as wants to board us!"

"Fool, why didn't you warn me?" Matthews turned toward the craft, shouted: "We're properly cleared for Africa! What's your business?"

"Suspected shanghaiing. Prepare to be boarded and searched!"

"Mate, put him below," said Matthews, indicating me. "And get us under full sail!"

"Aye, aye, sir!"

The bronze face lunged for me, but I was at the rail already.

"Chris Harmony!" I yelled. "Shanghaied and held against my will!"

On the small boat below I got the briefest glimpse of faces staring up: Sal, the Reverend Oakes, a stranger whom I took to be a marshal, several others. The mate lunged for me again, grappled me, but I wrenched free and planted my fist in his face. He grunted, swore, swiped at me, ran after me as I raced about the deck.

"Mutiny!" shouted Matthews. "Put that man in irons!"

Several crew members who had been watching all this, perplexed, stopped swabbing and gave chase.

"I'll board you!" yelled the marshal.

"A stowaway!" Matthews called down to him. "Inciting mutiny—he's got to be stopped!"

With the mate hot behind me, and in front of me several rough-looking men armed with belaying pins, I had only one choice. Darting to the rail, I leaped over it and plunged in the sea. A cold shock that went right through me, foam, a green blur; water in my nose, my throat. Gasping for air, I moved my arms and legs wildly, surfaced, knowing I'd be numbed in a minute. Shouts from the small craft greeted me, Sal's among them. A poor swimmer, I thrashed and splashed about, hampered by my clothing, made a bit of progress, grabbed at a line they threw me, missed it, felt myself going numb, sinking into blackness of night, but with a wild effort reached, grabbed at the line again, clutched it, felt myself being tugged toward the craft. Hands reached down, grabbed my clothes, my arms, my hair, and with a great heave hauled me up and threw me down sopping wet on the deck. I was stunned.

"Get him to the cabin!" ordered Oakes. "Get him into some warm, dry clothes, and fast!"

Sal rushed to me, but the others pushed her aside and picked me up. I was shivering, my teeth chattering, as they bore me into the cabin.

"Ahoy, *Dolphin*!" the marshal yelled again, but the brig, now under full sail, was pulling steadily away.

In the cabin two men pulled my wet clothes off, dried me with towels, tossed some oddments of clothing over me that didn't fit but at least felt warm and dry, then wrapped me in a blanket. My teeth were still chattering; huddled, I sat there, couldn't speak. Only when they dabbed my face with a cloth that came away spotted with blood did I realize that I'd been hit. The whole business seemed unreal.

"Here, mate, here's some java." One of the men held out a mug of steaming black coffee.

I nodded my thanks, took it, sipped. As heat flowed through my body, I trembled less.

"Hits the spot, don't it?"

I nodded, kept on sipping. I drank the whole mug, then another, before the trembling subsided.

"That sister of yours sure is something," said the other man. "Insisted on coming, and when we tossed you the line, she hauled away like the rest of us."

"She even brandished a revolver," said the first man., "till the Rev made her put it away."

I nodded, smiled a bit, still couldn't speak.

Sal and the Reverend Oakes now appeared in the cabin. She rushed to me and hugged me, tears in her eyes.

"Well, Mr. Chris," said Oakes, tall and sturdy, grinning between his sideburns, "you've had a bit of an adventure."

I nodded, still dazed. "How…?"

"How did we know?" said Oakes. "Your sister came knocking on the Mission door past midnight and roused us all up with her news."

"I got Mr. da Cunha to take me there in his carriage," said Sal. "He refused at first—the waterfront's no place for a lady and all that—but I insisted and he finally agreed. He had nothing to do with the kidnapping, showed up right after it happened."

"It smacked of shanghaiing," said Oakes. "My boys knew what ships would be leaving port in the morning, and when they mentioned the brig *Dolphin*, William Matthews, master, cleared for Africa, we knew that was the one. First thing this morning we hired a pilot boat and intercepted her in the Outer Bay. You know the rest."

"But the *Dolphin* got away," said Sal. "The marshal isn't too happy."

"Neither is Captain Matthews," said Oakes. "He'll have a lot of explaining to do to whoever wanted you out of the way."

"Uncle Jake!" said Sal. "Who else? Chris, don't you agree?"

I nodded.

"Don't make him talk now, miss," said Oakes. "He's had a nasty time, capped by a dip in the sea. Get him home now, keep him warm; talk later. That chill could bring on pneumonia."

As soon as the boat docked on South Street, there being no cab in sight, Oakes hailed a passing cart and paid the driver to take Sal and me home. I stammered a few words of thanks to them all, before they hurried me off. At home Sal all but threw me into bed. Ma was out. Since she thought I was sleeping late after the ball, when Ma came home Sal told her I'd woken up with a chill and was spending the day in bed; we'd tell her the whole story later. There was still a hint of cold in my bones, so when Ma brought me a hot cup of chamomile tea, I gulped it down, and didn't even resist two spoonfuls of Dr. Bunting's Universal Restorative, which tasted like tar and molasses.

After two days the chill was completely gone; no pneumonia. All jumbled up in my mind were Kathleen and me whirling in a waltz, Captain Matthews's hard, mean look, the cold shock of the sea, my bleeding lip, Zanzibar. Slowly, I ordered my thoughts. Someone—maybe a lot of someones—had wanted me out of the way. But here I was. What next?

First, fending off more spoonfuls of the Restorative, I had to convince Ma I was healing—in fact, healed. The puffed lip, I explained, had resulted from a fall, nothing more; she gave a look, said nothing. Then, up again, I conferred at once with Sal.

"Who knows what happened?" I asked.

"Just me, the deputy marshal, Reverend Oakes, and his boys. The Reverend told his boys not to talk."

"Did anybody see me at the dock?"

"I doubt it. There weren't many people around, and we hustled you off right away."

"And young da Cunha?"

"He knows you were kidnapped; he doesn't know you're back."

"So whoever wanted me shanghaied probably thinks it came off as planned."

"I suppose so, until they hear otherwise from Matthews."

"Which will take some time. Perfect! I'm going to lie low between now and New Year's, won't stick my nose out of the house."

"Why?"

"On New Year's Day they'll all be at Mrs. Rivington's. And I'll turn up, unannounced. I want to see their faces when I do. The ones who think I'm en route to Zanzibar will give themselves away. Great fun!" But I wasn't smiling.

"We know who's behind it: Uncle Jake."

"Maybe, but maybe some others, too. Maybe Dwight. Maybe Martinez. Maybe the Biggses. Maybe all of them."

"Mrs. Rivington?"

"Maybe."

"I can't believe it!"

"Maybe not. I'll look, I'll listen. I should learn a lot."

"And then?"

"It's my turn to make someone pay. They'll wish they'd never messed with me. I'll make them sweat and scream."

"You really mean it, don't you?"

"You bet!"

"Well, Merry Christmas."

"And Happy New Year to all."

31

Dear Chris,

Here we are in front of Petersburg, where we dug trenches with bayonets, tin cups, and plates, and piled up rails and logs for a parapet. Sharpshooters' bullets whiz and zing past our ears, and mortar shells make fiery trails through the air. We'd be bored here in these hot dirty trenches, if we didn't know we could be killed at any moment, which somehow livens things up.

Chris, it's a mean, long war. After battle I've seen dead men bloated up big as a horse, lots of them with their brains splashed out. I've heard the screams from the surgeons' tent, and seen the sawbones with their bloody pus-stained coats, and the severed arms and legs tossed out there in the open, where a bunch of wild hogs chomped them down. We're doing all this to save the Union, but it's near bust because of the South and their slaves. God damn the slave masters and slave catchers, and the slave ships and their filthy owners and crews, who made all this happen, I'd like to roast their guts!

Chris, I'm going to stick it out. For all its stinking faults, we've got the best government the sun ever shone on, and I'm going to help hold it together, even if I shit in my britches and eat hard crackers for a year. God bless this goddam country, I'll give my life for it if I have to. Keep well, study hard, write! Your tired, bored, crazy, loving brother,

Nathan

Rereading Nathan's last letter, written two days before he was killed, I had tears in my eyes. And I felt small: what was my war, compared to his? And yet, wasn't it the same war after all? He damned the slave ships and their owners along with everyone else who made slavery possible, and I now felt the same, and my war—our war—wasn't over. I was spoiling for a fight.

"If they all think you're en route to Zanzibar," said Sal, "what should I do in public? Weep bitter tears? Say the police are investigating? Rant and rave? What?"

"Pull a long face and don't say a word. When I go to Mrs. Rivington's, I want to knock them off their beam."

Our Christmas was quiet, as always; from Dwight and Uncle Jake, not a peep. They did remember us with presents; Ma was happy enough with her cashmere shawl, and Sal with her gilt comb from Paris, but if I was bound for Zanzibar, what was the point of a gold toothpick and a pair of elegant kid gloves? "They're playing dumb," whispered Sal. "Pretending they don't know." Ma, of course, still wasn't aware of my adventure.

When, having donned my best frock coat and some checked trousers that I thought rather dashing, I set out in the early afternoon of New Year's Day, Ma and Sal were arranging a feast of goodies on a table in the parlor. They anticipated twenty or thirty callers, mostly husbands of Ma's lady friends at church, several neighbors, and a contingent of what I termed Sal's "admirers" (a word she loathed), with Dan Hunter and Gorilla Gus leading the pack. Sal was excited less at the thought of her callers than by the mere fact that, after a two-year lapse, the Harmonys were again receiving.

Most of the early afternoon I spent calling on our neighbors, knowing I would never encounter Dwight or Uncle Jake in their parlors. There was a bit more risk in calling on the dancing class girls and their mamas, since Dwight also knew them, but by making these visits from mid-afternoon on I managed to avoid him, as he had already come and gone, saving what he considered the most interesting calls till last. It was early evening when I ascended the steep stoop of the Rivington brownstone on the Avenue, gave my wraps and card to the butler, and entered the parlor, where an even larger crowd of guests had gathered than I recalled from the year before. Mixed in with the regulars were some papas recruited from the ball. They were all babbling; at first my arrival went unnoticed.

"Why, Mr. Chris!" exclaimed Kathleen Rivington, all white silk and tulle, who came scurrying over to greet me. "I am delighted you have come. I was told you might be indisposed, but you look to be in the pink of health!"

As she spoke, the volume of babble dropped, and many eyes were on us.

"*Bon soir*, mademoiselle. I was indeed briefly indisposed, but the thought of Rivington hospitality and charm, and the viands that accompany it," (a new word, "viands"; I was proud of it) "have worked a wondrous recovery. I stand before you quite intact, and famished for a taste of your bodaciously delicious gingersnaps, especially if baked by you and offered from your very own fingers."

She smiled mischievously. "I hope, sir, that you will not be disappointed. We have gingersnaps galore, and baked by me, but as for the fingers," she lowered her voice a bit, "that depends on whether maman is looking. As she is right now."

"Welcome, Mr. Chris!" came Mrs. Rivington's resonant voice, cutting through the persisting low volume of talk. "You have not failed us after all—I am so glad! I'm afraid we had rather given you up."

She came forward in a violet dress trimmed with black lace, diamonds twinkling in her hair. With a quick glance I took in the faces watching us: Dwight and Uncle Jake, staring in astonishment; Señor Miguel Martinez and Jonathan and Peter Biggs, with a devilishly puzzled look; and others who were simply curious.

"One must never give up, Mrs. Rivington," I said as I clasped her hand. "I was booked for passage to Zanzibar, but changed my mind rather suddenly. So here I am instead!"

"I am truly delighted!" she announced in a voice that all could hear.

I was aware by now that we were both playing to an audience. She didn't approve of the recent shenanigans, was glad they had miscarried, wanted to register this with certain parties.

"Zanzibar?" said Kathleen. "That sounds like the end of the world."

"It just about is, mademoiselle. In the steamy hot wilds of Africa."

"Why would one ever want to go there?"

"Why indeed?" added Mrs. Rivington with a bite of irony.

"Perhaps a misplaced zest for adventure. Or an invitation not to be refused. But as I was leaving, I became so overcome with homesickness and a love of this city that I jumped overboard and splashed back to shore. Or rather, to a boat that brought me to shore."

"Overboard?" exclaimed Kathleen. "In this weather? You are joking, Mr. Chris!"

"Not at all, mademoiselle. Briefly, I tasted the delights of a dip in the Outer Bay. A smashing experience that chilled me to the quick!"

"You did not freeze?"

"Not quite. Friends pulled me out pretty fast. But my teeth chattered for days."

Mrs. Rivington heard this with wonder as keen as her daughter's. She was clearly shocked and annoyed.

"Jacob, it seems that your nephew has had quite an adventure!"

Uncle Jake approached, half masking his surprise and dismay. "Has he, now? Well, it runs in the family. We've all had adventures at sea and spin great yarns about them. Happy New Year, Chris! You're certainly looking fit."

"Adventure agrees with me, Uncle Jake. I plan to have more."

"Well, young pup, I'm sure that can be arranged."

"Happy New Year, Chris!" said Dwight sourly. "Any more travel plans soon?"

"Travel, no. I plan a different kind of exposure, and here's the man who can help. Happy New Year, Rob!"

Spruced up in his frock coat and cravat, Rob Peterson was looking on, obviously perplexed. He knew nothing of the shanghaiing. "Happy New Year, Chris. And how can I help you?"

"Another article in the *Chronicle*. With very specific facts and naming names, and soon!"

Rob brightened. "I'd like nothing better. It's all but written, and my managing editor says it's hot."

"An article on what?" asked Kathleen.

"Let it be a surprise." I'd renewed the threat, and thought that enough for the moment.

Looks were being exchanged among Dwight, Uncle Jake, and our hostess, though I couldn't decipher their meaning. Other guests, not following our talk, turned back to patter of their own.

"So, young Señor Chris, you have joined us once again to savor the company of our charming Doña Luisa. And her daughter too, of course. Which shows excellent taste. Happy New Year!"

Señor Miguel Martinez had approached, with his braided cuffs and hint of cologne.

"Happy New Year, Señor Martinez. It promises to be a year of surprises."

"So I gather. But then, life is full of surprises, is it not? Is your prospecting going well? Or your bug hunt, if you cling to that image?"

"Very well indeed, señor. I've learned a lot and will soon announce it to the world."

"I hope it will do some good. Truth, my young friend, is a sword that cuts many ways. It can slaughter friends as well as foes. It can even slice up the one who wields it. Sometimes it is wise—indeed, the very pinnacle of wisdom—to leave certain things unspoken. Why injure innocent lives and bring misfortune to oneself? Forgive the advice; I speak as a friend."

"You consider yourself my friend?"

"I aspire to that honor, both for our mutual benefit, and in remembrance of your illustrious grandfather, the esteemed Caleb Harmony."

"I see."

"Ah, the coldness in your tone! You do not accept my offer of friendship. A true *caballero* never refuses such an offer, when it is honest and sincere."

"A true *caballero* is never hasty, takes time to reflect."

"Very well, Señor Chris, reflect. Think long and hard and wisely. I ask no more."

With this, he bowed slightly and turned to other guests. I marveled at his ability to combine grace with guile, and to honey-coat a threat.

"Mr. Chris," said Kathleen, who had been chatting with other callers, "if you swam in the harbor recently so that your teeth were chattering, I insist that you partake of our coffee or tea. They will drive out any last trace of the chill."

"Gladly, Miss Kathleen, if I can have some of your gingersnaps, too."

"Certainly. Please come."

I was soon sipping a delicious hot mint tea and receiving from her fingers (maman being at the other end of the room) a sequence of gingersnaps that she popped in my mouth, while I endeavored, usually with success, to kiss her fingers as she did so.

"You are very naughty, Mr. Chris," she said with a smile. "You will compromise my reputation."

"A little compromise—just a teeny little bit—can enhance a young lady's reputation."

"You are very deep and subtle. But I have much to learn. This is the first time I have played hostess with maman in receiving a whole roomful of gentlemen callers. There are things I do not understand."

"Like what, Miss Kathleen?"

"Like when you and maman and your uncle and cousin were all talking together. You seemed to be saying more than you said. You seemed to be implying things, to be talking over the heads of the others. I was baffled."

"I apologize. I didn't mean to baffle you. Soon it will all be made clear."

"When Mr. Peterson's article is published?"

"That will explain a lot, though not everything. In time you will understand much. Too much, perhaps."

"Now you are being mysterious. There *is* a mystery, is there not? Something that you all know about, but I and other people do not."

"Miss Kathleen, this tea is delicious. Could I have some more, and a few more gingersnaps as well?"

"Now you are being evasive. I have been raised properly, perhaps too properly, but please do not think me a fool."

"Miss Kathleen, I swear that I do not think you a fool. You charm me; I delight in your company."

"That is very nice, Mr. Chris, but you are not frank with me, I sense it."

"Soon I will be only too frank."

"Is that a threat, sir, or a promise?"

"It is a statement of fact. Soon, Miss Kathleen, we will both need courage. I regret this, but that's how it is."

"Whatever you are talking about, I think I have a right to know. I am not a child."

"Miss Kathleen, your spunk becomes you."

"I do not know this word. What is spunk?"

"Spunk, mademoiselle, is pluck."

"Kathleen, my dear," called her mother, "please come and greet these guests."

Kathleen gave me a puzzled look, then went to join her mother, who was greeting a stream of late arrivals.

"Mr. Harmony, may I wish you the happiest of New Years."

Young Señor da Cunha had appeared, sporting his jeweled stickpin and velvet collar and cuffs.

"Thank you, señor, and I wish you the same. How our paths do cross!"

He had an earnest look. "Mr. Harmony, I know something of what happened to you, but not all. You disappeared, were taken advantage of, but survived. Am I right?"

"You are indeed."

"This business is alluded to but not spelled out. I confess I'm a bit confused."

"Your confusion does you honor, señor. It means you were in no way involved."

"Certainly not. We should be friends. Even if we both admire our hostess's charming daughter—she of the gingersnaps—we can still be friends."

He hadn't missed a thing. "Agreed!" I said, and clasped his hand. Another innocent who would soon be hurt.

I decided it was time to leave. Too many questions I couldn't answer, too many appeals that unsettled me.

"Leaving us?" said Mrs. Rivington, as I said my good-byes. "We have much to talk about. Let us meet again, and soon."

"I'd be delighted."

"Mr. Chris," said her daughter, "I hope that next time we can talk more frankly. There are things I think I should know."

"I'm sure there are, Miss Kathleen. Life is a learning experience."

"You see, maman, he is being mysterious again. And oh so very wise!"

Mrs. Rivington shot me an inquisitive look, said nothing, as I bowed slightly and left the room. I was quite aware of the daughter's eyes following me with puzzlement and a touch of annoyance. Decidedly, it was time to get out.

"Well, young pup, you do like springing surprises! We'll have to talk, and soon."

Uncle Jake had caught me at the cloakroom, where I was reclaiming my wraps.

"Fine, Uncle Jake. Say when."

"Tomorrow, in my office, at two."

"I'll be there, Uncle Jake."

"See that you are, Chris. See that you are."

I took my wraps, put them on. "By the way, Uncle Jake… "

"Yes?"

"Captain Matthews sends his regards."

He scowled; I left.

"So?"

Sal was waiting in the parlor, where she and Ma and Meg, having received some thirty-five callers, were clearing away the remains of the spread. I pulled her to one side.

"Uncle Jake and Dwight and Martinez, and probably Jonathan Biggs, were all in on it and quite surprised to see me. Mrs. Rivington knew about it, didn't approve, was genuinely glad to see me. Young da Cunha knew nothing about it at all. Likewise, I suspect, Peter Biggs."

I told her more, including my threat of another article in the *Chronicle* that would state facts, name names.

"Are they scared?"

"Yes, though they don't show it. That's why they want to see me. Uncle Jake tomorrow, Mrs. Rivington later this week."

"What'll happen?"

"They'll plead, threaten, squirm, offer deals."

"And you?"

"I've never had power before. I kind of like it."

"Meaning what?"

"I'll be ruthless."

32

"Come in, Chris. Right on the dot—good. Have a seat. Yes, it's time we talked. Louise says I should have talked to you long ago, but I'm more of a doer than a talker. So let's get right to it: what do you know?"

Tough and defiant as always, he eyed me across his desk. We were in his South Street office, door shut.

"Brig *Fearless* to the Leeward Coast, '43, 500 slaves to Havana. Schooner *Charity* to the Leeward Coast as the *Esperanza*, '54, loss of a third, 583 slaves to the north coast of Cuba. Yacht *Venture* to Havana, '59, renamed *La Nueva Paz*, from Cuba to Africa and back, various names, may still be in operation. The schooner *Mary D.*—"

"All right, you've made your point. That's not the half of it, but not bad for a start. Now, owners and masters, who can you name?"

"Jacob and Caleb Harmony. Hiram and Jonathan Biggs. William Matthews. Miguel Martinez and son. Innocencio José da Cunha and son, the son with the aliases Tejedor and Santos. Various others, and the so-called Prince of Slavers, Gideon Lynch. All documented with Custom House records, ships' papers, private correspondence, and the testimony of witnesses. Facts only, no risk of libel."

"Hmm. Well, you know a lot. Not everything, but a lot."

"And Mrs. Rivington."

His features tightened. "You would name her, too?"

"As Louise Lynch, interim operator of the *Venture*, 1859, between Jacob Harmony and Miguel Martinez of Havana. And perhaps some other ships, too; time will tell."

"Hmm." He was fingering his gold penknife, then suddenly he flung it away. "So you'll get this published and hurt your own family and the families of others, including innocents, come what may?"

"Come what may."

"Why? This all happened long ago. It's over and done with—finished! What's the point? It's senseless!"

"A lot of people made dirty money in a dirty trade. Now they're living high on the hog, clean, genteel, respectable. They should be exposed."

"Caleb Harmony went out of his way to treat the niggers decent: lots of space and air, plenty of good water, exercise on deck."

"A dirty trade."

"When his captains followed his instructions, the death rate was amazingly low. He should be honored for that, not denounced!"

"A dirty trade."

"You goddam little moralist! You don't know how the real world works. You think, feel, and imagine too much. You imagine things that maybe never happened, and if they did, it's irrelevant."

"I've answered your questions, Uncle Jake. Now you answer mine. Did you plan the murder of Jonas Ward?"

"God, no! I was out of town when it happened. When I learned of it, I was riled, and even more riled when I heard about the threats to you."

"Yes, 'no one touches a Harmony but me.' So who did it?"

"Some imbecile who hired a waterfront tough. Some goddam fool!"

"But you had me shanghaied."

"Damn right! I didn't want you hurt, just out of the way for a year or two, so you couldn't make trouble. So you could learn things that you can't get from books. To toughen you up and make a man of you, a Harmony. Afterward you'd have thanked me. Assuming you survived, that is."

"Louise Rivington didn't approve."

"Of course not. There's a hard way and a soft way to go at things. I like the hard way, she likes the soft."

"What would be the soft way?"

"A college graduate, and you haven't figured that out? Make nice with you and Sal, introduce you to her daughter, have dainty little games and such, get you all tangled up in their social life, so you'd think twice about mentioning her name in the press."

"I'm supposed to court her daughter and forget about her connection with the trade?"

"Clever, don't you think? Only a woman—a smart one—would come up with it. As for the daughter, you could do worse."

"Kathleen Rivington is my cousin."

He gave me a long, hard look. "So you know about that, too."

"I know a lot, and not all of it comes from books."

"You dirty little snooper! I owe you no explanation—none!"

"So the old salt Jacob Harmony, a blunt man tough as nails, fell for the lovely lady Louise."

For this, I expected a fist in my face. Instead, he softened, got nostalgic.

"Louise Lynch was the most fascinating woman I'd ever known, or have ever known since: young, but handsome, smart, and bold. What she saw in me I'll never know—a tough man, I suppose, with a good sharp smell of the sea. But married, of course, with two half-grown sons. It was awkward. Yet what we shared for a few short years was—damn it, I'm not slick with words! Well, it was confoundedly good. We charted the course we had to, we couldn't have done otherwise."

"How did Gideon Lynch look on this amour?"

"I thought he'd be furious, but he wasn't. An off-and-on-again lover, popping in from time to time, he could take, but not a full-time hubby. He wanted her all to himself."

This unexpected confidence disarmed me. Uncle Jake a lover! But I couldn't make fun of him. He was expressing deep feeling, nostalgia, regret.

"Does Kathleen know?"

"We decided not to tell her, invented a long deceased father. She's Louise's child far more than mine. She puts up with me as one of her mama's regulars, but she thinks me coarse, a boor. Which I am. Jolly old Uncle Jacob, who hangs around a bit too much. Not that I care, I don't."

I sensed deep hurt. "I'm sorry, Uncle Jake."

"Sorry for what?"

"For everything."

For a moment he looked wounded, vulnerable; I thought we might even be friends. Deep inside, this man was lonely. Tough, forceful, blunt, but achingly alone. What could I offer that he needed? Friendship? Understanding? I would try. But he shot me a quick, hard glance.

"I need no man's pity. And why am I telling *you* this—things that even my sons don't know? Chris, if you ever breathe a word of this to the girl, I swear I'll bust your skull!"

"I won't." And I meant it.

"Well, scholar, you think you're so smart. From the moment you started in on this family history, Louise Rivington and I were comparing notes."

"So whatever *you* knew, *she* knew, and whatever *she* knew, *you* knew."

"That's right, little genius. We've been sailing circles around you, and you didn't even know it."

"Maybe, but I've still learned a lot. That's why you're scared, the two of you."

"Scared? Of you?"

"Terrified."

"It'll take more than a puny little bookworm, a milksop who's never shipped out, to scare Jacob Harmony!"

"We'll find out soon enough, won't we, when you see your name in the *Chronicle.*"

"I can ride that out. Chris, I've never hated a Harmony before—unless myself as a lovesick dolt—but I can manage it now. I love a good hot hate. It whets my ginger, makes me sharp and snappy. So get your goddam article published, name all the names you like. See if I trim sail. I think you'll be surprised."

I stood up. "Fair enough."

"But do it soon, real soon."

"Why?"

"So we can both get started on our hate."

Again the parlor, with the low tea table between us, light filtering through the potted ferns hanging in a window, her smoky perfume blending with a scent of cedar and sandalwood. From his massive portrait over a fireplace, Geoffrey Lane stared down at us in his blue uniform with gold buttons and braid. She poured from a silver teapot; steam rose in little wisps and swirls, giving hints of a mellow sweetness.

"Well now, Mr. Chris, you've talked with Jacob, I gather?"

"Two days ago in his office."

"I'm sure he blustered."

"He declared war, said he liked a good hot hate."

"That's him all over. But we won't bluster, will we? Let's talk civilly and sanely."

"By all means. Will Kathleen be joining us?"

"She and Sal have been invited by your rival, Señor da Cunha, for a sleigh ride in the snowy Park."

"He's my rival?"

"I spoke facetiously. He obviously enjoys her company, as you do; a mother notices. But it's for you that she seems to care. I hope the feeling is mutual."

"She is utterly charming."

"She was raised to be. A perfect little moonbeam, or, as your sister would put it, a gumdrop."

"Kathleen is very different from you, Mrs. Rivington, but in her I discern traces of spunk. I think they'll develop with time."

"My daughter has spunk? What a novel idea! Your influence, I presume."

"Perhaps it's the Harmony in her."

Pouring another cup of tea, she stopped, then resumed pouring. "Ah, so you know about that."

"Not from snooping, I assure you. Sal and I saw the three of you together in the Park, and we knew, we simply *knew.*"

"That obvious?"

"Only to us. Probably to no one else."

"I hope not. Please don't tell her. I beg of you, don't."

"We shan't. I promise."

"She and her father don't get on. Jacob is a very strange man. Tender at times, but often curt and brisk."

"I've rarely seen him tender."

"I have, though he seldom shows it. When I met him I was young, quite guileless, impressionable, stupid."

"I thought your father raised you like a son."

"I knew all about business and ships, but nothing about society and men. Jacob was bold, brisk, raw: a man of few words, many deeds. I was, as they say, quite smitten."

"I can understand that."

"I can't. Not today. But the very things that repel me today attracted me back then: his vigor, his coarseness. He was married, but that didn't stop us, and my father managed to look the other way. And so..."

"Kathleen."

"Exactly. She doesn't know, doesn't particularly like him. He pretends it doesn't matter. But he has feelings and they run deep."

Fascinated by her confidences, I sat quietly, ignoring the tea and scones.

"Yes," she continued, "a strange man. I've seen him at his best and worst. To you, and you only, I shall speak frankly. With Jacob Harmony, on a few rare occasions, I experienced an intoxication, an excitement, a fulfillment such as I have not known since. He took me outside myself into a world I hadn't known existed, where I felt feelings I'd never felt before."

I sat there, stock-still. I had been told that only men had such feelings, that women were by nature too chaste, too refined. Respectable women, that is. Was Mrs. Rivington, as Ma would put it, a "bad" woman? I didn't believe it, couldn't. Glimpsing the breadth and depth of her experience—*their* experience—I felt clumsy, stupid, small. Did she intend this? What kind of a web was she weaving?

"Forgive the digression; let's get back to Kathleen. Her happiness concerns me greatly. That's why this article to appear in the *Chronicle* disturbs me."

"It won't mention the name Rivington or Lane."

"And Louise Lynch?"

"As interim owner of the *Venture*, 1859."

"Even that is a risk. I know better than to try to dissuade you. Couldn't you at least omit that name?"

"Absolutely not."

"It's so important?"

"Whoever was involved will be named. Including members of my own family. Even my father, who was never in the trade, but knew of it and never spoke out."

"How you judge!"

"A dirty trade. Those who got rich from it should be exposed."

"Like Geoffrey Lane?"

"Like Gideon Lynch."

"I suppose you see this brownstone as acquired with ill-gotten gains."

"In part. Like the one I live in. I have to face that every day. I don't enjoy it."

"You are ruthless even to yourself."

"I've vowed to be."

"Do you realize the consequences of publishing these facts? The full consequences?"

"I've thought of them often."

"Family names will be dishonored, reputations shattered. Innocent young people will feel its effects. Love and respect may yield to shame and hate. And for what?"

"For truth. For justice."

"Big words, very abstract."

"It was a dirty trade."

"You are so righteous!" Her eyes burned into mine.

"How could you do it? How could any of them? And why?"

"I never owned one of those ships. Not for long, anyway. I simply lent my name when it was needed. When Jacob or my father asked me to. You didn't know my father. He was loving, generous, shrewd, had a great sense of humor and total self-assurance. He radiated warmth and authority. I couldn't not do what he asked of me; it would have been unthinkable."

"That made you a part of it. A part of the deception."

"It was all so routine. Slavery was accepted; no one thought twice about it."

"No one?"

"Except for a handful of reformers who were dismissed as cranks and trouble-makers. Today I wouldn't do it, I swear I wouldn't, but back then things were different."

"You made money by trading in human beings who were shackled, branded, whipped, crowded, starved."

"Think of Kathleen! What if she should realize? What would she think of her grandfather? Of me?"

"She will adjust, just as I have. It will toughen her: teach her what the world is, and what people will do for money. It will be an education."

"Please don't! Please don't!"

I was amazed: this worldly, self-possessed woman, so poised, so shrewd, was begging me with tears in her eyes. I weakened, then with great effort, steeled myself.

"I have to! For my own self-respect, I have to!"

"You have no compassion!"

"How can the daughter of the Prince of Slavers talk about compassion?"

It struck home; she winced. We stared at each other. A flowery aroma rose from the poured cups of tea.

"Mrs. Rivington, I bear the burden of truth. I can't do otherwise."

Her features hardened. "Then you will never see Kathleen again."

I stood up. "That's the price I'll have to pay."

There was nothing more to say.

33

THE SLAVE TRADE IN NEW YORK
HOW IT WORKED
PROMINENT MERCHANTS NAMED
WHO KILLED JONAS WARD?
STARTLING REVELATIONS

Details of the nefarious prewar slave trade in this city, as carried on by prominent merchants of South Street and Pearl Street, can now be revealed, thanks to the tireless efforts of Christopher Harmony, a scion of one of the city's leading merchant families, who has survived death threats and an attempted shanghaiing to bring these facts to light. Thanks to Mr. Harmony's investigation, which cost at least one informant his life, this reporter has learned how that illegal trade flourished for so long in this city.

Mr. Harmony's continuing research may also bring answers to questions that have long haunted this city: What became of the racing yacht *Venture*? Who killed Jonas Ward? How could this foul trade have flourished here so long with impunity? Already Mr. Harmony has proven beyond doubt the complicity of his legendary grandfather Caleb Harmony, and his uncle Jacob Harmony, a prominent figure on South Street today. Also involved were their long-time associates the Biggses; the veteran ship's master William Matthews; members of the Martinez and da Cunha clans long established in this city; and the man who gloried in the name Prince of Slavers, Gideon Lynch. Why has Mr. Harmony persisted in this at times perilous adventure, which risks bringing shame and disgrace even to his very own kin?

> "It was a dirty trade," he explains. "Those involved in it ought to be exposed." Exposed they will be in this and subsequent articles giving names and dates. Let South Street and Pearl Street brace themselves: startling revelations are imminent.

"Wow!" said Sal. "Rob sure did make a story of it."

"As he would put it, a scorcher."

"And he promises at least two more."

"The *Fearless* this time, the *Charity* next, and finally the *Venture.* With more on Jonas Ward, my shanghaiing, and related matters."

"Well, it's finally out there for the world to read about. So what do we do next?"

"Wait."

"Wait for what?"

"Just wait."

"Excuse me, Master Chris," said Meg. "There's a Mr. da Coony as wants to see you. Looks to be in a peak of a dither."

In the vestibule I found Señor da Cunha, slim and elegant as always, but decidedly in a peak of a dither.

"Mr. Harmony, are you responsible for this infamous article," he thrust the *Chronicle* at me, "which alleges that my family was involved in the slave trade?"

"Obviously. It's all about my research."

He whipped out an elegant pair of black suede gloves and slapped my face with them. "I challenge you, sir, for impugning the honor of the da Cunhas. And next, I'll challenge the scribbler who wrote it."

I looked at him coolly. "Challenge all you like, señor, but we won't accept. We consider dueling outdated, barbaric, and silly."

"You refuse to duel me?"

"Absolutely. It's much too Old World fogy. But I'll spar with you for a round or two, if you like."

"Fisticuffs, sir, are beneath me. If you won't duel, you are not a gentleman."

"Señor da Cunha, you once offered me friendship, and *that* I can accept. Neither you nor I were ever involved in the slave trade. Let us vow to redeem our families' honor by exposing those who were, apologizing publicly, and rooting out its vestiges wherever we encounter them. That would be a true deed of honor."

"My family would never forgive me."

"Your family would be cleansed and redeemed."

"I cannot!"

"Then I can't help you."

"You push me to the brink of disgrace."

Spinning his trim young body about, he departed. What a performance!

Eager to check with Rob Peterson at the *Chronicle* about any incoming letters or threats, I set out pert and chipper. Halfway down the stoop I met Cousin Dwight, who was stomping up. Without a word he bashed me in the face, sent me reeling, then grabbed and pummeled me. Recoiling, I planted a left hook in the midst of his scowl. We grappled, fell, and rolled down the steps to the pavement, where we continued rolling about and trading punches and grunts. A crowd quickly gathered to watch the scuffle, so unheard of in genteel St. Mark's Place. Sal came rushing down the stoop, screaming at us to stop. Finally two policemen appeared and pulled us apart. Breathing heavily, we glared at each other, saying nothing. I was bruised and bleeding; Dwight's lip was awash in blood—a sight that I thought smashing.

"A family tiff," Sal explained to the knights of the locust. "I'll take my brother back in the house. Please, sirs, escort our cousin out of the neighborhood, so they can both simmer down."

The guardians of order nodded, led Dwight away; his coat was torn, he staggered.

Back in the house Sal dabbed my face, stopped the bleeding.

"Well," I said, "I guess that engagement is off. But boy, I sure did bash him!"

"Yeah. Now look at yourself in a mirror."

I did: bruises, a black eye.

Uncle Jake's response came two days later in the form of a letter to the *Sun*, the *Chronicle*'s arch rival. The wording was much too fancy for Jake, and there were many signatures, but the thrust of the letter was his.

To whom it may concern:

> The undersigned citizens of this city join their voices to protest the outrageous accusations made in an article published two days ago in the *Chronicle*, attempting to link some of the most reputable mercantile names in our city to the infamous slave trade of long ago. That trade is now a thing of the past, and to that past we relegate the memory of it. If a few local citizens committed a peccadillo or two in connection with it, that need not concern us now. What's done is done. Our city and nation have always flourished through the spirit of Go Ahead, looking to the future, not the past. Let us not be distracted by the attention-seeking mouthings of a young upstart with no mercantile experience who has yet to spend a full day at sea, and who, if he did so, would swoon like a damsel in the rigging, and heave his cookies into the deep. This city has attained, and will continue to attain, prosperity and glory through the hard work and heroism of its mariners and merchants, and not through the whimperings of a pantywaist, as conveyed to us through the scribblings of some petty ink-stained hack. Let us dismiss with scorn these base accusations and get on with our work.
>
> Jacob Harmony, Dwight Harmony, Hiram Biggs, Jonathan Biggs, Peter Biggs, Capt. William Matthews, Don Miguel Martinez, Don Innocencio José da Cunha III, Luis Santos, Capt. Jonathan Pell, James Fowler, Kenneth Stokes…

The names went on and on. Reading it, I felt sick. They'd made *me* the issue, shoving their guilt into the shadows. Uncle Jake's doing: his hate. "Swoon… heave his cookies… pantywaist…" Old wounds opened.

"This is outrageous!" said Sal. "Everything they've said is irrelevant!"

"But half of South Street signed it. Look at all those names—even the clerks at the chandlery!"

"I *am* looking. Hiram Biggs died last year, and William Matthews is on his merry way to Zanzibar."

"Who'll notice? I didn't. They've scuttled me, they've ripped me to shreds."

"Don't mix metaphors. Someone is bound to come to your defense."

"Who?"

"Wait. We'll see. But don't go out until that black eye heals. Don't give them the satisfaction."

"You should see Dwight."

"I've heard he may lose some teeth."

"I hope he loses all of them."

"Okay. But wait!"

A day later the *Chronicle* printed a letter from the Reverend Simeon Oakes of the South Street Mission, applauding my exposure of South Street involvement in the slave trade, and brief notes came to me from Junius Fox and two ministers, assuring me that the black community was behind me. But that was it.

And of course:

Dear Mr. Harmony,

I told you so!

—One Who Wished You Well

Harmony—

No one beleeves a pantiwaste. Ha!

—Rezoloot

Pantywaist! Hot memories assailed me: Dwight's taunts from years before. Grandpa Harmony taking us all on a sailboat out to Sandy Hook, with Dwight and Nathan and Sal helping him navigate, Rick cracking jokes, and me retching over the side all the way. Urged on by Grandpa, all the boys scrambling up a ship's rigging in a race, and me frozen not even a quarter of the way up, terrified at the thought of falling into the deep murky night of the sea, into extinction, into doom. Reliving it, I shuddered.

"Halloo, Chris! Halloo, Sal! Look who's back in town, just in time for the fireworks! Boy, Chris, have they done a job on you! Yes, I've seen Rob's article—he really fired a broadside!—and Pa's pantywaist letter, too. Wow, have you done damage! They're adrift, they're rudderless, we've got them on the rocks!"

"Listen, I'm the one on the rocks. And the one who got the broadside. I feel like it went right through me."

"You'll mend, Chris, you'll float free. Soon enough you'll be sailing with the wind abaft."

"So what's it like at Uncle Jake's?" asked Sal.

"The Skipper is in high glee, cackling like a hen that just laid a big, fat egg, the egg being that letter to the *Sun.* But Brother Dwight has the mopes. The engagement's off, and thanks to your knock-'em, sock-'em shindy, he's out one tooth in front. You should see him gap-toothed—he looks like a spook. Quite miffed he is; it spoils his image as a dandy. Now let's have a look at *you.* Hmm… several lovely shades of purple. What a scrap that must have been! Wish I'd been there, I might have landed a few in Dwight's sweet mug myself."

"So you see, Chris," said Sal, "Dwight's in far worse shape than you are. And he's lost Miss Van Whoozit to boot!"

"But nobody's called him a pantywaist in print."

"That's just Pa's bilge," said Rick. "He's hunkering down with the rest of them. Say, is your ma home? I'd better check in with her and see what's on for dinner. The very thought of roast turkey or a plum cake makes me drool!"

At dinner he regaled us as usual with tales of hurricanes and mutinies, bucko mates and leaky hulls, and other perils encountered on the great trackless deep. As belated Christmas presents he gave Sal castanets, Ma a cross ("Pure Mexican silver!"), and me an *idolita*, a tiny statuette of baked clay reclaimed from the soil of Mexico, which, he assured me, had figured in mysterious rituals centuries before the first white men trod the soil of the New World.

"Rick," said Ma over dessert, "you're a dear boy and you'll always have a place at our table, but you repeat yourself. You breeze in out of nowhere, spin marvelous yarns, shower us with gifts, liven things up, and then take off again without warning. Always the same, as if you were running from something, maybe from yourself. You need ballast. I want to see you slow down, change, and grow."

"I like Rick just the way he is!" protested Sal, but Rick had quickly sobered.

"Aunt Martha, you're dead right. What's with me, anyway? Let's have a talk, just the two of us, after dinner."

Which they did, shut up in the parlor, while Sal and I exchanged glances in the sitting room.

"But I *do* like him the way he is," she insisted.

"So do I, but Ma's right. Rick goes in circles—marvelous circles—but circles nonetheless. Even as a ship's master he's pretty much the same old Rick."

After the talk Rick paid us a quick good-bye. Something was up.

"Greetings and salutations, Mr. Harmony! I was just about to write you a note. So the first results of your research are made known, even to the point of naming names, and you find yourself like Caesar and his legions, besieged on all sides by the Gauls, as evidenced by that blackened eye."

"Purple, I'm told, several shades of it. And Caesar had a way of winning, while at the moment I seem to be routed. Instead of talking about complicity in the slave trade, everyone's talking about *me.* And what they're saying isn't very nice."

Professor Stevenson adjusted his wire-rimmed glasses, flicked a speck from his rumpled coat, looked at me.

"Your enemies are clever, no question. I anticipated a bit of to-do, but certainly no furor like this. *O tempora! O mores!*"

"My Uncle Jake is leading the charge. And believe me, he knows how."

"Ah yes, the stealer of chests."

"He also tried to have me shanghaied, says it would have done me a world of good."

"Shanghaied?" Framed by silver-gray muttonchops, his pink features registered astonishment.

I told him the whole story and filled him in on all that had happened since. He shook his head in near disbelief, muttering Latin phrases I couldn't make out.

"Pantywaist!" he finally exclaimed. "That's just a silly word, but you feel its sting. Well, better a pantywaist than a slaver. You haven't trafficked in your fellow human beings for gain."

"But, sir, what should I do? Answer my uncle blast for blast? Ignore him? What?"

"Crossing spears with him will only provoke more clashes, more hurling of insults. I can't tell you specifically what to do, Mr. Harmony; that must come from you. But I can tell you a story from my youth. Yes, Old Muttonchops was young once, *mirabile dictu*, and just as bookwormy and eager as you, and just as green. Would you like to hear?"

"Please, sir, yes. Anything that would help."

"At your age, Mr. Harmony, I knew in a vague way that I wanted to study how the great powers of Europe fought for control of this continent." He gestured toward the maps on the wall. "And how, out of that conflict, our republic was born. But I was a child of the eastern seaboard. I'd never seen the hinterland they fought over—those vast lands on the other side of the mountains, the West. So one day I said to myself: 'Get up! Get out there! Look and listen and learn!' I scraped together a few dollars—mighty few—packed a knapsack, and set out. I crossed the mountains on foot."

"You walked all the way?"

"Having little money, I had to. And I saw everything. The mountains in spring! Towering blue ridges, roses and azalea in bloom. Little inns where barefoot servant girls served you wild turkey and mountain venison. Waking to a cold dawn and setting out again, blithe and limber, on those steep, rutted trails, breathing the fresh mountain air."

"Sir, it sounds wonderful! What did you do, when you got out there over the mountains?"

"I looked and smelled and listened, stuck my hands in a rich, rock-free soil just meant for growing things, and even chewed sweet grasses. And worked! Chopping wood here, working as a farmhand there, doing whatever job came my way. I talked to everyone: farmers, teamsters, millers, backwoodsmen, wandering preachers, gamblers and whores—everyone! In just a year and a half I saw and heard enough to last me a lifetime!"

"But sir, you did come back."

"Oh yes, I came back to the East. But I'd seen wilderness and the West. I was ready to start my research. I'd learned from more than books."

"Professor Stevenson, should I go west?"

"Heavens no, dear boy, unless it answers your need. That was my solution; it may not be yours. Find out what you need, then do it. These are your young years—don't waste them. Just like me at your age, you need to broaden your experience, toughen up. Work or travel or think. Reach for something! Strive! Once you've done that, no one will call you a pantywaist, or if they do, you'll just laugh it off. Because you'll know the world and yourself. *Gnothi seauton,* know thyself! Lecture finished."

"Wow! Sir, you've given me a lot to think about."

"That's where you start, Mr. Harmony. Think! Think long, think hard! If you do, you'll be all right. Trust me: you'll be all right!"

I left his office all worked up. And I began to think.

34

Myself and young Ernest Stevenson, in dungarees and broad-brimmed hats, climbing higher and higher in the mountains on a narrow trail with steep soaring cliffs on one side, and on the other, a plunging ravine with tops of cedar and pine far below. Camping out at night, under a vast twinkling firmament of stars. Dawn: a ruddy glow. Setting off amid a fresh smell of sumac and oak. Higher, ever higher, toward the last towering ridge, its blue haze shot through with the gold of the sun.

"Your ma's right," Rick said to me and Sal. "I need ballast." Then to Sal: "A fellow like me needs the gentle influence of a mate. Are there any nice young ladies you could introduce me to?"

"Loads. Miss Twinkletoes Toothy Ruthie Moore, Miss Sarah Throgwhistle, Little Miss Constance Muffet." (The dancing school crowd, weighted with mamas, whom I'd exchanged pleasantries with on New Year's Day.)

"Rick," I put in, "they're fine young ladies, even if Sal persists in mangling their names."

"All right," said Sal to me. "That'll settle Rick. So what are *you* doing these days?"

"Thinking."

"That's all?"

"That's plenty: thinking."

Myself in the far, far West, in buckskin breeches fringed at the seams, panning for gold in a river, or chasing vast herds of buffalo stampeding across limitless plains... Starting a school for the children of ranchers, founding a newspaper, herding sheep in the Sierras. Talking to sodbusters, cowboys, dance hall girls, and Chinese cooks. Discerning on the distant horizon wigwams and wisps of smoke, while a guide whispers, "Arapaho… Kiowa… Cheyenne…"

From the Rivingtons, not a word. Had even Sal been banished from their premises?

Rick at church, worshipping in our pew, singing hymns with gusto, shunning his pa and Dwight, who glowered from a distance and barely nodded even to Ma.

Rick keeping company with respectable young ladies, making the smallest of small talk, and vowing, when the good weather came, to join them in the niceties of lawn tennis and croquet.

Rick accepting Ma's renewed invitation to move into Nathan's room, adorning it with his clutter, minus his collection of photographs (I'd seen them more than once) of leggy females. An intrusion that irked me just a mite, since I viewed Nathan's room as a shrine.

"A new Rick!" Sal said to me. "He's done sowing wild oats. He's walking the straight and narrow."

"Don't mix metaphors."

"And what about you? Still thinking?"

"Still thinking."

"Those must be some thoughts!"

Dear Chris,

I had my battle and you have yours. Give it to 'em, bucko—I know you'll come through. Pa and I are behind you, you won't let us down. Yes, Pa is here too, and Grandpa Harmony as well. He's sorry, Chris, real sorry. Forgive. Let Rick have my room. I don't need it and he's a capital fellow. Who needs a shrine? You have me in your heart. That means a lot to me. It would bring tears to my eyes, but here no one cries. It's calm here, weirdly quiet and strange. We can see you, but only from a distance, as if looking through a thick glass pane. Got to go now—taps. Your loving brother,

Nathan

A note from Rob Peterson:

"No more articles on the slave trade—that's the word from the owner. Don't know why. I feel squelched. My editor is riled, but you don't talk back to the owner. Maybe someday, but no time soon. Sorry. —Rob."

Rick to me: "I've been knocking around the waterfront and talking with the Reverend Oakes. It's funny, but about the trade and all, a lot of them don't care. Ancient history; let sleeping dogs lie. A few exceptions like Oakes and his boys and some others, but most of them just shrug. Someone was scared enough to murder Jonas Ward, but now, when the news comes out, names and all, on South Street it's greeted with a yawn. And your name there is poison: a snitch. For now, keep away!"

Professor Stevenson to me: "You see, Mr. Harmony, this is the so-called Age of Flash. High ideals and noble effort got all used up in the war. The Union's saved and the slaves are free, so let's make money and kick up our heels, have fun. A familiar problem for historians: we know a lot, but no one wants to hear it. In time, all this will change. The shame of the slave trade will register, but it may take years, decades. Meanwhile, keep on thinking, think till you reach a decision. Think, Mr. Harmony, think!"

Neber worked a day in your life... NEGRO DOGS. Branded on his forehead SLAVE.

Papa Bear, Mama Bear, Baby Bear. I love a good hot hate. You have no compassion! Please do not think me a fool.

We have the burden of truth. Justice! Justice! Justice! To be free!

Sal to me: "I finally called on the Rivingtons. They're gone, no forwarding address, vanished. Beyond that, the butler wouldn't say a word."

But a note came in the mail.

Dear Mr. Chris,

I know it is not proper for a young lady to write a young gentleman; forgive the indiscretion. Maman suddenly announced that she must inspect some property in Martinique and of course she is taking me with her. Just when I was getting used to New York and making such good friends! Was it that article? I saw it—a wonderful article! It did not mention her. Why should she be upset? There is so much I do not know.

Maman expects to be in Martinique many months, she does not say how long. Then we may go to Paris, if all there is finally in order. I do not know if or when we will return to New York. Imagine that big house standing empty, except for the servants—no parties, no receptions, nothing! I do not understand.

Mr. Chris, I am afraid this is adieu. Not au revoir, but adieu. That article shows you have courage and a great desire to speak the truth, come what may. That is admirable; keep at it. I shall always think of the things that, in New York, might have been. I shall never forget how you waltzed me as I have never been waltzed in my life. But perhaps I say too much. What a bore it is to be proper! Adieu, Mr. Chris. Your friend,

Kathleen Rivington

Reading this, I choked up, fought back tears.

Your young years—don't waste them. Reach for something! Strive! You'll know the world and yourself. Think long, think hard. Think!

The solution, when it came, was thunderingly simple. For the first time in months, I felt on even keel.

"Still thinking?" Sal said.

"No, I've thought my thought."

"Oh?"

"And reached my decision."

"Meaning…?"

"I'm going to sea."

35

Yes, I'm shipping out. Even with the advent of steam, sailing vessels still course the seas. Rick has offered to go with me for at least the first stage of the voyage, but I'm determined to do it alone. After three days, he assures me, I'll get my sea legs. And climbing the rigging should be no problem for me now as an adult; I'm a Harmony, I know I can do it. The Reverend Oakes will find me a ship with a good master and mate, and no connection with Jacob Harmony; they can be as tough as they like, as long as they're decent and fair. Embarking with a good heart and a willing mind, I'll holystone and swab the deck with the best of them, and scramble all over the rigging as needed. Whatever weather comes—storm blasts, hurricanes, roaring seas—I'll endure it.

In time, I'll see all those distant ports that Caleb Harmony spoke of, whose names have danced in my mind ever since: Havana, Rio, Buenos Aires, Valparaiso, Callao, Guayaquil. And maybe the Sandwich Islands, Macao, and Canton. I'll get to know them not as dreamlike places of legend, but as the raw, gritty ports they really are, and I'll know as well the hard task of getting there and back. And I'll come to know the men I ship with, and come to know myself.

My enemies will gloat, thinking themselves free of me at last, but I'll return, having acquired the one thing I lacked for my project: firsthand knowledge of ships and the sea. The essential documents will be waiting for me, secure in two large safe deposit boxes in the vault of a bank. I'll pick up my research and go on with it, surer of myself, patient, and determined something fierce. I'll learn all I need to learn, then share it with the world. If the world doesn't want to listen, I'll make it listen. And if no publisher offers, I'll publish it myself.

Ever since the day I discovered that last entry in my father's diary, and went on to sift the contents of Caleb Harmony's chest, I've been troubled by dark knowledge that tantalized, obsessed, horrified me. I can see the slaves being marched in chains to the coast, being herded on board and branded, being locked by hundreds in the hold. I hear their moans, their weeping for their lost homeland and kin, their pleas for water, their screams if the ship catches fire. I smell the stink of the hold, and the chloride of lime that is meant to, but cannot, cleanse it. In the streets of old New York I hear Mingo and Quanimo and their friends plotting a fearful vengeance, and Simon Congo's shrieks of agony as they roast him alive but cannot smother his cry: "To be free! To be free! To be free!"

I hear the pen of the commission merchant scratching foolscap, as he fills out the bill of lading acknowledging receipt, by the grace of God, of so many hundred slaves, duly marked and numbered, in sound and healthy condition or not, for which he invokes the blessed name of Our Savior. I read the sale notice for the wench who will make a good drudge, and the posted reward for the runaway girl with irons on her ankles, whip scars on her back, and a padlocked chain around her neck, who prays a lot.

I see the merchants who profited from this trade, with their braided cuffs and hint of cologne. Their fancy carriages shine in the sun, their gardens invite the soft laughter and genteel to-do of lawn tennis, the gentle disputes and clicks of croquet. In their gas-lit parlors I feel the upholstery of silk and brocade, smell camphor and sandalwood, a smoky perfume. Their gilt-framed portraits stare down grandly from the walls; they sleep in bedrooms adorned with old maps and prints of ships, and ivory chess sets and delicate figurines.

This I cannot forget.

I leave with gifts aplenty: from Rick, Bowditch's *Practical Navigator* and, slyly with a wink, another packet of condoms; from Ma, a small Bible and her blessing; from Sal, a journal that I intend to write in daily.

Rick now works in a ship chandlery—not his father's—and keeps steady company with Miss Twinkletoes Moore; they're all but engaged. He tells me that it's tough, giving up his ladyloves and the ardent, but I think he'll make it through. Though courted by Dan Hunter and Gorilla Gus Miller, Sal attended a lecture and now proclaims herself a suffragist, whatever that is, causing Ma shock and chagrin; she has also kept up her shooting. I wish them all well. Reports come to us that Uncle Jake has been invited to join the Chamber of Commerce; Dwight has a new front tooth.

When Sal and I told Ma about the attempted shanghaiing, she listened quietly, intently, without a great show of emotion. Then, having pondered for a few minutes, she announced,

"Jacob will never set foot in this house again, nor will Dwight. What they did was unforgivable." The finality of her words was chilling.

"I'm going to sea, Grandpa. I'm finally shipping out."

"A true Harmony! I'm proud of you, real proud."

"But I'll come back and go on with the history. I'll expose them all, the Harmonys included."

"Doing that, you'll redeem us, you'll be worthy of the Harmony name at its best."

"But I'm ashamed, Grandpa."

"Your shame is a credit to you, Chris. You're honest, you don't shirk the truth."

"How about you, Grandpa? Do you shirk the truth?"

"No. Not now. Not any more."

"You admit you did what you did?"

"I admit it and regret it. I was blind, callous, stupid. Your judgment is my punishment. But say I don't disgust you. Say that you forgive me. It's terrible when the young judge the old. It hurts so bad. I need your love, Chris, I need it very much."

"It's not easy, Grandpa, knowing what I know."

"You know the worst, the very worst. Look past it, if you can."

"Grandpa…"

"Chris?"

"I forgive you."

"Thank you, Chris. That means so much, so very much."

"Who am I to judge? I'm young; I haven't had time to make mistakes. Someday

I may need forgiveness, too. I hope I get it."

"You will, Chris. You will."

"I need it even now. I've been hugely cruel. Say you forgive me, Grandpa. Say it, Grandpa. Please!"

"Of course, I forgive you, Chris. My little bookworm, finally going to sea."

"I miss you, Grandpa. I want to hear more stories."

"Not now, Chris. Someday when we're together again."

"Promise?"

"I promise. I have lots of stories—lots. I'll wait for you. It will be such fun."

"I love you, Grandpa."

"And I love you. But I've got to be going now."

"Not yet, Grandpa. Just one story now. Just one. Please!"

"Chris, you've got your own life to get on with. Don't let an old man keep you from it."

"Don't go!"

"Godspeed, Chris, Godspeed!"

OTHER
ANAPHORA LITERARY
PRESS TITLES

PLJ: Interviews with Gene Ambaum and Corban Addison: VII:3, Fall 2015
Editor: Anna Faktorovich

Architecture of Being
By: Bruce Colbert

The Encyclopedic Philosophy of Michel Serres
By: Keith Moser

Forever Gentleman
By: Roland Colton

Janet Yellen
By: Marie Bussing-Burks

Diseases, Disorders, and Diagnoses of Historical Individuals
By: William J. Maloney

Armageddon at Maidan
By: Vasyl Baziv

Vovochka
By: Alexander J. Motyl

CPSIA information can be obtained
at www.ICGtesting.com
Printed in the USA
FFOW02n1144300717
38216FF

9 781681 143675